MISCALCULATIONS

MISCALCULATIONS

Elizabeth Mansfield

JOVE BOOKS, NEW YORK

MISCALCULATIONS

A Jove Book / published by arrangement with
the author

PRINTING HISTORY
Jove edition / June 2000

ISBN: 0-7394-1091-1

A JOVE BOOK®
Jove Books are published by The Berkley Publishing Group,
a division of Penguin Putnam Inc.,
375 Hudson Street, New York, New York 10014.
JOVE and the "J" design
are trademarks belonging to Penguin Putnam Inc.

PRINTED IN THE UNITED STATES OF AMERICA

A NOTE TO THE READER

Our heroine, Jane Douglas, is earning twenty pounds per annum when our story begins. In American money at the time, it would have equaled ninety dollars. The average American income at that time was one hundred and ten dollars. Since the British per-capita income was about 20 percent higher than the American, you can see that Jane's salary was quite low.

The British pound in 1810 was equivalent to about thirty-three current American dollars. Thus, when Luke loses seven hundred pounds in one evening, it amounts to more than twenty-three thousand dollars by today's standards. Quite shocking! No wonder his mother is appalled.

But then, his mother has a bill from her milliner for one hundred and twenty-six pounds, over four thousand dollars in today's terms. Some might consider such an expenditure for hats just as appalling.

PROLOGUE

No one who watched Lord Kettering smile and exchange pleasantries with his acquaintants as he descended the long stairway of Brooke's club would have guessed that he was churning with torment inside. Indeed, his close friend, Taffy Fitzgerald, who knew that the occurrence upstairs in the gaming room must have disturbed him, could detect no outward sign of perturbation. *The fellow's amazing,* he thought in admiration as he followed the Viscount Kettering down the stairs. *Such control! Such sang-froid! It's extraordinary!*

Theophilus "Taffy" Fitzgerald was not the only one looking admiringly at Lord Kettering. A good number of the younger set on their way up the stairs (fellows who thought it dashing to begin their gambling just when the older men were giving up) and several of the elderly gentlemen reclining on their easy chairs in the lounge down below gazed at him enviously. Lucian Hammond, Lord Kettering (Luke to his intimates), was an outstanding example of the group of young men known as Corinthians, and thus he attracted deferential glances not only from those who aspired to the group but to those who'd outlived it. To be called a Corinthian required a self-confident carriage, an elegance of dress, an insouciant manner, a talent for all the manly arts (like boxing, riding, fencing, and cards), and a penchant for taking risks. But the final gloss—the embellishment that all but a very few of that select set could consistently achieve—was a sportsmanlike disregard for the *outcome* of those risks. In all of these qualities, Lord Kettering was known to excel.

As he descended the exquisite staircase of the highest-stake gambling club of London in the wee hours of the morning, after having spent most of the night at one of the green-baize-covered gaming tables, he showed not a sign of weariness or disrepair. His dark hair was in the perfect state of calculated disarray; his face (kept from being too handsome by a square jaw and lean cheeks) glowed with the healthy ruddiness of a man who spent a good deal of time outdoors; the points of his collar were as stiffly starched as they'd been when he set out eight hours earlier; the tight-fitting breeches that covered his muscular legs were uncreased; and his boots still had the unblemished gleam they'd had when his valet's gloved hands had pulled them on. *It's no wonder,* Taffy thought, *that everyone throws him those envious glances.* Nature and breeding had given Luke every advantage. Taffy himself, even though Luke was his best friend in the world, was often envious. Two stone heavier and four inches shorter than his friend, he'd have given much to have Luke's tall frame and slim hips.

"I say, Kettering," someone shouted from the depths

of an armchair near the fireplace of the front room, "is it true that Moncton bested you again?"

Luke, not slowing his progress toward the doorway, waved his arm in the direction of the query with a dismissive gesture. "It only means, Foster, that I'm lucky in love," he said with a laugh.

It was not until he'd stepped out of the club into the darkness of St. James Street that Luke's smile died away. He even permitted himself to rub the bridge of his nose before setting off down the street. Taffy recognized the gesture as a small but certain sign of distress. "Why did you do it, Luke?" he asked as he fell into step alongside him.

"Do what?"

"Let Monk get away with cheating you."

Luke threw his friend a quick glance "You saw him cheat?"

"Yes, I did. The great Sir Rodney Moncton palmed an ace. Why did you let him get away with it?"

Luke frowned. "I suspected it, but I wasn't certain. I didn't actually see it. I suppose you think I'm the worst damned cod's head that ever was."

"Yes, you are," Taffy said in solemn agreement. "You should've been on the lookout."

"Do you think I don't know that?" He shook his head in self-disgust. "Damnation, I can't explain why I let him get away with it."

"Do you think your reluctance has something to do with Dolly Naismith?"

Luke stopped short. "Of course not. What has she to do with it?"

"I've often thought you feel guilty about her."

"What on earth do you mean? Guilty of what?"

"You stole her affections when she was under his protection, didn't you? You know she's the reason Moncton hates you so."

"I didn't steal her. She came to me of her own volition. So why should I feel guilty?"

Taffy shrugged. "I'm only theorizing. You've bested him on horseback, you've bested him in fencing, and you've bested him in *amour*. In short, in everything but cards. Perhaps you couldn't bring yourself to destroy this last prop to his self-esteem."

Luke studied his friend with a look of amused respect. "Bless me, Taffy, but you sound positively professorish. I've never before heard you 'theorize' on people's hidden motives. You have depths I never expected. I'm impressed."

Taffy colored with pleasure. "Ain't so deep," he said deprecatingly. "It was obvious you had to have a reason for letting yourself fall into debt to the fellow when you suspected he was cheating."

At the word *debt*, all amusement faded from Luke's eyes. "I must have turned jingle-witted. Betting two hundred pounds when I was already down a monkey."

"Good God!" Taffy stopped in his tracks. "Do you mean to say you owe the fellow *seven hundred?*"

The actual sound of the total debt made Luke wince. "And how I'm to pay the damned makebait I just don't know," he muttered glumly.

"I could lend you sixty," Taffy offered. "And Ferdie Shelford can probably raise the rest. . . ."

"More than six hundred? I doubt it. Thank you for

the offer, Taffy, but it doesn't really help. I'd have to pay both of you sooner or later."

"That's true. I can only spare it till the end of the month. I know you don't like to do it, Luke, but I'm afraid you'll have to ask your mother again."

"I know. Dash it, the very thought twists my innards into knots."

"I don't see why, old fellow. It's your own money, after all."

"It doesn't feel like mine when I have to ask permission like some deuced schoolboy begging for a raise in his allowance."

"Your father must have been a dastard to have left your inheritance so tightly tied up," Taffy muttered.

"No, he wasn't," Luke admitted honestly. "He believed I had so much to learn about managing money that it would take until I was thirty-five to be fit for the responsibility. And if he could have seen the idiotic way I behaved tonight, he would have felt himself completely justified."

Taffy nodded wisely. "Fathers always believe their sons can't manage money."

"But it seems he was right in my case." Luke kicked at a pebble, overwhelmed with self-loathing. "If I could let myself be manipulated by Monk so easily, perhaps I *deserve* to be treated like a schoolboy."

"Perhaps you ought to give up cards."

"No, not yet. I've bested Monk on horseback, with the foils, and on the cricket field, but when it comes to cards, he makes a Tom Doodle of me."

"Only because you let him cheat," Taffy pointed out.

"Tonight, perhaps. But I have no reason to believe he

ever did it before." He sighed deeply. "Once, just once, I'd like to . . ." But he didn't finish the sentence.

The two men walked on in silence. When they reached Taffy's digs, they shook hands. "Are you sure you don't want to borrow my sixty?" Taffy asked.

"Yes, I'm sure. But thanks for the offer, old fellow. As much as it pains me to do it, I shall have to write to Mama." He turned to depart for his own house. "I only hope she doesn't ask me why I need it," he tossed over his shoulder as he walked away. "If I have to tell her, she will think her son a complete ass. And so I am."

"Yes, there's no denying it," his good friend called after him. "That's just what you are. A complete ass."

ONE

At daybreak Jane Douglas woke to a most unusual feeling of warmth. Since she was almost always cold in the mornings (being the only one in the family who could bear sleeping in an attic room that was icy cold in all but midsummer, when it was, of course, stiflingly hot), she breathed in the mild, springlike air that had leaked in through the cracks in the window-frame with real pleasure. After a spell of such frigid weather that one's breath turned to icy droplets in the air, the rise in temperature on this late-February morning felt almost balmy. Jane snuggled into her pillow, letting the unaccustomed warmth thaw her bones. She meant only to spend a few moments in this indulgence, but when she next opened her eyes she knew at once, by the bright light that seeped in at the edges of the draperies, that more than a few moments had gone by. "Heavens!" she exclaimed in alarm. "How long have I slept?"

From the angle of the light rays, she knew it must be after eight, the hour she usually arrived at her post at

Kettering Castle. Although her employer, Lady Martha Hammond, Viscountess Kettering of Kettering Castle, Cheshire, rarely put in an appearance before eight-thirty, Jane was expected to have sorted through the mail by then. Sometimes, of course, her ladyship would not come down until nine, but there was no reason to suppose that today would be such a day. Besides, if it was now as late as eight-thirty, Jane was not likely to cross the threshold of the castle by nine. She would never make it!

She threw off the coverings, leaped up, and rushed to perform her ablutions. Thrusting her hands into the icy water in the lavabo was enough to wipe away the last of the warm feeling she'd experienced under the covers. But icy water was the least of her worries. She hurried through her washing-up and dressed with all the speed that a heavy linsey-woolsey dress with eighteen buttons down the back permitted. *These back-buttoned gowns,* she thought in annoyance, *should be made only for women who can afford to employ abigails to dress them.*

As she ran down the narrow stairway which led from the attic to the tiny entry hall of the cottage, she heard the mantel clock strike the hour. She paused on the stairs and counted. Good God, *nine!* Even if she didn't allow herself a bite of breakfast, by the time she ran the more-than-two-miles to the castle, she'd be an hour-and-a-half late.

She crossed the hallway to the dining room in a mere three strides, for the area was tiny, a narrow passageway separating the dining room from the other front room that served as both a sitting and drawing room. The entire cottage was tiny. It consisted of only five rooms:

the sitting and dining rooms in front, two bedrooms in the rear, and her own bedroom in the attic. The kitchen was housed in a small outbuilding at the back. For a family of three females of meager income, this arrangement would have been considered adequate, but Jane, her mother, and her sister were gentlewomen who'd been accustomed to better accommodations. Jane's father, an army officer who'd been second son of a baron, had had an income large enough to support them all in modestly comfortable circumstances, but when, two years ago, he'd died suddenly of heart failure, they discovered that he was hugely in debt. By the time the creditors were appeased, there was nothing left but a paltry annuity of forty-nine pounds. Jane, realizing the inadequacy of the annuity to support three females, had answered an advertisement for a secretary-bookkeeper (male, of course) and had convinced Lady Martha to hire her. With the post secure, she'd searched out living quarters in the vicinity of Kettering Castle and found this cottage for rent. Over her family's loud objections, she'd moved them in. Though they couldn't deny the necessity, they'd never quite forgiven her.

She entered the dining room hurriedly. Her sister Adela, sitting at the dining table casually sipping tea, looked up at her in surprise. "*Jane!* Goodness, aren't you late? I thought you'd gone already, so I ate up all the eggs."

"That's quite all right," Jane assured her. "I've no time for breakfast. Where's Mama? Has she eaten already?"

"She remains abed. She says she has the headache."

"Again?" Jane winced. Her mother's physical complaints were too frequent and too frivolous for her daughters to be seriously concerned about her health, but they had long since fallen into the habit of indulging their mother's wish to spend most of her waking hours languidly propped up on her pillows with a cold cloth over her eyes. No arguments of theirs, nor of the several doctors who'd been consulted over the years, had ever convinced their mother that she would feel a great deal better if she spent at least some part of the day on her feet. But it did no good to suggest that she'd find greater enjoyment in life if she'd try to view the world from an erect posture, so they'd given up trying.

Jane now shrugged helplessly and, as she ran quickly out to the entryway, said to her sister over her shoulder, "Then you'll have to take breakfast to her, Adela. I must run off at once."

"But, Jane, I can't," the younger girl protested, her pretty bow-shaped mouth compressed into a pout. "I'm promised to Geraldine this morning. We're to go riding. She's lending me Chantey, the sweetest little mare."

Jane, who'd already snatched up her shawl from the coatrack, reappeared in the dining room doorway, frowning at her sister in annoyance. "You will go riding, my dear, only *after* you've brought Mama her breakfast and done the beds!"

"The beds!" Adela rose from her chair angrily. "Why can't Mrs. Appleby do the beds?"

"Mrs. Appleby has enough to do today, what with all the laundry to be washed and hung, the sitting room carpet to be aired, and luncheon and dinner to prepare."

"But—!"

"Don't argue with me, Adela. I've no time for it. Say

good day to Mama for me and explain that I overslept. I'll be in to see her this afternoon, as soon as her ladyship lets me go."

Jane threw the shawl over her shoulders, caught up her bonnet—a shabby little straw concoction with three wilted flowers dangling from its crown—and dashed out the door, tying on the bonnet as she ran. She could hear her sister complaining loudly behind her that it wasn't fair that all the beds were left to her to do. "And besides," the girl whined from the doorway, "I don't see why we can't hire a housemaid to assist Mrs. Appleby."

Jane did not turn or alter her speed. *All the beds,* she repeated to herself in disgust. There were only two! And as for hiring a housemaid, it took all her talent at management to contrive to pay Mrs. Appleby her meager wages. The rent on the cottage, the cost of food, and Mrs. Appleby's wages used up most of the pay Jane received from Lady Martha, with their annuity going as far as it could to assuage her sister's and her mother's constant demands for gowns, medicines, sweets, and fripperies. There was certainly no money left for a housemaid, even a half-day. Nor would one be needed, if only Adela did her share instead of whiling away her hours in daydreaming, in searching the back issues of the Ladies Book for new fashions, or in coaxing the neighbor's boy to drive her into town in his curricle so that she could visit her friend Geraldine and spend long hours shopping for knickknacks, gossiping about other girls, or evaluating every young man in the vicinity as a prospective romance.

As Jane ran along the road to the castle, breathless and despairing, she revengefully imagined a scene in which she announced to her lazy, self-indulgent family that she'd lost her post. *Therefore, Mama,* she envisioned herself declaring, *you must get up and replace Mrs. Appleby in the kitchen, for I can no longer pay her wages. And as for you, Adela, unless you have a swain who is willing to offer for you, you must apply to the castle for a position as a housemaid, if you want to continue to eat. So there!*

The scenario was not as far-fetched as it might seem, Jane realized glumly. If her ladyship should be too displeased by her dreadful lateness this morning, she could very well be sacked. "Then where will you be, Adela, you spoilt little wet-goose?" Jane muttered under her breath.

She had no breath left with which to mutter anything by the time she ran up the stone steps to the castle's wide front door. Mr. Massey, the butler, opened it before she knocked. "Where've you been?" he muttered, sotto voce. "She's in a lather."

"Is she?" Jane pulled off her bonnet and shawl as she ran across the enormous circular foyer. "Has she been down long?"

The butler hurried alongside her and took her things. "More'n an hour. Would you credit it that the one morning you're late, she'd rise early?"

" 'Tis typical of the ironies of life," Jane replied and paused to catch her breath. She put a hand to her wind-blown hair before setting off in a run down the long hallway toward the library where her work area was housed.

"I'll send up some tea and scones for you, Miss Jane,"

the butler said, looking after her with sympathy. "You look as if you need them."

"Thank you, Mr. Massey, I do," she threw over her shoulder as she hurried away from him down the hall, "but not right away. Let her ladyship cool down first."

But Lady Martha was not in a lather. She was peering out the window, wringing her hands. At nine o'clock she'd been angry, but by this time, at nine-thirty, the anger had been replaced by deep concern. Her secretary-bookkeeper, the astounding, mathematically gifted Jane Douglas, on whom she'd come to rely completely, had never before kept her waiting. For two years now, every weekday morning, rain or shine, the girl would be waiting for her at the library desk, a folder of papers all ready for her inspection. Something dire must have occurred, her ladyship decided worriedly, to have kept the girl from her post.

At the sound of the door being opened she whirled around. "Jane!" she exclaimed in relief. "You had me in a fret! I was afraid something dreadful had happened to you . . . that you'd been set upon by footpads or fallen under a carriage . . ."

Jane couldn't help laughing as she dropped a bobbing curtsy. "Sorry, your ladyship. I only wish my excuse was half so good. I overslept."

Lady Martha's motherly expression died, and her back stiffened. The Dowager Viscountess of Kettering was an imposing figure of a woman even when calm—tall, full-bosomed, with silver-gray hair plaited in a coronet around a well-shaped head—but when she drew herself up in disapproval she was awe-inspiring. "Overslept?" she echoed coldly.

"Yes, ma'am. I'm afraid so."

Her ladyship's arched eyebrows rose. "Over*slept?*" she repeated in an even colder tone. "Is that your excuse?"

"No, ma'am, it's not an excuse. It's simply the truth."

"You seem to take it very lightly."

"No, my lady, I don't. Not at all."

Lady Martha studied her for some sign of remorse. Jane, though modest in stature, was a beguiling creature whose queenly carriage made her seem taller than she was. She stood proudly erect just inside the doorway, her shoulders back, her hands at her sides, her head high, her lovely complexion only slightly flushed, and her dark eyes meeting her mistress's with a bright, straightforward, steady gaze. The only signs of discomfiture were a slight breathlessness and an unusual disorder of her thick auburn hair, which, instead of being neatly pinned into a bun at the nape of her neck in her usual style, had been tied back somewhat hastily with a bit of ribbon and was now hanging in windblown profusion down her back. In short, she seemed quite unshaken, as if she'd done nothing wrong. The young woman's equanimity, her ladyship thought, was decidedly inappropriate under the circumstances. Her ladyship was irked by it. "I am very displeased, Miss Douglas, very. Overslept, indeed. That it's the truth only makes it worse. Oversleeping is not a practice I can readily condone. It is a sign that you do not hold your post in proper esteem. I think you are taking advantage of my affection for you."

Jane opened her mouth to repeat that she was sorry but immediately shut it again. Her pride had been offended by her mistress's scold, and she could not bring herself to say the words her ladyship evidently expected to hear. Everything Lady Martha had just said was unfair. Jane had never been late before, had never overslept, while Lady Martha herself often slept late and kept *her* waiting. And why should she hold her post in esteem when her ladyship, in spite of her oft-expressed admiration for her secretary's talent at calculation, nevertheless only paid her a servant's wage, not much greater than that of an upstairs maid (and lower, Jane had learned, than either the cook's or the housekeeper's)? If that was evidence of her ladyship's affection, that affection was a poor thing indeed. Jane lifted her chin and eyed her employer with a direct gaze. "I esteem my post in direct proportion to *your* esteem for it," she said proudly.

Her ladyship frowned. "And what do you mean by that, pray?"

"I mean, ma'am, that I esteem it twenty pounds per annum's worth, neither a penny more nor a penny less."

Lady Martha gasped. "Are you suggesting, Miss Impudence, that your lateness is due to a dissatisfaction with your salary?"

"No, I'm not. My dissatisfaction with my salary has nothing to do with the matter. My lateness is due to having overslept, that's all."

The older woman, startled at this turn of direction in the exchange, peered at the girl intently. "But you *are* dissatisfied with your salary, I take it."

"It is not an amount to bring much satisfaction," was Jane's blunt response.

Her ladyship's eyes fell. "I had every intention of offering you a rise in salary. And a generous gift next Boxing Day."

"Boxing Day is ten months off," Jane couldn't help retorting. "And I don't believe you've ever given my salary a second thought, once the original agreement was made."

"Jane Douglas," her ladyship cried in offense, "are you calling me a *liar?*"

"Yes, I am," Jane said flatly.

"Your impudence is beyond anything I've ever heard!" Lady Martha put a hand to her bosom as if to quiet a trembling heart. "I should have followed my original intention and hired a man," she muttered. "No man would have the temerity to throw such an accusation in my face."

"No man would have the courage," Jane said promptly. "And what's more, no man would have accepted a twenty-pound-per-annum salary."

"Hummph!" was her ladyship's only retort.

Jane studied her mistress with head cocked. "Do you know, it occurs to me that you would rather have had a lie from me this morning than the truth?"

"What on earth do you mean?"

"If only I'd lied and said I *was* set upon by footpads, you'd have overwhelmed me with kindness."

Lady Martha's mouth dropped open. She gasped audibly and stared at the girl whose impudence evidently knew no bounds. But after a moment she put a shaking hand to her mouth. "Goodness me," she admitted in surprise, "I do believe I would have."

"Beset by footpads, indeed," Jane added, a light of amusement appearing in her eyes. "Who would believe that footpads would be skulking about at nine in the morning?"

Her ladyship sank down on the nearest chair. "I am a foolish old woman." She sighed.

"Yes, but only sometimes." Jane smiled down at her, unable to keep from feeling a strong fondness for the woman. Lady Martha was a strange sort—sometimes thoughtless, yet often kind; sometimes foolish, yet often sensible; sometimes penurious, yet often surprisingly generous. "Well, ma'am," she asked after an extended period of silence, "are you going to sack me?"

Her ladyship looked up in surprise. "For oversleeping?"

Jane shrugged. "Or for impudence. Or both."

"Don't be silly. How would I get on without you? But I hope you will not expect me to give you a rise in salary today."

Jane laughed. "I suppose you cannot be expected to reward me on the very day I've been guilty of oversleeping and impudence. But I hope you'll give the matter of my wages some thought."

"Hmmm." Her ladyship neither agreed nor refused but merely made a noncommittal nod. After another momentary pause, however, she fixed her eyes on the girl with a look both quizzical and admiring. "You, Jane Douglas, are an extraordinary young woman."

"Yes, ma'am. So you've said more than once."

"And I'll say it again. Extraordinary. Out of the common way. In fact, almost bizarre."

"Thank you, my lady. I shall take that as a compliment, although I'm not at all certain it is. In any case, ma'am, shall we get to the mail?"

TWO

❧

Jane Douglas could indeed be called extraordinary. She'd been unique since childhood. Her father had been the first to recognize it. When she was three years old, he'd watched her as she sat before the fire playing a clapping game all by herself. "Papa," the child had asked, smiling up at him and clapping out the numbers, "doth thwee an' thwee an' thwee an' one make ten?"

Her father had gaped at her in astonishment. "It does indeed," he'd said, gulping down his Adam's apple. Then he'd wheeled about to where his wife lay on a chaise longue with a wet cloth over her brow. "Mavis, did you hear that?" he'd cried. "The child is remarkable! She reckoned that three threes and one makes ten! That means she's taught herself both addition and division, when even *boys* that age have barely learned to count!"

"Mmmm," his wife had murmured languidly.

"Dash it, Mavis, are you listening?" the excited fellow had shouted. "I think our daughter may be a genius at numbers!"

But Mavis Douglas, the mother of the possible genius, had merely lifted the cloth from one eye and squinted up at him. "Numbers, eh?" she'd muttered. "Much good that'll do her."

The mother was right. A talent for numbers was not a quality likely to do a girl much good. Although in the years that followed Jane did indeed exhibit a remarkable skill at things involving calculation (things like playing copper loo and whist, grasping the theory of musical notation, or understanding books on astronomy), she soon discovered that a mathematical bent was not an advantage in the arena where young women needed most to excel—the arena in which they competed to attract gentlemen. Most men tended to back away when they discovered that Jane could do sums in her head more quickly and accurately than they could do them on paper. Despite her lovely face and shapely form, men were not attracted to a mind sharper than their own.

But her talent *did* stand her in good stead in another way: it strengthened her character. Her manner of thinking was so logical that, even while she was still in the schoolroom, people who knew her brought their problems to her, problems both financial and personal. The quickness of her understanding, and the lucidity with which she could analyze them, made talking things over with her useful to everyone. Servants, friends, and even her parents instinctively turned to her for advice. Not surprisingly, this had an effect on her development. The respect that people around her felt for her gave her a confidence in herself that was rare in females of her age.

But the best use of her talent came when her family was beset with their financial emergency. That was when her mathematical mind rewarded her in a most practical way. In her interview with Lady Martha for the post of secretary-bookkeeper, she was easily able to demonstrate to her ladyship that she would be as capable in the position as the best-qualified male. Without once putting pen to paper, she proved her talent with three observations: first, she made an accurate estimate of the cost of running the castle by merely walking through the kitchens; next, she found an error in the bailiff's ledger by merely passing her eye over the page; and, finally, she disagreed with her ladyship about the payment of a bill. Lady Martha asked if she should pay her milliner the amount of one hundred and twenty-six pounds all at once or follow the milliner's suggestion of making six more "modest" monthly payments of twenty-four pounds. "Oh, pay her off at once," Jane had urged.

Her ladyship had raised her brows at that. "I realize that if I pay the bill monthly, I'll be paying a bit more in the end," she said, "but surely it's better to stretch the payments out than to pay in a lump."

"You'd be paying a great deal more than a bit, ma'am," Jane had pointed out. "It comes to *eighteen pounds* more. That's more than fourteen percent in interest. When most banks will lend money at two percent, a fourteen percent interest charge is worse than usurious. It's outrageous."

Lady Martha had hired her on the spot.

Her ladyship was remembering that interview as she sat before the library windows reading her letters. Jane had irked her this morning, but it was more her own fault than the girl's. If truth be told, hiring Jane Douglas was the wisest decision she'd ever made. Ever since Jane had come, the household had been running smoothly. The books were in order, the staff's wages were paid on time, household arguments were settled amicably and fairly, and all the business questions that her man from the City, Mr. Fairleigh, placed before her were now being handled by Jane with admirable results. (Mr. Fairleigh had even confided to her ladyship that he'd try to steal Jane away from her to work in his office, except that hiring a woman as a "man of business" would make him a laughingstock on the street.) She *would* give the girl a rise in salary, her ladyship decided. Even if she earned more than the expensive French cook, Jane was worth it.

With a decisive nod, she turned her attention to her letters. On top of the pile were two invitations for dinner from nearby gentry. She would accept only one. "Here, Jane," she said, passing the notes over to the girl at the desk, "write an acceptance to Squire Greenfield and an excuse to Lady Oldham. Dinner at the squire's table can be jolly, but Lady Oldham's a garrulous bore who never permits her guests to get in a word."

Jane, struggling to decipher the scrawl on a bill from a London wine-merchant, murmured an absent "Yes, ma'am," and set the invitations aside.

Meanwhile, Lady Martha stared worriedly at her next letter. She'd recognized the hand. "This is from Luke," she muttered as she broke the seal. "You don't suppose . . ." Her eyes ran quickly over the page. "Yes, dash it, he's done it *again!*"

Jane looked up. "Fallen into debt again, has he?"

"He's asking for another *thousand!*" Her ladyship put

a shaking hand to her forehead. "Didn't I send him a thousand just a short while ago?"

"A thousand just after the New Year," Jane answered promptly, "and six hundred two weeks ago."

"Good God!" Her ladyship winced in horror. "He's dissipated a fortune in less than two months!"

"So it would seem," Jane said, returning to her writing.

"Is that all you can say?" Lady Martha demanded irritably. " '*So it would seem'?*"

"It is not my place to say anything," Jane said, demurely calm.

"Hummph! You certainly didn't worry about your 'place' when you sauced me this morning."

"That was different. I had to protect myself."

"Well, I give you leave to speak your mind in this case. I need your views in this matter."

Jane eyed her suspiciously. "Are you certain, ma'am? You may not find comfort in my views."

Lady Martha sighed. "I am not looking for comfort. I'm looking for a solution. I think I need some of your honesty and logic."

"Then, ma'am, here it is. It seems to me that your son Luke is a wastrel and an incorrigible gambler."

"Does it indeed?" her ladyship snapped icily.

"You said you wanted honesty, did you not? You yourself told me of some of his wild exploits. The time he raced a gelding through Covent Garden and overturned two flower stalls and a vegetable cart in the process. And the shocking occasion when he instigated a fencing match with—who was it you said, the young Lord Ponsonby?—and they engaged in swordplay throughout Lady Ponsonby's mansion, causing all sorts of damage. And the ridiculous wager on a turtle race—"

"Yes, enough!" The older woman made a protective movement of her hand, as if trying to ward off the truth. "I grant you the point. He's a wastrel and a gambler."

"Yet," Jane went on, "I don't think he's altogether to blame for his profligacy."

This caught Lady Martha's full attention. "Don't you?" she asked, head cocked. "Then who is? His friends? Or are you trying to say that *I'm* somehow to blame?"

"Perhaps in a way you are. I wonder if his profligacy comes from a resentment of the fact that his mother has control of his fortune."

"That was his father's condition in the will. I had nothing to do with it. The late Viscount Kettering did not have confidence in his son's discretion. And, as it has turned out, he was quite right. Luke has no discretion in money matters."

"But he's never been given the responsibility of *dealing* with money matters. Perhaps if he had . . ."

"Are you saying—after calling him a wastrel and a gambler—that I should turn over to him all control over his wealth?"

"Why not? You can do it if you see fit, can't you?"

"Yes, I suppose so." Lady Martha's brow wrinkled as she considered the matter. "The will provides that the time to turn over control is at my discretion until he reaches the age of thirty-five, at which time it becomes his. But—"

"He is now thirty-one, is he not? The fortune becomes his in a mere four years. At that time, will-you, nill-you, he will do one of two things: either dissipate what is left, or decide to act responsibly. If he's going to dissipate it, what does it matter that you've managed to stave off the disaster by a few years? On the other hand, if you show some confidence in him by giving him the reins *now*, he may live up to your belief in him and behave like a man of sense."

Her ladyship blinked thoughtfully. "What an interesting idea," she said after a long pause. "It is certainly worth considering."

"Yes, ma'am," Jane said and returned to her work.

"Of course, he knows nothing of managing a large fortune," the older woman murmured, half to herself. "He will need someone to advise him."

"Mr. Fairleigh is up to the task," Jane said, not looking up.

"Yes, on large matters, like investments. And he deals well with the bailiff on land-management matters. But the everyday sorts of decisions . . ." She got up and began to pace. "He'd need a man of business, or a secretary . . . or someone—"

"Yes, ma'am," Jane said absently, engrossed in her writing. "That's a good idea."

Suddenly her ladyship stopped in her tracks. "Someone like *you*, Jane!"

Jane looked up. "Ma'am?"

"Why not?" Lady Martha strode back to the desk and leaned over it. "Why couldn't you go to London and do the job yourself?"

Jane blinked in amusement. "Me?"

"Yes, you. You're the perfect solution."

"But, your ladyship, that's ridiculous."

"Why?"

"There are a dozen reasons why. For one thing, he will want a male secretary. I'm a female. For another, I know nothing of London or the kind of life his sort lives. And even if the idea were not preposterous, I have my family—"

"Yes, of course. It *is* preposterous," her ladyship agreed, her face falling. She sighed, turned from the desk, and walked slowly back toward her chair. "Of course, I could *demand* that he hire you . . . as a condition of the agreement, you see. And I could stay with you in town for a while, to help you become acclimated."

"Please, ma'am, stop. It is not an option to be considered."

"What if you went for only a month or two? Your family can certainly spare you for a couple of months."

"No, ma'am, they can't."

"One month, then. Just enough time for you to set things going . . . procedures, ledgers, and the like. And to hire someone for him . . ."

"Sorry, ma'am, I just can't—"

"And of course I'd give you a rise in salary. A big rise. Double!"

Jane stared at her. "*Double? For the year?* And I need remain in London for only a month?"

Lady Martha's eyes gleamed triumphantly. "Double. And a lovely gift on Boxing Day. Agreed?"

Jane drew in a deep breath. Forty pounds per annum was almost as much as the salary of the French cook! "Very well, ma'am. Agreed. Though I haven't a doubt in the world that I shall come to regret it."

THREE

Luke, sitting stiffly in the corner of his carriage, was trying to ignore Dolly's flirtatious overtures. It had been a dreadful evening, and his desire for her had considerably diminished during the course of it. He usually found Dolly's bright green eyes, spectacular shape, and lively spirit enchanting, but tonight he'd found her nothing but irritating.

From the moment of his calling for her at the doorway of the building on Curzon Street in which he'd established her, things had gone awry. First she'd appeared in a gown too shockingly décolleté for an evening at the opera at Drury Lane. Then she'd blithely announced that she'd embarked on a project of redecorating the apartments he'd rented for her, which meant not only that he could expect an exorbitant bill for the work but that the place was not at present in a condition for his viewing. "I can spend the night with you in Charles Street instead," she whispered into his ear with what, in other circumstances, he would have considered a tantalizing giggle. It was not tantalizing tonight.

The fact was that, as much as he enjoyed spending an hour or so in her arms, he did not enjoy a whole night of it in his own home. He did not like a female intrusion into his own abode, he did not like having to face her over breakfast, and he did not like his servants knowing so much about his affairs. But since it didn't seem gentlemanly to reject her offer, he ordered his coachman to make a stop at his home before going on to the theater in order to tell his butler to prepare a room for a guest.

They were already late for the theater. Instead of asking the coachman to carry the message to his butler, he leaped from the carriage himself, ran up the outer stairs, and gave the order to his butler in as few words as possible.

Parks, a rotund fellow whose triple chins tended to quiver whenever he was upset, nevertheless always tried to appear impassive, as the perfect butler should. However, he could not hide his surprise now. "A guest, my lord?" he asked. "Tonight?"

"Tonight," Luke snapped, turning back to the stairs.

"A female guest?"

The note of disapproval in the butler's tone, though slight, was enough to irritate Luke. He glowered at the fellow. "Yes, dammit, a female guest," he muttered and started back down.

Parks followed at his heels. "Miss Naismith, I take it?"

Luke threw him an icy look but didn't bother to answer.

"I shall wait up for you, my lord," Parks said, running past him and opening the carriage door for him.

"Thank you," Luke muttered as he climbed up, but he could feel the butler's unspoken smirk. Parks would have great fun this evening sharing this delicious gossip with all the servants, Luke was sure of that. As he sank back onto the cushions, the feeling of irritation spread through his innards like a chill.

But there was worse to come. As soon as they entered the theater, they came face to face with Moncton with a new *cher amie* on his arm (the woman dressed, by the way, in a perfectly respectable gown). Dolly preened and paraded Luke about like a trophy, making clear by her manner that she wanted Moncton's new doxie (and everyone else) to know she'd snared the better prize. It took all of Luke's self-control to hide his embarrassment.

Dolly's reaction to the opera, too, had been irritating. Luke had been dismayed by the performance—a popularized version of *Don Giovanni* that had, he felt, cheapened Mozart's lovely score. Dolly, however, had been enchanted by it—further evidence, if that were needed, of her lack of discrimination. And finally, after he'd endured the entire performance for her sake, she insisted on their going on to Limner's for a noisy, badly prepared dinner.

The result of this accumulation of vexations was an unaccustomed coldness in his reaction to her blandishments. Here in the carriage Dolly herself could feel it. "Oh, my sweet love," she murmured, snuggling up to him and running a gloved finger along his jaw, "are you in a pet?"

"I am never in a 'pet,' " he said, holding her off. "Pets

are foolish little female tempers. Men do not indulge in them."

"Pooh," she said, snuggling closer. "They do indeed indulge in them. All the time. You are doing it now, even if you choose to call it something else, like . . . like . . . a 'huff.' " She looked up at him with an appealing little smile. "You are in a huff, then, aren't you?"

He found himself softening. "No," he said with a small twitch of his lips. "A huff is as feminine as a pet. Let us say I'm in high dudgeon."

She giggled appreciately and threw her arms around his neck. "Call it anything you like, so long as you get over it before we get home," she said and kissed his mouth.

By the time the carriage came to a stop at his town house on Charles Street, he had indeed gotten over it. His desire for her had welled up as strongly as ever. *Blast it,* he said to himself as he jumped down from the carriage, *I may as well enjoy the next hour, even if I hate myself in the morning,* and he held up his arms to her.

She leaped into them with an eager cry and nuzzled his neck. Filled with renewed energy, he would not put her down. He turned to carry her up the stairs, but as he put his foot on the first step he heard someone call, "M'lord!"

He looked up to see Parks running down the steps at a dangerous pace, his chins and his corpulent middle shaking and his eyes wide with alarm. "Wait, m'lord," the butler gasped. "There's something you should know before you come up."

"Something I should know?" Luke asked in confusion. "What on earth—?"

"It's Lady Martha. She's *come!*"

Luke gaped at him. *"Mother? Here? Now?"*

"Yes, my lord."

"But she never wrote that she was coming—"

"No, my lord, I know. I tried to urge her to go to bed, but she wouldn't go before seeing you."

"Damnation! Of all the inconvenient—"

"Yes, m'lord. That's why I came out to warn you." The butler glanced up worriedly at the lighted windows on the first floor. "I left her in the front sitting room drinking tea. She insisted on waiting there."

Luke looked up, too. *Good God,* he thought, *Mama could be looking out at me right now—through those very windows.*

All his desire for Dolly died at once. Quickly he turned and lifted his burden back into the coach. "Sorry, m'dear," he said to his startled paramour, "but our rendezvous must be postponed. I'll have to send you home." Then, waiting only till the carriage trundled off down the drive, he turned and ran up to face whatever trouble was waiting for him.

As soon as Luke appeared in the sitting room doorway, his mother put down her cup, rose from her chair, and smiled at him fondly. He expelled a relieved breath; she evidently had not seen his arrival. "Mama," he exclaimed, holding out his arms, "what a wonderful surprise!"

"Luke, dearest boy!" She threw her arms about his neck in an embrace to which he responded warmly. Then she stepped back and surveyed him from top to toe. "Except for windblown hair and a disordered neckcloth, you look none the worse for the wear and tear of your dissipated life," she murmured in approval of his appearance.

"You are looking in the prime yourself, Mama," Luke said, hastily making an adjustment to his neckcloth. "But what on earth brings you here without a word of warning? Is anything wrong?"

"Nothing's wrong. In fact, I come bringing news I think you'll be delighted to hear. But first let me introduce you to my companion." She made a gesture indicating that someone was behind him.

"Companion?" He had not been aware of anyone else's presence. He turned round in surprise.

The young woman who rose from a chair in the corner was not tall, but her slim figure and erect carriage made her seem so. She had the bearing of a noblewoman, but her clothes belied that impression. Under a shabby bonnet, her dark hair was drawn back so that very little of it was revealed. Her dress was a dull gray color, as if many times washed, with a high neck and a white tucker, like the dress of a governess. Luke immediately concluded that the woman was an abigail whom his mother had brought with her. But his mother was at that moment introducing her. "Miss Douglas, this is my son, Lucian Hammond, Viscount Kettering. Luke, this is Miss Jane Douglas."

Was it likely, Luke asked himself, *that his mother would make so formal an introduction to a mere abigail?* The matter was puzzling.

The young woman curtsied and said in a melodious voice, "Lord Kettering, good evening."

Luke bowed in return. "Miss Douglas," he murmured and threw his mother a questioning look.

"Jane has come with me from Cheshire," Lady Martha remarked.

This was no help at all to the puzzle. "Oh?" he asked cautiously.

"Why don't we all sit down," her ladyship suggested, "so that I can explain why we came."

Miss Douglas shook her head. "Perhaps you should explain to his lordship in private. If I may be shown to my quarters—?"

"Quarters?" Luke echoed, feeling utterly bewildered.

"Ring for Parks," her ladyship said. "He'll know where to put her."

When the butler had been told what was needed, Luke could see that the fellow was as bemused by the puzzle as he was. Was this stranger a servant or a guest? "Shall I give her the room I prepared for your . . . for the . . . um . . . guest you were expecting?" Parks asked in an aside to him.

But her ladyship heard him. "Were you expecting a guest, Luke?"

"Yes, Mama, but . . . something came up."

"He's not coming, then?" she prodded.

"No, he's . . . er . . . no."

Something in his voice made his mother peer at him.

Jane Douglas, too, must have heard something hesitant in his voice. "You needn't be polite for my sake," she assured her host. "If you *are* expecting a guest, please don't give me his room. I shall be perfectly comfortable in the servants' wing."

"This house has plenty of bedrooms," her ladyship put in quickly. "If the fellow—whoever he might be—

should appear, he can certainly be accommodated. Which room have you made up, Parks?"

"The Rose Bedroom," Parks said smoothly. "The one across the hall from his lordship's and just down the hall from your own."

"That will do for tonight," Lady Martha said. "We can make more permanent arrangements tomorrow."

Luke nodded his acquiescence to the butler, who bowed and led the young lady to the door. At the doorway she turned and curtsied. "Good night, my lady. My lord."

"Sleep well, Jane," Lady Martha said fondly.

"I hope you find the accommodations satisfactory," his lordship added.

Miss Douglas simply nodded and departed.

As soon as she was gone, Luke turned to his mother. *"Permanent arrangements?"* he asked, eyebrows raised. "What's this about, Mama?"

"I might ask you the same." She fixed him with a suspicious eye. "Who is this mysterious guest who failed to appear?"

"No one who need trouble you," her son assured her, "so please, Mama, sit down and tell me why you've come so far, without a word of warning and in the company of a dowdy creature who wants to bed down in the servants' quarters."

"Dowdy, indeed!" her ladyship said in offense. "I'll have you know that Jane Douglas is quite special. Unique. A rare gem."

"You don't say," Luke said, his tone mocking.

His mother threw him a look of disgust. "I won't bother to defend her," she said, seating herself. "You'll discover her remarkable qualities soon enough."

"Will I?" He pulled up a chair and sat down facing her. "So you *do* intend to install her here permanently. In what capacity, may I ask? As my governess? A new cook? Or do you wish me to adopt her?"

"Be still, you idiot. Let's have none of your nonsense. I have something serious to discuss with you."

"Very well, my dear, discuss away."

"It concerns your finances."

Luke winced. "I was afraid it might."

His mother leaned forward and patted his hand. "You know I love you, dearest, and want nothing more than your happiness . . ."

"Heavens," he muttered, eyeing her askance, "what a beginning. I tremble to hear the rest."

"It won't be so very dreadful, I promise. But I must start with the ugly fact that you are dissipating your fortune. You received sixteen hundred pounds from me in the last month, and now I have a letter asking for more. You must see that you cannot go on this way."

He sighed and hung his head. "Yes, I do see that."

"You get a very generous allowance, yet you've never managed to live within it."

He got up and began to pace around the room. "That allowance is like a blasted straight-waistcoat. Damnation, Mama, it gives a fellow no room at all to . . . to maneuver."

"To maneuver?"

"To manipulate funds . . . to contrive . . . to employ some financial strategy. A fellow likes to feel he can stretch the bounds sometimes and make it up later. If one has control of one's own funds, one can maneuver.

This way, having to come begging to you when I've broken the bounds . . . well, it's humiliating."

His mother surveyed him critically. "Manipulate? Break the bounds? Your argument doesn't sound the least bit logical to me."

He opened his mouth to defend himself, but the urge immediately died. He shook his head ruefully. "It's not very logical to me, either," he admitted.

Lady Martha smiled. "Don't look so downcast, my boy. I do agree that you have reason to feel constrained. Therefore I've decided that it's time to turn over your inheritance to your own control."

He could not believe his ears. "*What* did you say?"

"You heard me well enough. I've even informed Mr. Fairleigh of my intentions," she said, smiling complacently.

"Mama! You don't mean it!"

"I mean every word."

He blinked at her, speechless. With the few words he'd just heard, his prospects had completely changed. The dreadful burden of debt could now slide from his shoulders. It was too good to be true!

But it *was* too good to be true. He'd just gotten himself into the worst financial muddle of his life. Why had his mother chosen this particular moment—four years before she had to—to surrender the reins to him? He eyed her suspiciously. "But, Mama . . . *why?*"

"Because Jane thinks I should."

"*Jane?* Jane who—? Do you mean the Friday-faced chit we just sent to bed? What has she to do with it?"

"She has everything to do with it. She pointed out to me that the responsibility of handling the money yourself may be the very way to teach you what you haven't seemed able to learn so far—how to handle your finances with maturity."

Luke's face lit up with delight. "Well, bravo for good old Jane!" he shouted. "And for you, too!" Pulling his mother up to her feet, he wheeled her about in a wild dance.

It took some doing, but she managed to squirm out of his grasp. "There is, of course, one small condition," she said when she'd caught her breath.

He stopped in his tracks. His eyebrows rose. "Of course. I should have guessed." Naturally there would be a stumbling block of some sort. It had been too easy. "One *small* condition, eh? And that is—?"

"That one month from today you can show me that you've organized your finances and have incurred no new debt."

He glared at her. "All that in one month?"

"Yes. It won't be difficult, I promise you. I've provided you with the best possible assistance in the matter."

"What assistance?"

"Jane. All you must do is take Jane on."

"Take her *on?* What the devil does that mean?"

"Hire her. Employ her."

"*Employ* her?" He stared at his mother as if she'd taken leave of her senses. "I don't understand you, Mama. In what capacity am I to employ her?"

"It's simple. As your man of business."

FOUR

Jane took a candle from the butler, stepped over the threshold of her temporary bedroom, shut the door firmly, and leaned back against it with a deep expulsion of breath. She was grateful for the door's support, for her knees were still weak. It was the sight of Lucian Hammond that had undone her. She'd taken one look at him and had felt her insides melt.

It was a completely unfamiliar phenomenon. She'd never experienced anything even remotely like it. When he'd come striding into the sitting room, filling it with a kind of masculine excitement—his brow creased, his hair disheveled, his dark eyes questioning—she believed she'd never seen anyone so exciting. Her impulsive response surprised her. He was handsome, yes—firm chin and jaw, expressive mouth, intelligent eyes, broad shoulders, and shapely body—but she'd met handsome men before. What was it about him that had stirred her so?

She had no answer. This feeling could not be what her silly sister would call love at first sight. Jane was not the sort to indulge in such foolishness. Whatever one felt at first sight could never be love. Love, she was certain (though she'd never experienced it herself), was too serious and complex an emotion to overwhelm one in a moment. It was something that evolved . . . that developed gradually, as slowly as time permitted one to discover those qualities in the other that would make him beloved. One had to be completely unreasonable to tumble into love while one was ignorant of the other's character . . . in a moment . . . with a single glance. Unreasonable! And Jane was, if anything, a reasonable woman.

Besides, she didn't even like him. His sort—the kind of man who spent all his time in sporting, gambling, wenching, and other depraved amusements—had always been an anathema to her. It was reasonable, therefore, to surmise that what she felt was an aberration . . . a momentary loss of sense. It would pass, as dizziness passes, or nausea. Probably it would be gone by morning. When she saw his lordship again in the light of day, she would surely see him for what he was: a self-indulgent Corinthian. And this feeling she was experiencing—whatever it was—would be gone.

With the matter thus decided, she lifted her candle and looked about her. Even in the dim light she could see it was a large room, larger than any she'd ever slept in. A banked fire glowed in the fireplace. She went up to it and poked it into a blaze. As soon as her eyes adjusted to its brightness, she gaped at her surroundings. No wonder it was called the Rose Bedroom. Soft pink wallpaper lent a reddish-amber glow to the entire room. The paper was flocked with a delicate floral design that was repeated in the chintz of a loveseat near the fire and the weave of the sheer fabric of the bedhangings. The four-posted bed itself was magnificent. It stood against the wall to her left, so large and high that a stepstool was required to climb up to it. The bed quite took her breath away. The hangings, the comforter folded at the foot (so soft it must have been filled with eiderdown), the mattress as thick as a half-dozen featherbeds, the dozen or more pillows clad in pristine white with embroidered trimmings, all combined to make it seem fit for no less than a royal princess.

But there was more to delight the eye. The bed was flanked with side tables bearing charming china figurines—shepherdesses with beribboned bonnets and harlequins with masks over their eyes. Over the fireplace the mantel, too, held a figurine, in addition to an ormolu clock and two silver candlesticks. And in the wall opposite the fireplace, a doorway led to a dressing room.

Jane carried her candle to the doorway to peer inside. She discovered a chamber as lovely as the bedroom, with a chaise longue on one side, an elegant washstand on the other, and, in between, a long, marble-topped dressing table with an enormous mirror above. Jane gazed around her in delight. It was a charming place in which to dress.

She carried her candle to the dressing table to examine all the wonders that had been laid upon it—an abundance of combs, brushes, perfume bottles, cruets filled with mysterious fluids, vials of lotions and oils, embroidered hand towels, and aromatic soaps. Her sister Adela would have fallen into transports at the sight.

As Jane sniffed into a Chinese box containing a fragrant powder, it suddenly occurred to her to wonder why the items on this table were so explicitly feminine. Hadn't the butler said he'd prepared this room for the guest his lordship was expecting? Wouldn't shaving soap and a razor have been more appropriate than perfumed powders? Unless—

She gasped. Good God! Was the guest Luke Hammond had expected a *woman?* Had she and her ladyship interrupted an *assignation?*

She had a vivid memory of how Luke Hammond had looked when he came in—his hair tousled, his forehead wrinkled, his expression troubled. His demeanor had certainly been that of a man who'd narrowly escaped being caught in some sort of guilty pastime. The more she thought of it, the more positive she became that her surmise was correct. He *had* planned an assignation. Her stomach churned in revulsion.

She turned back to the bedroom, the candle trembling in her hand. That blackguard! The man was just what she'd imagined before she'd met him—a wastrel, a ne'er-do-well, a gambler, and a lecher. And to think she'd imagined herself taken with him!

She gave a short, ironic laugh. The feeling had certainly been of short duration. Love at first sight indeed! She quite despised him now.

Well, she consoled herself, there was no need to feel downhearted. The man of the house might be a disappointment, but there was still the bed. Surely that could not disappoint.

She stripped off her dress as quickly as the back buttons permitted, and pulled off her stockings and shoes. Dressed only in her chemise and underdrawers, she clambered up the stepstool and flung herself upon the bed, sinking into the most voluptuous mattress she'd ever encountered. Then, pulling the eiderdown comforter up to her neck, she snuggled into the mound of pillows and sighed with pleasure. This was luxury. Tomorrow, no doubt, she would be consigned to a mere featherbed on a narrow cot in the servants' wing. But tonight was hers!

FIVE

⌘✿⌘

The bed did not disappoint. Jane enjoyed a delicious, deep, uninterrupted sleep. Embedded in luxurious softness, she awoke reluctantly, groaning at the rude intrusion of the morning light. It took a moment or two to remember where she was, but when she did, the sense of delightful voluptuousness vanished. What time was it? she wondered in alarm. Would she be late for her very first interview with her new employer?

She threw aside the comforter and leaped from the warmth of her eiderdown wrapping into the cold air of the bedroom. No housemaid, she realized, had yet appeared to poke up the fire. Perhaps she hadn't overslept after all. One quick look at the clock on the mantel proved she was right. It was not yet seven.

As she dressed, she became aware of a new sensation—she was ravenous. Perhaps it was not too late to join the staff for breakfast. She did not yet know her way about the house, but she was sure she could find the way to the servants' dining hall. All she had to do was to locate the back stairs and follow the sounds of clinking dishes and low voices.

The route to her destination was just what she'd anticipated, but she did not anticipate what followed. First of all, the servants' hall itself was larger than she'd expected, and there were more than a dozen people sitting round a long table. The staff seemed to be almost as numerous as that at Kettering, a house perhaps four times as large as this one. To run this twenty-room town house, there were at least a dozen in staff—two footmen, the butler, two or three other men, and at least half a dozen females. *Lord Kettering*, she said to herself, *is very well cared for indeed!*

And so was his staff. That was her second surprise. The table was laden with platters of the most tantalizing food. It seemed quite like a festive banquet—shirred eggs, sliced ham, soused herring, and piles of biscuits and buns. Her already eager appetite was painfully whetted.

While she stood on the threshold, hesitating, they began to notice her. A hush fell over the room. Jane, embarrassed, took a step back. One after the other the servants rose uneasily to their feet. Jane raised a restraining hand. "No, please," she urged, "you needn't stand for me."

As they awkwardly sat down again, she turned to the housemaid nearest her. "Can you show me where I might sit?" she asked.

"Y' don't wish t' eat *here*, miss," the maid answered, bobbing shyly. "The family takes their breakfast upstairs in the mornin' room."

"Yes," Jane tried to explain, "but I'm not family."

"You be a guest, ben't ye?" a footman asked, getting to his feet again. "I'll be 'appy t' show you the way."

"I'm not really—" Jane began in explanation.

She was interrupted by a woman who was seated at the head of the table. "You see, miss," she explained, rising, "the family doesn't usually come down before nine." Older than the others, she was evidently in charge. Jane surmised that she was the housekeeper. "We'll send up some breakfast for you at once, if you like."

Jane sighed and shook her head. They were finding her intrusive. "No, don't bother," she said, deciding not to disrupt their regular routine. "I'll wait for the family." And she turned reluctantly away from the delicious aromas.

"T'ain't no bother, miss," the housekeeper called after her, but Jane had already started up the stairs.

A tall clock at the top of the stairs chimed eight. She had a whole hour to wait. Feeling hungry and very much alone, she wandered about the marble-floored foyer, peering up at the paintings that adorned the walls. Then she decided to examine the rooms that opened on to it. As she was crossing the hallway, she came face to face with a man hurrying toward the magnificent stairway that curved gracefully up to the second floor, his eyes fixed on the half-dozen starched white linen neckcloths that hung over his arm. He did not notice her until he almost collided with her. At the sight of her he jumped in surprise. "I beg pardon, miss," he said in hurried alarm. "I didn't expect . . . that is, I know I should be usin' the back stairs, but there ain't us'ally anyone in the hall at this hour. I'm Varney, his lordship's valet, y'see, an' he's waitin'—"

"You needn't mind me, Mr. Varney," Jane assured him and stepped aside to let him pass.

The fellow smiled in relief and scurried off. *If Lord Kettering's valet is rushing about with neckcloths,* Jane reasoned, *it means that his lordship is awake and—oh, joyful prospect!—that breakfast will follow shortly.*

After she'd examined a large drawing room, two small sitting rooms, and the morning room, she discovered the library. It was a beautiful, high-ceilinged room with a highly polished parquet floor, a huge fireplace flanked by two leather armchairs, and, opposite, a wall of tall windows facing the rear garden. The other walls were covered, floor to ceiling, with heavily laden bookshelves. Jane's eyes widened with admiration. Her father had had what he'd called a library, with a collection of three hundred books. Here there seemed to be thousands.

The thought of her father's books made her sigh. His books should now have been hers, but they'd all been seized by the creditors with the rest of his property. She had never ceased to regret the loss.

How fortunate Lord Kettering is, she thought, *to have so impressive a library.* Did he appreciate this treasure that was housed under his roof? "Not very likely," she said aloud. It must have been the former Viscount Kettering who'd collected these books. Certainly the present viscount, preoccupied as he was with wenching and gaming, was not given to such intellectual pursuits.

Jane, on the other hand, was delighted to have discovered this room. This library was just the place for her to divert her mind from her pangs of hunger. She began to look over the titles. She discovered that the shelves contained a huge collection of Latin and Greek

classics, a section devoted to biblical and religious trea-
tises, and another on histories. And this was only part
of the collection. One could spend a lifetime in this
room, she thought, and not read everything.

As her eyes rose to the higher shelves, she glimpsed,
quite near the top, a book that looked familiar. Her father
had had a red-leather volume—a great favorite of hers—
that he'd mended with a mismatched patch on the spine.
The off-color patch on the spine of the book on the shelf
above was a perfect duplicate of the one she remembered. Could it possibly be the same book? Could a book
from her father's collection have somehow found its way
here?

Excitedly she pulled over the ladder that rode on rail-
ings along the upper shelves and mounted it to get a
closer look. She climbed six rungs of the ladder but
found the book still out of her reach. A bit nervously,
she glanced down to see how high she'd come. The floor
looked much farther away than she'd expected. However, since she'd come so far, she would be not only
foolish but cowardly to retreat before achieving her ob-
jective. Only one more rung would do it.

Carefully she climbed another step. Clinging to the
ladder with one hand, she extended her other arm and,
with her index finger, managed to pull the book out an
inch or so. If she stood on tiptoe, she reasoned, she could
manage to get a real grasp on the spine. But just as she
raised herself on her toes and reached up for it, a loud
masculine voice below her exclaimed, "So *here's* where
you've been hiding." Startled, she turned so abruptly that
the ladder slid from under her. Suddenly there was noth-

ing underfoot. The air was whistling past her ears. She was falling.

Sheer, icy terror enveloped her. The seventh rung had been frighteningly high. She was surely doomed, if not to death, then to broken bones and a cracked skull. A scream escaped from her throat, but before the cry had fully emerged, she felt herself thump against something that was not the wooden floor but a solid human body. Her tumble through the air was miraculously halted. It was a moment before she realized she'd been caught by two strong arms.

But the terror was not yet over. The weight and force of her fall caused her rescuer to totter back. Another frightening moment passed before he managed to regain his balance. Once his footing was secure, she was able to look up. The face looking down at her belonged to Lord Kettering.

"Good God," he gasped, trying to catch his breath, "but there's more heft to you than meets the eye."

The sense of gratitude that had welled up in her immediately died. "If the heft is too great, my lord, then I suggest you put me down," she said with asperity.

His eyebrows rose, and he smiled with a wry amusement. "You are *welcome*, ma'am, I'm sure."

She felt herself color at his mild reproof. "I'm . . . sorry. I do thank you."

"You should. I saved you from what could have been a nasty fall."

"Yes, I . . . I . . . know. I'm truly grateful."

She wondered why he did not put her down. All at once she became acutely aware of the closeness of his chest and arms and of the fact that she was clutching him tightly round his neck. He could probably hear her heart beating. Grateful as she was for his rescue, she could not forget who this man was. She was not the sort of female who would permit herself to be held in the arms of a man she knew to be a libertine. Besides, it was necessary to her dignity to put him in his place. Withdrawing her arms, she eyed him coldly. "If I'm as heavy as you say, my lord, I can't help wondering why you are still holding me."

His eyes glinted into hers. "Not too heavy, I assure you. Quite a delectable armful, if truth be told." Nevertheless, he set her on her feet.

Completely discomposed by his pleasantry, she turned away and busied herself smoothing her skirts. He, meanwhile, knelt down and retrieved the book that had taken the fall in her place. "Is this what you went to so much trouble to get? Malory's *Morte D'Arthur*?"

She nodded but kept her face averted. "My father used to read it to me when I was a child. I haven't seen it since he . . . for many years."

"Don't tell me you managed to read the title from way down here."

"No, it was the patch. See it there? Papa's book had a patch just like that."

Lord Kettering examined the spine. "This is the Caxton edition—rather rare, I believe. There cannot be two Caxton Malorys with identical patches. Do you think this can possibly be—?" He opened the book and looked inside the cover. "Good God! Was your father Glenville Douglas?"

"Yes!" Jane peered at the book over his shoulder. "Oh, my! That's Papa's bookplate!"

His lordship gave a short laugh. "My father collected most of these books. Do you suppose he stole it from yours?"

"Oh, no, you mustn't believe that," Jane assured him. "My father was almost impoverished when he died. The books and everything else went to his creditors, who must have put everything up for sale. I'm sure this volume came to your father's hands quite legitimately."

"I'm relieved to hear it. Nevertheless"—he closed the volume and handed it to her—"it gives me great pleasure to restore it to you."

She thrust her hands behind her and backed away. "No, no, I couldn't—"

"Please. I'm sure it's more precious to you than to me."

Jane could not disagree. It *was* precious to her. She took it in her hands and stared down at it, moved almost to tears to be holding again a book that brought back so many happy memories. His lordship, libertine though he was, had made a very generous gesture. "This is most kind of you, my lord," she murmured in a choked voice. "I do thank you . . . again."

His lordship had stepped away and, with head cocked and a speculative look in his eyes, was studying her from top to toe. "It seems, ma'am, that my mother was not far off in describing you. Unusual, she said. I think that a young woman who reads Malory and who is a genius at numbers is decidedly unusual."

"Your mother exaggerates, my lord. I have a facility for reckoning, that is all."

"Have you, indeed? Evidently Mama is convinced that

your 'facility' is enough to straighten out the muddle of my finances."

"I don't believe the task will require a genius."

"You think it will be easy, then?"

"Yes, I do. I've already observed one small extravagance that can easily be corrected."

"Already? May I ask what it is?"

"Of course, my lord. I saw your valet this morning, with at least six neckcloths on his arm. I understand that a modish Corinthian is required to make a to-do of folding his neckcloths, but half a dozen every morning does seem to me to be excessive."

He raised an eyebrow in a manner she found almost forbidding. "What a paltry beginning!" he said coldly. "If I made myself more adept at folding, and cut the number down to two, it would save not so much as a groat."

She refused to let herself be cowed. "I don't claim the saving would be great, my lord, but it would be more than a groat. If six neckcloths are relaundered daily, they soon need replacement, do they not? I suspect your haberdasher charges five shillings for a linen neckcloth—"

"More likely ten," the Viscount admitted.

"Ten! Shocking! Then, assuming you replace neckcloths at the rate of a dozen a year—and by your expression I suspect the number is much greater—if you cut back by two-thirds, you will have saved four pounds."

"Four pounds per annum," he mocked. "A great sum indeed."

"Surely you've heard your mother say, 'Little, and often, fills the purse.' "

"At my time of life I do not need to be guided by clichés from my mother. Nor do I wish to concern myself with petty economies."

She lowered her head. "As you wish, my lord."

"None of this is as I wish, but I must accept it. How shall we begin, Miss Douglas? Do you wish to count my underdrawers?"

She ignored his sarcasm. "Perhaps the first thing is to find me a quiet place in which to work."

"How about right here? This room is not much used."

"I didn't think it was," she murmured dryly.

He heard the implied aspersion, and the forbidding eyebrow rose again. Jane braced herself for a tongue-lashing, but after a moment of silence he evidently decided to ignore the slur. "Will that writing table do for your purposes?" he inquired.

"Of course. Though it is much too fine."

"Then that's settled. What next?"

"I think the next problem is for you to establish my place in the household. The servants refuse to believe I'm part of the staff, though I don't understand why. My appearance and dress are surely no better than theirs."

"I understand it. It's your carriage."

"My carriage?"

"Your carriage, your manner, your entire demeanor." A flicker of amusement shone in his eyes. "Don't you realize, ma'am, that you walk as if you were the Queen of all the Russias?"

She stiffened in offense. "Don't be ridiculous."

That made him guffaw. "There, you see? Not one of my staff would dare to tell me not to be ridiculous."

Her cheeks grew hot. "I beg your pardon, my lord.

Your mother permits me great liberties in my manner of speech. I'm afraid I'm quite spoilt. But to return to the matter at hand, I think you should instruct your butler to inform the staff that I shall be among them for a month."

His lordship looked puzzled. "Do you live with the servants at Kettering?"

"No, my lord. I live with my own family nearby. I believe I am what is called a 'live-out.' "

"Mmm." His lordship stroked his chin. "But you're not really a servant, are you? When Mr. Fairleigh visits, I don't put him in the servants' quarters. Mama called you my 'man of business,' a position quite like Mr. Fairleigh's. Therefore, I don't see why you can't stay where you are."

Her eyes widened in surprise. "In the Rose Bedroom?"

"Yes. It's only for a month, after all."

"But surely you must wish that room for your . . . um . . . guests."

He showed not a glimmer of understanding her hint. He merely shrugged. "We have plenty of rooms."

"Nonetheless, that room is not appropriate for a 'man of business' who is not a man," she persisted. "It would not be . . . seemly."

"Seemly?" He peered at her for a moment, and then raised that forbidding eyebrow. "Ah, I see. You are suggesting that the room is too near the master's bedroom, are you not?" His voice was suddenly colder. Icy, in fact. "That the proximity might tempt the master to pay a *late-night visit?*"

She would not permit herself to be intimidated by his

tone. She put up her chin. "Such things have been known to occur."

"They have," he snapped, "but not in this house! I am not the sort to take advantage of persons in my employ."

She fixed him with a level look. "I have yet no way of ascertaining *what* sort you are, my lord."

Her retort caught him by surprise. He gave a little hiccough of amusement but immediately afterward took offense. How dared this creature question his character! "You, ma'am," he said, "have much too saucy a tongue. I begin to think I agreed to my mother's plan too soon."

She did not answer. He strode over to the window and back again, trying to calm his temper. He had not the slightest notion of how to handle this outspoken female. He glanced over at her, his brow knit. She stood just where he'd left her, calmly waiting, apparently untroubled by the altercation. Perplexed, he took a deep breath. "Very well, ma'am, I shall give you the point," he muttered.

"The point?"

"I will let you win this round. We shall leave the matter of your accommodations to my mother. Does that suit you?"

"Yes, my lord. She will know what is appropriate."

"Good. Then I suggest we postpone further discussion until she is with us." With that, he nodded brusquely and went to the door.

"My lord?" Her voice sounded, to her own ears, a bit desperate.

He turned. "Yes?"

"There is one thing I must ask you to do for me."

He looked at her suspiciously. "Can't it wait?"

"I'd be most grateful if you could deal with it now."

"Something important?"

"It is to me."

He sighed in annoyance but surrendered. "Very well then, what is it?"

She gave him a pleading look. "Can you *please* arrange for me to get some breakfast?"

SIX

Lady Martha did not emerge from her bedroom until half-past ten, by which time Jane had long since finished a sumptuous breakfast (which she'd eaten in lonely splendor in the morning room), and Luke (who never ate before midmorning) had returned from his daily canter through St. James Park. He was making his way upstairs to change out of his riding habit when Parks informed him that his mother was at this very moment breakfasting alone. Changing his direction, he strode into the morning room. "I must speak to you, Mama," he said, waving Parks out of the room.

"You might say good morning first," his mother reprimanded.

"Very well, then, good morning," he obliged, and he helped himself to a hearty serving of York ham and eggs before seating himself opposite her.

"Thank you. I suppose it is too much to expect you to be properly dressed at the table."

"Much too much," he retorted.

She sighed. "Incorrigible, as always." Nevertheless, she serenely poured herself a cup of tea. "Well, go on. What is it you want to say to me?"

Luke sat back in his seat and fixed his eyes on her. "Your idea is preposterous," he announced bluntly.

"What idea?" Raising her brow innocently, Lady Martha returned his look.

"The idea of my employing your blasted bluestocking as my business adviser. The position is completely inappropriate for such a woman."

"Bluestocking? What on earth do you mean by that appellation? That she's too bookish?"

"*Prudish* is closer to my meaning. The girl is a prig."

Lady Martha glared at him. "What nonsense! My Jane hasn't a prudish bone in her body."

"You are in no position to know that," her son declared.

"And you are?"

"As a man, it is easier for me to judge that sort of thing."

Lady Martha put down her cup, her expression puzzled. "I don't see why you say that. Unless—" She peered at her son suspiciously. "Good God, Luke, don't tell me you attempted an indecent assault on the girl!"

"Mama!" He slammed down his fork. "What do you take me for?"

"I take you for the libertine that you are."

He drew himself up and glowered. "If you believe, my dear, that I would *ever* take advantage of a female in my employ, you know me as little as your bluestocking does!"

"Oh, pooh! Come down from your high ropes, you

lunkhead! I *am* your mother, after all, and quite fond of you."

"Hummph! You've a fine way of showing it. Calling me a libertine, indeed. Very motherly, I must say."

"Being motherly doesn't necessarily mean being blind to your faults. But we were speaking of Jane. If you found the girl to be a bluestocking, *something* must have occurred between you—"

"Something for which *I'm* to blame, is that it?" he demanded sarcastically.

"Something that made her react in a manner you interpreted as priggish."

"She reacted priggishly to my suggestion that she remain housed in the Rose Bedroom."

This surprised her ladyship. "Really? Why on earth should she—?"

"You may well ask. It seems she feared the proximity to my rooms made her vulnerable to any lustful midnight wanderings in which I might indulge." As he rose to fill his cup from the carafe of coffee on the buffet, he muttered *sotto voce*, "The damnable chit flatters herself."

His mother, deep in thought, did not hear him. "She is not completely misguided," she remarked. "The Rose Bedroom is not a fitting place to house a member of the staff."

"Oh?" His brow wrinkled in a troubled frown. "Was I wrong to offer it? I only thought she shouldn't be asked to room with the servants. She seems a little high in the instep for that."

"She is not at all high in the instep. I don't know how you've received so completely erroneous an impression. But as for housing her, we can install her in your old governess's room. That will do nicely, I think."

"*I* think," Luke countered, "that we should forget your plan altogether. Why don't we simply send Miss Jane Douglas back to Cheshire? I can quite easily find myself a man to handle for me what your Jane does for you at Kettering Hall."

"You *won't* find such a man. I tell you, Luke, my Jane is quite extraordinary."

"She has a talent for reckoning, I know. She told me that herself. But I'm certain that many a man can be found with an equal talent."

Lady Martha shook her head. "You're quite wrong. But I shan't bandy words with you, Luke. I've made up my mind, and I will *not* change the terms of our agreement. Either you agree to all of it, or it is void."

Luke frowned in frustration. He could not let his fortune—so close to coming under his control—out of his hands again. How could his mother permit a mere servant girl to become the sticking point in this matter? "Please, Mama," he urged, "don't be inflexible in this matter. It's not only the matter of her prudery. She is insolent and stubborn and very quick to make judgments that are detrimental to me. Can't you see that this girl and I will never get along?"

"No, I don't see that at all. You hardly know her. It seems to me that you're the one who's quick to make detrimental judgments."

"Dash it, Mama, how can we come to such an impasse over a mere—?"

The sound of the door opening stopped his tongue and caused both their heads to turn. Jane Douglas stood in the doorway.

Lady Martha, alarmed that the girl might have over-heard some of their conversation, flushed. "Jane, my dear," she said awkwardly, attempting to smile, "do come in."

"Oh!" Jane, noticing his lordship for the first time, froze in the doorway. "I thought you were alone, ma'am." She glanced quickly at him and then dropped her eyes. "I wanted to speak to you, but it can wait." And she took a step backward over the threshold.

"No need to wait," Luke snapped, striding to the door. "I was just leaving." He brushed by her, adding, "It seems I've been wasting my time here anyway. You win, Mama." And he shut the door sharply behind him.

Jane looked after him in surprise. "I'm sorry, ma'am. I hope I did not interrupt something important."

"No, not at all." Her ladyship, relieved that Jane showed no sign of having heard anything and that her son had accepted her ultimatum, now was able to smile up at the younger woman with real sincerity. "Do take something from the buffet, my dear, and join me at the table."

"No, thank you, ma'am," Jane said, standing her ground. "I've already breakfasted. I've only come to say that I made a serious mistake in agreeing to take this temporary post, and I wish you will permit me to leave London and return to Cheshire at once."

Her ladyship winced. *Not you, too!* she cried to her-self. Then she took a strong sip of her tea. "You have a good reason, I suppose?"

"Yes, I do. I've discovered that I can do nothing to assist your son with his finances. Or with anything else, for that matter."

"Did something occur to bring you to that conclusion?"

Jane shook her head. "Only that we had a few moments to converse this morning, a conversation that proved to me we could not . . . er . . . get on."

"A few moments of conversation? Are you saying that you managed to uncover the complexities of a man's character so quickly?"

"I ascertained enough to convince me that my remaining would be a waste of time."

"Can you tell me just what it was you ascertained that convinced you?"

Jane hesitated. "You're his mother, ma'am. I should not like to offend—"

"I promise to take no offense. You know I'm not unaware of Luke's faults."

"Yes, I know. You've often discussed with me his profligacy and irresponsibility. But—"

Lady Martha cut the girl short. "It was to improve him in those regards that I brought you here, was it not? You knew that before we agreed on the terms."

"Yes, but I did not know the extent of them. I now realize that I can have no good influence over his behavior."

"And what made you realize that, may I ask?"

Jane did not know how to answer. "I . . . he . . ." She expelled a helpless breath. "How can I make any headway if he has taken me in such dislike?"

"Has he? What makes you think—? Has he been rude to you?"

"No, not at all. He's been very polite. In fact, quite generous."

"Generous?"

Jane's eyes fell. "He . . . gave me a book. As a gift."

"Did he, indeed?" Lady Martha studied Jane's face with interest. "A gift, you say? I would not take that as a mark of dislike."

"Well, that was before . . ." Her voice faded away.

"Before—?"

Jane shook her head. "No, never mind. I can't explain."

"It seems to me, my dear," her ladyship said, "that you, of all people, are not being logical. If a man is very polite to you, offers to house you in the Rose Bedroom, and even gives you a gift, it hardly seems logical to suppose him to dislike you."

"No, it doesn't seem logical," Jane had to agree. "It is not something I can prove rationally, with numbers. But one can make judgments from instinct, too."

"But without rational proof, how can you be sure your instincts are sound?" her ladyship pressed.

"I . . . don't know," Jane admitted reluctantly. "But I am sure that I don't want to go on with this."

Lady Martha took another sip of her tea and, thus fortified, set down the cup. "We had an agreement," she said firmly.

"Yes, but—"

"I am not an ogre, Jane. I cannot force you to honor your word. But I can point out the consequences if you break it."

Jane, knowing that her life's situation depended on the good offices of this woman, tried without success to keep her voice from quivering. "C-consequences?"

Her ladyship did not mince words. "Not only will you

lose your rise in salary but your post in my house."

The girl put up her chin. "I don't see why this matter should have anything to do with my post in your house."

"You cannot expect me to employ a person whose word I can no longer trust."

"Oh. I see." Jane, recognizing defeat, sank down upon the nearest chair. "You've given me no choice," she said glumly. "I must go on with this, then."

Lady Martha reached across the table and squeezed the young woman's hand. "Don't fall into the dismals, my dear. It's only for a month, after all."

"Yes, you're right." Jane put her shoulders back and rose from her chair. "I suppose I shall survive a month."

Her ladyship watched her go to the door. "We've had your things sent up to a very pleasant room on the third floor. And you're to take your meals in the family dining rooms, at whatever hours suit you. So you see, we are trying to do everything to make your stay comfortable."

Jane bobbed a little curtsy. "Thank you, ma'am. As you pointed out, I've given my word. I shall do my best. But I hope you will not place the blame at my door if this little experiment of yours proves—as I'm sure it will—to be an utter failure."

SEVEN

❦

As she reentered the Rose Bedroom, Jane felt a tinge of regret. No more would she be surrounded with such luxury. This was the last time she'd see this room. Before she gathered up her things, she looked around at the elegant appointments that had been hers for one night—the flocked wallpaper, the china figurines, the ormolu clock, the lovely, sheer fabric that decorated the posts of the magnificent bed. That bed had been heavenly. She'd never experienced a night of such sumptuous luxury. *It's just as well I'm leaving this room,* she thought. *If I spent another night on that bed, I might never be able to pull myself out of it in the morning.*

On an impulse she threw herself down on it, just to feel its softness once more. But she'd barely laid her head on the satiny pillow when the door opened. "Oh, dear!" she cried, sitting up abruptly. "Who—?"

"It's on'y me, ma'am," said a timid voice from the doorway. "I'm Meggie. I hope I ain't disturbin' ye."

"No, no," Jane said, blushing in embarrassment as she

met the eye of the young housemaid standing at the door. "I was only . . . that is, I . . ."

"I cin come back later, ma'am," the girl said. "They sent me t' show ye yer room upstairs."

"Oh, I see." Jane scrambled off the bed hurriedly and straightened her skirts. "Thank you, Meggie, I'm quite ready."

"Ye needn't disturb yer rest, ma'am," the girl insisted. "I cin come back later."

"I wasn't resting. I was . . . well, I was just being childish. Enjoying the luxury of that featherbed."

The housemaid nodded. "I know whut ye mean. I tried it once when they let me do up this room. It's mostly Mrs. 'Awkins job to do the fam'ly bedrooms, but once when they was all busy, they let me do it." She grinned at Jane conspiratorially. "It's a grand bed, fer certain."

"Yes," Jane said, gathering up her clothes and stuffing them into her shabby portmanteau, "a grand bed."

Meggie insisted on carrying the portmanteau upstairs. The third floor was very quiet, the rooms evidently not in use. "Where does the staff sleep?" Jane asked the maid.

"We all 'ave rooms in the back wing," Meggie explained, starting to unpack the portmanteau. "This 'ere floor was fer the governess an' the tutors, back in the ol' days."

"You needn't do that, Meggie," Jane said, taking over the unpacking. "I'm just a servant here, like you."

"I don' know about that, ma'am," the girl replied. "They said I was to do fer you whatever you need."

"Thank you, but I don't need anything. And please, Meggie, don't call me ma'am. My name is Jane."

Meggie accepted Jane's attempts at informality with a smile, but she nevertheless dropped Jane a curtsy before departing.

I'm afraid I'll always be neither fish nor fowl in this household, Jane thought with a sigh.

Alone in her new quarters, she looked about her. Lady Martha had been right; the room was very pleasant. Although only a fraction of the size of the Rose Bedroom, it had two dormer windows with padded sills for seating, a good-sized bed, a table with a mirror and a lavabo, a small bookcase containing a handful of books, and a cupboard. After she'd stowed away her things, Jane looked at the books. They were, for the most part, children's books—fairy tales, Aesop's Fables, Mother Goose, copy books, and a children's Bible. As she leafed through the well-worn Aesop, a folded sheet of paper fell to the floor. She picked it up and unfolded it. It was a letter written in a childish hand. The first line, Dear Simmy, was crossed out. Then it went on:

Dear Miss Simmons,

Parks told me that yestiday was your birthday. Why did you not tell me? I am very sorry not to have given you this on the propur day. I hope you will like this good-luck tokin, even tho it is late. I whitled it myself from a peice of a doorknob from the old stabel door. It is supose to be Cupid, the God of Love. I am sory the nose broke off. Mama gave me the chane, so you may wear it round your neck if you wish. Happy birthday.
Yours, Lucian Hammond.

Jane, charmed, read it over twice. His lordship must have written it when he was no more than seven or eight. Miss Simmons must have been his governess, whom he'd affectionately called Simmy. What a lovable child he seemed to have been! What on earth, she wondered, had made him change to a gambler, a wastrel, and a libertine? She sank down on a window seat and stared at the childish handwriting. Even the misspellings were endearing. So sweetly innocent he once had been. It was enough to break one's heart.

EIGHT

⌒⋙❦⋘⌒

Lady Martha, having succeeded in coercing both her son and her protégé into accepting her terms, lost no time in sealing the bargain. Dressed in a mauve satin walking dress, a hat with six enormous peacock feathers dangling from its brim, and her newest pair of white gloves, she accompanied her son to the offices of Mr. Fairleigh in the City, where they would sign the documents required to surrender control of his fortune into Luke's hands. "This is a very special day," she told her son when he made a mocking comment about her hat, "and I want to be properly costumed for it."

Mr. Fairleigh and his clerk ushered them into his offices with appropriate fanfare, but the business of signing took no more than a quarter of an hour. It took no more than another quarter hour, however, before her ladyship was regretting her decision.

The start of the meeting was very pleasant for all concerned. And for Luke it was a splendid event. As he signed the last paper, he looked at Fairleigh eagerly.

"When does this go into effect?" he asked.

"Oh, immediately, my lord," Mr. Fairleigh declared. "Immediately. Although you do understand that, if the report of your financial activities is not satisfactory to her, Lady Martha may still revoke your rights at the end of one month."

"Yes, I understand," Luke murmured, staring down in awe at the documents that would so drastically change his life. "But in the meantime, I may use my entire inheritance as I see fit?"

"Yes, quite so."

Mr. Fairleigh, a lawyer as well as a financial adviser, was a portly, bald-headed fellow whose demeanor, even when he had to give a client bad news, was invariably cheerful. On this happy occasion, he exuded geniality from every pore. "A momentous day!" he kept declaring as the papers were passed from hand to hand. "Such a momentous day!"

In order to celebrate, he ordered his clerk to bring in a bottle of port and three glasses. As soon as the liquor was poured, he raised his glass and offered a toast. "May good fortune always be yours," he said, grinning broadly and slapping Luke on the back.

"And so it will be, Luke, my love," his mother added, her feathers bobbing with every earnest nod of her head, "if you but remember that moderation in prosperity staves off adversity."

"Oh, yes!" the smiling lawyer agreed. "Quite true, quite! Your dear father often used to say that riches have wings and too easily fly away. He understood that prudence is the greatest asset to wealth."

"Did he, indeed?" Luke took a sip of his port to suppress a laugh. "I seem to remember another of his say-ings: 'Wealth is not his who *gets* it but his who *enjoys* it.' "

"You *would* remember that," his mother muttered dryly.

"Of course you will enjoy it," Mr. Fairleigh said, "but within moderation. Moderation must be the key." He drained his glass and licked his lips before proceeding. "After all, we don't want anything to stand in the way of your mother's final signature at the end of the . . . er . . . shall we call it probationary period?"

"Yes," Lady Martha said. "That's just what it is. A probationary period."

The lawyer, gathering up the papers, looked up to ask, "Am I correct in assuming you will not require an in-crease in your monthly expenses?"

"I don't know," Luke answered. "We shall see. But I should like to make a withdrawal right now, if you please."

"Right now?" Mr. Fairleigh's smile wavered only slightly. "Ah, yes, I understand. Naturally you would wish a little something for a celebration this evening. Quite understandable, quite. A token of your inheritance to lavish on some amusement to mark this day." His smile restored, he looked up at Luke eagerly. "I believe fifty pounds will be a most enjoyable, if moderate, amount for the purpose—?"

Lady Martha's dangling feathers came upright as her chin lifted. "Fifty pounds? Good God, that is far beyond moderation for an evening's frivolity! Twenty-five would be more than adequate for any sort of dissipa-tion."

But Luke shook his head. "I'm afraid, Mr. Fairleigh," he said as he put down his glass, "that I shall require a thousand."

His mother gasped. "*A thousand?*" That was when she felt the first misgiving.

"A thousand, yes," Luke said firmly.

"But did you not mean it only as a celebratory token?" the astounded lawyer asked. "To enjoy for some festivity this evening?"

"That is just what I intend," Luke said, holding out his hand.

Mr. Fairleigh, his smile making an abrupt disappearance, hesitated and glanced over at Lady Martha. Her ladyship, stiffening so angrily that the feathers trembled, opened her mouth to object, but Luke held up a restraining hand. "Am I correct in believing that the papers we just signed permit this decision to be my own, at least for this month? That I might demand from you any amount up to the sum total on this document, and that I might throw it to the four winds if I wish? Is that not so, Mr. Fairleigh?"

"Yes, your lordship, it is your right," the portly man gulped, "but—"

"Come now, Luke," his mother snapped, "must you behave like a jackanapes? Throw it to the winds, indeed!"

"I'm trying to make a point, Mama. I've stated an amount for a withdrawal. I expect my wishes to be honored. What is the purpose of this experiment if I still must explain or apologize for any demands I might make?"

Her ladyship, admitting to herself that he was right,

threw up her hands. "Very well! Do as you wish. For the next thirty days I have no control over what you do."

The lawyer lowered his eyes. "A thousand, then?" he asked.

"Yes. In ten-pound notes if you please."

While Mr. Fairleigh left them to count out the cash, Luke and his mother waited in silence. Luke could barely restrain his grin, but Lady Martha had to struggle to keep from expressing her extreme displeasure. *What a piece of effrontery,* she thought. *One thousand pounds!* This unwonted extravagance seemed proof that, Miss Douglas's advice notwithstanding, her son would always be a spendthrift.

Mr. Fairleigh, making a brave attempt to restore his cheerfulness, returned with a pile of a hundred ten-pound notes in his hand. "Will this be satisfactory?" he asked his lordship, casting a wary eye on the mother.

Luke took the bills in his hand. "Very satisfactory," he said.

"I hope you don't *really* plan to use it all in one evening," the lawyer said in a tone implying that his lordship had surely been joking.

"Yes, I do," Luke said, looking down at the bills with a gleam.

His mother could restrain herself no longer. "What on earth can it possibly be that would tempt you to fritter away such an amount in one evening?" she demanded, feeling helpless. "It's a woman, isn't it? Some bit of muslin on whom you'll squander all that?"

"See here, Mama," he said, frowning down at her in annoyance, "have you turned over my inheritance to me only to keep demanding an accounting of how I spend it?"

She made a gesture of surrender with one white-gloved hand. "No, of course not," she admitted, realizing that she had no course but to abide by her agreement. She lowered her hat so that the many feathers hid her eyes. "I'm . . . sorry."

Her retraction softened him. "That's better," he said, letting a little smile show. "And since you've apologized so nicely, I'll admit to you that this money will *not* be squandered on a woman. Does that please you?"

"No, it doesn't," his mother snapped. "However you intend to squander it appears dreadful to me. Do you truly believe such wastefulness will give you enjoyment?"

"Take my word, Mama," he said, lifting the lowered brim of her hat and placing a fond kiss on her cheek, "that I shall enjoy it very much indeed."

NINE

As soon as she returned to Charles Street, Lady Martha
tossed aside her bonnet (which, because of its associa-
tion with the unpleasant afternoon she'd just endured,
she intended never to wear again) and stormed up to her
bedroom, pausing only to order Parks to send Jane to
her. Parks found the girl in the library, sorting through
a pile of unpaid bills that he'd handed to her earlier, in
response to her request to examine the household accounts. Since it was he who handled the household accounts for his lordship, he was somewhat put out at the
request, the possibility occurring to him that he might
be superceded. However, this was not the time to inquire
into that matter. "Her ladyship wants you, ma'am," he
said. "Right away. She's up in her bedroom."

"Thank you, Mr. Parks." With a sigh Jane rose from
the desk. "I told you, didn't I, that you and the rest of
the staff needn't call me ma'am?"

The butler shook his head. "It doesn't seem fitting to

call you by your first name. How about . . . what if we call you Miss Douglas?"

"If you wish," Jane said, going to the door, "but at Kettering Hall everyone calls me Miss Jane."

The butler considered the suggestion for a moment. "Very well," he said at last. "Miss Jane it is, then. I'll tell the staff."

As she hurried down the corridor toward the stairs, Jane reflected on this exchange with the butler. From his manner it seemed as if Lord Kettering had been right in his assessment of her demeanor. He'd implied that her manner was arrogant. And Parks's reaction to using her name seemed to support that view. Yet, if there was really something arrogant in her carriage, why wasn't the staff at Kettering put off by it?

The butler, following her down the hall, suddenly cut into her thoughts. "I'd take care, Miss Jane, if I was you," he warned.

She turned to him. "Take care?"

"It seemed to me her ladyship was in a real taking."

"Was she?" She threw the butler a grateful smile. "Thank you, Mr. Parks. I'll take care."

The smile remained on her face as she ran up the stairs. Parks's warning was the first sign of friendship from the fellow. Perhaps she *didn't* carry herself like the Queen of all the Russias after all. Perhaps his toplofty lordship was wrong about her.

But as she approached Lady Martha's bedroom her smile died. *What's happened to put her ladyship in a "taking" this time?* she wondered as she tapped at the door.

Responding to a curt summons to come in, Jane

stepped inside and discovered that the room was in confusion. The bed was covered with scattered items of clothing, the abigail was busily rolling up pairs of gloves and putting them into a straw bandbox, and her ladyship was sitting at her dressing table, holding a silver-framed miniature in one hand and dabbing at her eyes with the other. "Are you packing?" Jane asked, surprised.

"Yes," her ladyship said, lowering the little painting to her lap and looking up at Jane, "I've decided to return to Cheshire this very day."

Jane was appalled. "But, ma'am, you *can't!* You promised to stay with me for a fortnight at least!"

"I'm sorry, Jane. It's just . . . impossible. I cannot abide watching my son dissipate his fortune, as he seems intent on doing. And I dislike living in London. I always have. Too much noise and bustle. I long for home."

"So do I, your ladyship, so do I." Jane gave her mistress a pained look. "Does that mean nothing to you?"

Lady Martha, sighing guiltily, dabbed at her eyes again. "I know the sacrifice I'm asking you to make," she admitted.

Jane was not moved by her mistress's tears. She knew they came easily to Lady Martha. Instead, she felt a wave of anger well up in her. "How is it, ma'am, that you can expect me to keep *my* word but have no compunction in breaking *yours?*"

Her ladyship hung her head. " 'Tis a privilege of age," she muttered.

"Huh! A privilege of *wealth,* if we're to be honest."

Lady Martha's head came up at once. "Save your sharp retorts for my son," she said in reproach. "He needs them more than I do."

Jane turned away, unwilling to show how upset she was at the prospect of being left in this house without the support of the one person who wanted her there. "It seems you both deserve a sharp tongue," she muttered.

Lady Martha made a gesture of helplessness. "I'm sorry, my dear. I admit I'm deserting you. But you are so capable and clever. I know you'll manage well. All you need do is show me at the end of the month that he's curbed his gambling and kept his expenses within some sort of reasonable limit. But even if you don't succeed at prodding my son into some sense of responsibility, I'll not blame you. I'm sure you'll have tried your best."

"I don't need butter-sauce poured over me, ma'am. I need your help."

"I can give you no help. My son has just proved to me that he doesn't care a fig for my opinions."

"What makes you think he'll care a fig for mine?"

"I don't know if he will or not," her ladyship conceded, "but I'm convinced you are Luke's only hope." Emotion overcame her again, and, her eyes filling with tears, she lifted the silver-framed miniature from her lap. "Look at this," she said, gazing at the painting fondly. "This is Luke at nineteen. Rowlandson limned it." She handed the miniature to Jane. "Wasn't he a handsome boy? He is still devilishly good-looking. Whenever I go to a ball where he's present, I notice how all the women flock round him."

"Yes, he is," Jane said, studying the tiny face. "Very handsome."

"I used to wish he would marry, that the influence of a good woman would improve him," his mother said sadly, "but now I'm convinced that he'd only choose the wrong sort."

Jane continued to stare at the painting. The face was strikingly attractive, and the eyes looking back at her were clear and honest. It was not the face of a man without character. "I think, ma'am, that you belittle him," she said softly. "I'm still convinced that he will grow into maturity, now that you've given him a chance to earn his independence." She handed the miniature back. "But saddling him with my presence will only make him feel you still don't trust him enough."

"He knows I don't trust him. But I trust you, Jane. Something tells me that you're what he needs to make a good start with his new responsibilities."

Jane, realizing that further argument would be useless, gave up. "Very well, ma'am, since you give me no choice, I shall keep my word and stay. May I ask you a favor in return?"

"Yes, of course, if I can. What is it?"

"Will you ask one of the maids at Kettering to look in on my mother and sister and let me know how they do? I worry a great deal about them."

"But why should you? Didn't you tell me you used some of your rise in salary to hire a town girl to work for your mother?"

"Yes, to assist Mrs. Applegate with the housework in the afternoons."

"Mrs. Applegate? Who is she?"

"Our housekeeper."

"You have a housekeeper in your tiny cottage?" her ladyship asked, surprised. Servants were not supposed to keep servants.

"Yes. She works a few hours in the mornings, when I'm at the Hall with you. My mother is not well, you see, and needs assistance."

"But what about your sister? I seem to remember . . . ah, yes. Adela, isn't it? Why doesn't she—?"

"My sister is young. Only seventeen." Jane dropped her eyes from her ladyship's keen questioning. "Not yet up to her adult responsibilities."

"I see. So you've hired a village girl to take your place in the afternoons, is that it?"

"Yes. I tried to make adequate preparations for my absence, but I'd be much easier in my mind if I knew things were going well with my family."

"Yes, of course. I'll visit them myself," her ladyship promised, "and I'll write to you."

"Thank you, ma'am." Jane went to the door and curtsied. "I hope you have a pleasant journey back."

"Wait," Lady Martha said, rising and going to the door. "Jane, my dear," she said, placing her arm pleadingly on the girl's shoulder, "do your best with my Luke. That's all I can ask for. I shan't blame you if you fail. Whatever happens, you will still have your place in my employ."

"Will I?"

"My word on it. And I promise one thing more. My undying gratitude."

TEN

Luke, having not the slightest inkling that his mother was at that moment leaving the house, picked up Taffy in his curricle and drove off toward Brooke's club. Taffy noted with some surprise that Luke was humming merrily as he guided his pair of grays through the crooked streets. This cheerful demeanor was a decided alteration in his friend's previous frame of mind; only a fortnight before Luke had been sunk in the dismals. "Something's changed," he remarked, searching his friend's face for a clue. "What's passed since I saw you last?"

"Everything's changed," Luke said, trying to keep from grinning.

"Oh? Don't tell me your Mama came through for you again."

"In the very best of ways." Luke, keeping his hands on the reins, lifted his elbow to make his coat pocket accessible to Taffy. "Put your hand in my pocket!"

Taffy did so, and removed from the coat pocket a

thick roll of bills. He gasped. "Is this the seven hundred you owe?"

"A thousand," Luke said, tossing off the number with a feigned nonchalance.

"A *thousand?* I say! Your mama has become unusually generous, hasn't she?"

"You won't believe this, Taffy," Luke said, letting his grin break out at last, "but she has taken steps to sign my inheritance to me in one month's time."

Taffy's mouth dropped open. "Bless my soul! *All* of it?"

"Every penny."

The enormity of the news left Taffy momentarily speechless. Then, chortling with delight, he pounded Luke on his back and shouted in enthusiastic glee, "Good for you, old fellow, good for you!"

"Well, don't fly into alt," Luke said, flicking the reins. "I'm on a month's probation, so we shouldn't toss hats in the air just yet."

"Merely the thought of seeing Monk's face when you pay him off is enough to send me into alt," Taffy insisted excitedly. "I overheard him bragging to Stanford that he'd probably forced you to go to a cent-per-cent."

"I was afraid I'd have to," Luke said, his smile fading. "Getting myself into the clutches of a moneylender has always been a nightmare to m—"

Something he saw on the street just ahead of them startled him. "Ho, there!" he cried out in fury to a barely discernable figure, "just what are you about, you damnable cur?" With a sudden pull-back of the reins, he drew the curricle to an abrupt stop.

As Taffy gaped in confusion, Luke leaped out of the

curricle. "If there's anything I can't abide it's a cawker who abuses his horse!" he muttered to Taffy over his shoulder. "Hold the reins for me, will you, Taffy?" And he ran across the street to where a man stood beating a bony nag that apparently was refusing to pull the cart to which it was hitched. "Stop it!" Luke ordered, grasping the man's arm. "Can't you see the poor beast is on his last legs?"

The horse-beater turned round. Luke, his free arm raised and his fingers tightened into fists to administer a blow, was startled into immobility by the look of the man. He was a poor, unshaven, shaggy fellow and had tears running down his sunken cheeks. " 'E winna move!" he moaned in despair.

"Of course he won't move," Luke said, his anger somewhat assuaged by the misery in the man's face. "He's all skin and bones. He has no strength left."

"Do ye think I dinna know it?" The man lifted the back of a dirty hand to rub away the tears from his cheeks. "I ha' no likin' t' whip 'er, poor Tessie."

"Then why are you doing it? You've probably been pushing the poor animal beyond her limits all day."

"Wha' cin a poor drayman do, sir, I asks ye?" the fellow pleaded. "I mus' deliver the cattle t' the market, mustn't I? But I swear I never whipped 'er before."

"Then why now?"

" 'Cause I mus' get 'ome!" The man's tears began to flow again. "It's already dark, an' my little un's all alone. She'll be cryin' er eyes out fer me." He turned to the horse and looked the animal in its eyes. "Please, Tessie, ol' girl, jus' one more time!" he begged.

"Are you saying you've a child waiting for you who's uncared for?" Luke asked suspiciously.

"Aye, sir," the man said. "There ain't no one but me, see? My woman, she died o' the cholera las' winter, an' our girl—she's on'y eight, a good little poppet she is— she cin manage by 'ersel well enough by day, but she's fearful at night. I always make it 'ome by dark, but Tessie's sore tuckered today." He looked at the horse in heartbroken defeat. "It's been dark two hours already, an' I 'ave moren' an hour's ride still to go."

Luke studied the man's face for a moment and then walked quickly back to his curricule. Before Taffy's astonished eyes, he unhitched one of his grays and led the horse to the cart. "I say, Luke, what on earth are you up to?" he called out.

Luke only waved back. The drayman gaped in amazement as Luke released the old nag from his bonds and hitched up the gray. "There," he said to the drayman when he was done. "It's a trade. My gray for your nag. But you must promise me you'll never raise a whip to him."

"Ye're givin' me yer lovely horse?" the man whispered, awestruck. "I mus' be dreamin'!"

"A gift for your little poppet. Now, go on home." He took hold of the nag's bridle, led the horse to his curricle, and tied her to the back.

The drayman followed, dropped to his knees beside Luke, and tried to kiss his hand. "Bless you, sir, bless you," he wept, but Luke snatched his hand away and jumped up onto the curricle. "Go on home," he called and drove off down the street.

"Are you mad?" Taffy demanded when the drayman

and his cart were out of sight. "You've given away half of your best pair!"

"I know," Luke said ruefully, trying to keep the curricle balanced with one off-center horse. "But the fellow had to get home to his little poppet. Poor Tessie behind us could never have pulled that cart for an hour."

Taffy turned around and looked at the animal. "What are you going to do with her?" he asked.

"I'll have her taken to Kettering, where she can die a peaceful death."

Taffy peered at his friend with a combination of admiration and dismay. "I've never witnessed a more bubbleheaded act. I don't think anyone else I know could have done it. You, Luke Hammond, are too deucedly good-hearted."

"What rubbish!" Luke said disparagingly. "Good-hearted, indeed. You make me sound like a blasted altruist."

"And so you are. Good-hearted as could be."

"Good God, Taffy!" Luke exclaimed, appalled, "I hope you don't intend to say that to anyone else. If word should get around that I'm good-hearted, I'd never live it down."

It was too difficult to proceed with an off-center horse before and a tired nag behind. Luke turned back to his stable and, after instructing his gaping groomsman on what to do with poor Tessie, he and Taffy set off again for the club, this time on foot. "Let's go and find Monk," Taffy said, hurrying his step. "After you've settled with him, you two ought to play another game. I have a feeling you might win it all back before the night is over."

They found Moncton playing faro at one of the round green-baize-covered tables in the Great Subscription Room. It would be hard to miss him. Sir Rodney Moncton stood out in a crowd, not only for his impressive size—six feet two in his stockinged feet, with an immense breadth of shoulder to match—but for his head of long jet-black hair dramatically emphasized by a streak of white at the peak of his forehead that split and fell from a center part and framed his face. His size and a tendency to glower made his aspect forbidding; Sir Rodney was not a man one would easily provoke.

Luke came up behind him and tapped him on the shoulder. "Here, Monk," he said without preamble, "your ill-gotten gains. All seven hundred." And he let the ten-pound notes flutter one by one to the table in front of the fellow.

If there was a flicker of guilt in Moncton's eyes, it was not apparent to anyone at the table. "*Well*-gotten, I would say," he retorted over his shoulder.

"Two or three of us know that *ill-gotten* is the more apt expression," Taffy said bravely, his tone hinting at deeper implications.

Although some of the players at the table exchanged significant glances, Monk chose to ignore the slur. "The payment is more prompt than I expected," he said, gathering up the notes. "Tell me, Luke, did you have to pawn the family silver?"

Luke laughed. "Not for so paltry a sum, I assure you." And with casual indifference, he turned away to exchange greetings with a friend at the adjoining table.

Moncton noticed, however, that Luke still held a good pile of notes in his hand. He rose from the table, pocketed his chips, and clapped Luke on the shoulder. "How about a game of piquet, just the two of us?"

Taffy looked at Luke expectantly. "There's a free table, over there," he pointed out, starting to cross the room.

"Yes, I . . ." Luke began, but suddenly hesitated.

"You may even win back the seven hundred," Monk said in a tone that belied his words.

Taffy chortled. "That's just what we have in mind."

But Luke was staring down at the three hundred pounds still in his hand. Would he be as lucky as he felt? he wondered. He'd often felt lucky early in the evening, but later the cards had proved otherwise. Would he be squandering this three hundred—and perhaps more—as heedlessly as he'd squandered the seven hundred he'd just dropped in Moncton's lap? Was gambling away this three hundred pounds a sensible beginning to this month-long probation?

Another question popped into his mind. Why had he demanded a thousand from Mr. Fairleigh instead of the seven hundred he needed to pay the debt? Was it because he wanted another chance to best Moncton? Or was the real reason merely to shock his mother and that infuriating female man-of-affairs she'd brought with her? Was he as beetleheaded as his behavior seemed to suggest?

It suddenly struck him that he didn't really want to spend the first evening of his newly acquired independence frittering away a piece of his inheritance, even this small one. "On second thought," he said, looking up at Moncton thoughtfully, "I think I'll let you enjoy holding on to the money for a while." Pocketing his remaining bills, he waved goodbye to Monk and the open-mouthed Taffy.

"Don't you want to play?" asked his astonished friend.

"Some other time," Luke said.

There was something lighthearted in his step as he took his leave.

It was not yet ten when he arrived home. Parks, not expecting him so early, was nowhere in evidence. Luke threw his hat and cane on a chair, took a lighted candle from the hall table, and started toward the stairs. Then he saw a dim light shining under the library door and changed his direction. He threw open the door, hoping to see his mother. She was not there, but he was not surprised to see Miss Douglas working at the library table. "Is this not a late hour for you?" he asked.

She started. "My lord! I thought . . . is this not early for you?"

"I asked first."

"I knew I wouldn't sleep," she explained. "Your mother's departure has upset me."

"My mother's *departure?*" He gaped at her in astonishment. "What are you saying? Where has she gone?"

"Home, my lord. To Cheshire. Didn't she tell you?"

"No, not a word." He felt not only surprise but a sharp disappointment; he'd intended to apologize to her for his behavior that afternoon. "Damnation, I could strangle her! Why did she leave so abruptly?"

"I couldn't say, my lord. I believe she does not like being in town."

"No, she never did like staying in London, even when

my father was alive." He stalked over to the fireplace and stared into the flames. "But it's not London that drove her away," he muttered glumly. "I think my behavior today must have overset her."

"Did it?" Jane asked innocently.

He swung around and peered through the dim light at the girl at the writing desk. "You are being very coy. She told you all about it, didn't she?"

"Told me what, my lord?"

"That I behaved badly at the lawyer's office."

"She didn't say anything to me about the events at the lawyer's office. *Did* you behave badly?"

"It depends on one's point of view." He strode across the room to take a closer look at her. "But you *knew* all this! I can see it in your face."

"I knew nothing. But I guessed from Lady Martha's manner that something troublesome had occurred."

"Yes, something troublesome occurred. But what is more troublesome, my girl, is that my mother treats me like a child!"

"Perhaps it's because you sometimes behave like a child."

He stiffened. "Neither you nor my mother can have the slightest notion of how I behave!" he spat out. "You are not here often enough to make a judgment."

"But there are signs . . ."

"What signs?"

"Your constant requests to her for funds, for one thing. These unpaid bills for another." She held up the papers she'd been studying. "Some of these are months old."

He was silenced. Unable to think of a rejoinder, he stomped back to the fireplace.

She got out of her chair. "Would you like me to leave you alone, my lord?"

"No, I shall be going myself in a moment." He kicked a log, causing a shower of sparks to fly up in the air. "She should not have left so soon," he muttered to himself.

"No, she should not," Jane agreed.

He wheeled on her. "And she should not have left you behind to spy on me."

"I'm not here to spy. I'm here to assist you in managing your new financial responsibilities."

"Why should you—and my mother—assume that I cannot manage them on my own?"

"Only because you haven't yet demonstrated that you can do so."

He turned away and stared into the flames again. "You are very glib, Miss Douglas. You have an answer for everything."

"Do I? You surely must know, my lord, that you needn't put up with me if my presence is annoying to you. This is your house. You are the master here. All you have to do to rid yourself of me is to order me to go."

"As easy as that, eh?" He turned to look at her, a gleam of amusement appearing in his eyes. "And should you *like* to be dismissed, Miss Douglas? How would such an act affect you? Would it be a blow?"

She met his eyes with a level look in her own. "I should survive, my lord."

He laughed. "I believe you would. But I don't intend

to exercise my right to dismiss you quite yet. And in the meantime, here are three hundred pounds. Use the money to pay off whatever bills you can."

Jane took the money and gazed at it in surprise. "Did you win this playing at hazard this evening, my lord?"

He cocked an eyebrow at her suspiciously. "What, ma'am, can you possibly know of hazard?"

"A good deal. I know, for instance, that an intelligent player can do better at hazard than at faro, which is strictly a game of chance."

This caught his full attention. "Oh? And how is that?"

"Surely a gambler of your stamp knows this without my telling him. At faro the cards are dealt purely at random. But at hazard, you throw a pair of six-sided dice. Certain mathematical deductions can be made from that."

"Can they indeed?"

Now she looked at him suspiciously. "You're cozzening me, are you not, my lord? Surely you knew that."

"I know that some numbers can be thrown more easily than others—that you're twice as likely to throw a seven as a four, for example—but how did you know?"

"My father taught me to play when I was young. As a mathematical puzzle, you see."

"No, I don't see. How is it a mathematical puzzle?"

"Well, you can calculate the odds. Just as you did when you said you're twice as likely to throw a seven as a four."

"Yes, but I don't know why."

"It's simple, really," she explained. "In each throw of a pair of dice, there are thirty-six possibilities. To make seven, you can throw either a four-and-three, a five-and-two, or a six-and-one. That gives you six chances in thirty-six. But to make four, you can only throw a three-and-one or a two-and-two. That gives you only three chances in thirty-six, making it twice as likely to throw a seven as a four."

He gaped at her, impressed. "Remarkable!" he exclaimed. "My mother was right. You *are* remarkable."

"There is nothing remarkable about simple calculation," she said, a blush suddenly rising in her cheeks.

"I think, ma'am, that you should not denigrate what is a very real, and very admirable, talent."

"Thank you. But, if we may change the subject from my talents to yours, you haven't answered my question. Did you win this money at the gaming table tonight?"

"No. I didn't play tonight."

"Oh?" A small smile lit her face. "It's too bad your mother didn't stay a bit to hear that. She would have been pleased."

"By the fact that I didn't gamble it away?"

"Yes, of course."

"I wouldn't place too much significance on it, Miss Douglas," he said as he sauntered from the room. "I fully intend to return to the gaming tables tomorrow. To play hazard."

ELEVEN

When Jane attempted to pay the bills the next day, she ran headlong into her first problem. Parks refused to give her the household ledgers. "But how am I to record these payments," she asked, "if you don't let me have the account book?"

"His lordship always leaves all financial matters to me," the butler said belligerently.

"Evidently not always," Jane retorted, unaccustomed to such a tone of voice from one of the staff. At Kettering Castle she'd always been treated with respect. But the moment the words had left her tongue she regretted saying them. It was not her purpose to be at odds with the butler. Rather, she hoped to make a friend of him. With Lady Martha gone, she felt the need of support from someone else of influence. "You see, Mr. Parks," she said in a softer voice, "last night his lordship ordered me to pay some of these bills. He left me the money to do it, too."

"He did?" Parks was taken aback. "He didn't say anything about it to me."

"I don't think he's required to ask your permission," Jane pointed out as gently as she could.

"Well, I ain't handing over any account books to you without his permission, so there!" the butler declared stubbornly.

Jane continued to try to be conciliatory. "It's not as if I'm taking over your responsibilities," she explained. "I'm only here temporarily. To set up a new accounting system, you see."

"I don't see why we need a new system when the old one works just fine. You'll get nothing more from me until his lordship gives me orders." With that, he turned on his heel and marched out of the library in a manner that was decidedly out of countenance.

Jane watched him go, a sigh of discouragement welling up in her. But after a moment, she decided to put the problem out of her mind. *Lord Kettering will surely explain to Parks just what I'm here to accomplish,* she told herself, *so there's no need for me to feel concern.* Once Parks understood her situation, she was certain she and the butler could come to friendly terms. In the meanwhile, she busied herself addressing envelopes to those merchants whose bills she could pay.

That evening, the first since Lady Martha had left, Jane ate a lonely dinner at the long, empty table of the family dining room. She had just risen from her chair when his lordship, only partially dressed in his evening clothes—in shirtsleeves, with his neckcloth undone, and without his coat—burst into the room. "Dash it, ma'am, must you disrupt my entire household?" he demanded.

Her eyes widened. "*I?* What—?"

"Parks is beside himself! Burst in on me in my dressing room just before I'd even chosen my waistcoat! He threatens to leave his post at once!"

"Leave his post? Good God, why?"

"It seems you told him that I no longer find him trustworthy. How dare you take it upon yourself to say such a thing to him?"

"I said no such thing," the girl declared, jumping to her feet. "Mr. Parks exaggerates out of all proportion. I merely asked for the household account book."

"What?" Luke blinked in confusion. "The household account book?"

"Yes. I asked to see it. Mr. Parks refused. I think he assumed he was being relieved of the responsibility of keeping the accounts."

Luke eyed her suspiciously. "What did you want the book for?"

"You gave me three hundred pounds last evening. Shouldn't the payments I make with that money be entered into the book?"

"Well, confound it, let *him* enter them if it means so much to him! What difference does it make? Must I be bothered with such trivialities?"

"It makes a difference, my lord. A difference far from trivial. You see, Mr. Parks does not know why I'm here. He should be made to understand that all the household accounts—in fact, everything having to do with your finances—must be turned over to me if I'm to accomplish what I've been brought here to do."

"Then, dash it, why don't *you* explain it to him?"

"I've tried. He will not take my word. It's up to you, my lord, to tell him."

Luke glared at her. "Up to me? Are you daring to educate me on what you judge are my responsibilities?"

"I would not put it in those words, perhaps, but—"

"Then let me put it in other words," he snapped. "You're telling me what to do, is that not so?"

"I suppose . . ."

"Giving me orders! I'll have you know, my girl, that I will not brook being told what to do by a mere chit in my employ!"

"I don't see how I can avoid telling you what to do," she explained with calm logic, "when it is necessary for something to be done, and you're not doing it."

Luke, uncomfortably aware that he was being irrational, found the reasonableness of both her tone and her words the last straw. "*Damnation*," he swore, grasping her by the shoulders so furiously she was almost lifted from the floor, "must you always have a ready answer on your tongue? Am I expected to endure having my household at sixes and sevens so long as you are under my roof?"

Jane stared up at him, aghast. He was going to shake her! Instead of the fury she ought to have felt for his rude, unwarranted behavior, she experienced the same weakness in her knees that had struck her when she'd caught her first glimpse of him. The pressure of his grip on her arms, the angry glitter in his eyes, the unruly curl of hair that hung over his forehead, the closeness of his face to hers—so close she could feel the heat that emanated from his skin—all combined to cause a strange turmoil inside her. She recognized that it was an attraction . . . an attraction so strong it frightened her.

This, she thought, *is a completely senseless reaction.* She should be furious with him. And, being a sensible woman, she could not permit herself to encourage this weakness in herself, much less this ill-temper in him. He was behaving like a brute, and that she could not permit. She wrenched herself from his hold and turned away, fearful that he might see in her face something of what she was feeling. "Am I, my lord, expected to endure being spoken to and manhandled in this way?" she managed, trying by careful enunciation to hide her breathlessness.

"I'm sorry," he said, thrusting back his disordered hair and trying to regain control of his temper. "I didn't mean to . . . I shouldn't have . . ."

"No, you shouldn't have." She rubbed her arms, feeling bruised. "It was . . . brutish."

"Well, dash it," he retorted, "no one in my employ has ever before dared to contradict my every word, as you do."

"I am not in your employ. Your mother is my employer. Therefore, I shall not find it necessary to give you notice that I am leaving. I shall merely remove myself from this house first thing in the morning." She put her chin up and tried, despite her still-trembling knees, to march purposefully to the door.

"Miss Douglas?" His voice was contrite.

She paused but did not turn. "Yes, my lord?"

"I apologize. Forgive my brutishness. I don't usually manhandle the females on my staff. It's only that . . . you do seem to have a way of raising my hackles."

"Then it's just as well I'm leaving."

Luke suddenly realized he did not want her to leave. He needed her; his mother had not been wrong about that. He had only a month to show his mother he could manage his finances, but what did he know about household accounts, ledgers, investments, and the like? But it wasn't only self-interest that made him wish to keep her here. He was shamed by his behavior. Never in his life before had he handled a woman roughly. Repentant, but nevertheless fully aware of his superior position in this household, he crossed the room to the door and faced her. "Come now, Miss Douglas, don't be difficult," he said with a conciliatory smile. "I apologized, did I not? And very contritely, too."

"You are blocking my way, my lord."

"What if I explain to Parks the conditions of your employment, just as you asked me to?" His lips curved up in a wry—and, to her, very appealing—smile. "Complete surrender. Will that make you relent?"

Steeling herself against the temptation toward additional weakness, she shook her head firmly. "I'm afraid not."

"You are a stubborn creature, ma'am. Will you not believe that I'm truly sorry? I wish I could think of stronger words to say it."

"I hardly think words are adequate," she said coldly.

"But I've offered more than words. I've completely surrendered." He was beginning to enjoy this exchange. She was a challenge to him. It was as good as a game. "Isn't there *something* I can do to make amends?" he asked with a sudden grin. "Sell one of my horses? Cut down on the number of my neckcloths? Go up to the old schoolroom and write 'I will never again manhandle

Miss Douglas' twenty times on my slate?"

She did not smile back. "I don't doubt that your boyish charm can be quite effective, my lord, but I fear that I'm no more susceptible to boyish charm than I am to being manhandled. I'd be obliged if you would step aside."

Defeated, he shrugged and did as she asked. As she brushed past him, he murmured, "Mama will be disappointed."

"Yes, she will," Jane agreed, crossing over the threshold without a backward look, "but she'll forgive you, I'm sure."

"No, she won't," he said ruefully. "I don't think she's susceptible to my boyish charm, either."

"You're probably right," Jane threw back over her shoulder as she made for the stairs. "Boyish charm only goes so far."

But oh, blast you, Luke Hammond, she thought as she climbed on still-shaking knees up to the third floor, *your boyish charm goes far enough! And, for my peace of mind, much too far for me.*

TWELVE

Jane woke early after a fretful sleep. She'd been troubled by dreams in which she was trapped in a succession of strange rooms. One of the rooms had contained an enormous bed that was too high to climb upon and that kept growing higher. Another was a library in which every book had a patch on the spine. All of the rooms had several doors, but she'd been unable to open any of them. It had been a dreadful night.

When she rose and threw aside the curtains, she discovered to her dismay that the shrubbery below her window was iced with sleet. Worse, the icy rain was still falling. *Of course,* she thought, her lip curling bitterly, *it would be sleeting!* She'd have to carry her portmanteau through this downpour to the nearest hostelry (goodness knew how far!), where she could catch a stagecoach. She would probably be chilled to the bone by the time she boarded. This ill luck was all of a piece with her entire London experience. It had been unfortunate from the first.

She wondered, as she packed her meager possessions, if she had enough money for the stagecoach fare. It hadn't occurred to her to ask Lady Martha for a part of her salary; she hadn't anticipated the need for expense money. Worried, she paused in her packing and went to her purse. The few coins in her possession came to four shillings and tuppence. She hoped that would be enough to take her back to Cheshire. If it wasn't, she would take the stage as far as she could, and, wherever it was, she'd find herself some sort of employment to earn the rest of the fare.

As she turned to resume packing, her eye fell on the leather-bound Malory that his lordship had given her. How generous he'd appeared to be that day in the library! He hadn't seemed like the same man yesterday, when he'd grasped her upper arms with such force she felt bruised. "Drat him," she muttered aloud, "I'd like to throw his blasted gift back in his face!" Of course she wouldn't do it. She was too much the lady. But at least she'd leave it behind for him to find. It would convey the message that she'd take nothing from him, nothing at all.

She placed the book conspicuously on the dressing table, strapped up her portmanteau, put on her bonnet and shawl, and, with the luggage under her arm, went from the room. She'd just gone a few steps, however, when she turned, ran back, and snatched up the book. She had to keep it after all; it held too many memories, and not all of them of her father.

She slipped the book into the reticule that hung from her waist and started for the back stairs. But before reaching them, she changed her mind about that, too. *I am not some frightened housemaid stealing away in shame because I'd broken a china vase,* she told herself, *and I will not behave like one.* With chin high, she turned and marched down the front stairway, just as she imagined any man-of-affairs might do, especially one in high dudgeon, as she was.

Her air of bravery was wasted—there was no one about. It was just past seven; the staff was probably still at breakfast. But when she reached the front door, she heard her name being called. She turned to find Mr. Parks hurrying toward her across the marble floor of the foyer. In his arms were three large ledger books. "Miss Jane, please wait!" he called nervously.

She waited. He was quite breathless when he came up to her. "Thank goodness I caught you," he gasped. "If you'd left, I'd be in the soup for sure."

"What are you talking about, Mr. Parks?" Jane asked, puzzled. "What has my going to do with you?"

"Everything! Put down your portmanteau, miss, please!" The man appeared to be distraught. "Here, I've brought you the ledgers. I'm truly sorry I didn't give them to you yesterday, when you first asked. Truly sorry."

"You needn't apologize to me," Jane said, trying to console him. "You were only defending your position here. I quite understand. Believe me, Mr. Parks, my leaving is not your fault."

She turned again to the door, but the butler blocked her way. "Please, Miss Jane, you mustn't go! If you do, I'm finished."

"Finished? I don't know what you mean."

"His lordship gave me a royal tongue-lashing yesterday. Said you would not be leaving if I hadn't set up your bristles, and that if I didn't set things to rights, I'd be sacked forthwith."

Jane gaped at him. "Sacked?"

"Those were his very words—'sacked forthwith.' "

"Do you mean *discharged?*"

The butler nodded glumly. "Before the day is out."

"I don't believe it!" Jane exclaimed. "His lordship wouldn't stoop to such . . . such . . ."

"Believe me, he would and he did."

Jane blinked at him, trying to make sense of what she'd heard. "Why, he's trying to intimidate *me* by threatening *you*," she said after a moment. "That's nothing but simple blackmail!"

"I wouldn't call it simple," Parks muttered.

"But it *is* blackmail, and I don't intend to submit to it." Furious, she threw down her portmanteau. "Don't let anyone take this back upstairs," she instructed the butler. "I shall be leaving shortly." And she strode to the stairway.

"Wait, Miss Jane!" the butler cried, dropping the ledgers and running after her in alarm. "Where are you going?"

"I'm going up to face him," she said, mounting the stairs. "Don't worry, Mr. Parks. While I have a breath in my body, I'll not let you lose your post."

"Miss Jane, *no!* He's probably still asleep!"

But she'd already rounded the landing and disappeared from sight. The poor fellow, more discomposed than ever, sat down on the stairs, dropped his head in his hands, and groaned.

Upstairs, Jane stalked down the corridor to the master

bedroom and knocked loudly. In a few moments the door was opened a crack and the valet peeped out. "Ssssh!" he hissed. "His lordship's asleep."

"Yes, Varney, so I supposed," Jane said in a loud, clear voice. "Then I suggest you wake him."

"Are you loony?" the valet asked in a tense whisper. "I ain't ever supposed to wake 'im."

"Today we shall break the rules. Go in and tell him Miss Douglas must see him at once."

"Well, I ain't goin' to do it," was Varney's hissed response, "an' that's final."

"Then I shall," Jane declared, pushing the door open and striding past the astounded valet.

"Wha's the to-do?" came a sleepy voice from the far side of the darkened room.

Jane's eyes could just make out the shape of the bed. "I must speak to you, my lord," she said to the dark shadows.

There was a rustle of bedclothes. "Who's there?"

The valet hurried past her. "It's Miss Douglas, m'lord. I couldn't keep 'er out."

"Miss *Douglas?* Damnation, man, open the curtains. I can't see a thing!"

In a few seconds, a ray of gray light filtered in. As the valet ran from one window to the next, throwing open the draperies, Jane finally was able to see the man. He was sitting up in bed, wearing a ruffled nightshirt and a bewildered expression on his sleep-lined face. He squinted at her. "It *is* Miss Douglas," he muttered in disbelief.

They stared at each other for a moment as his lordship tried to shake his still-sleepy brain into functioning.

"What's that tapping sound?" he asked thickly, running his fingers through his disordered locks.

"It's sleet, my lord," Jane offered. "Blowing against the panes."

"Is it? Blast! I wanted to go riding this morning." He rubbed his eyes and then peered at her. "Is there some reason, ma'am, why you're standing here in my bedroom?"

"I *tried* to prevent—" the valet began, hovering about the bed nervously.

But Jane interrupted him. "A very good reason, my lord. I came to demand that you retract your threat against Mr. Parks."

"What threat? What the devil are you babbling about?"

"You told him you would discharge him—*sack him forthwith*, I believe were your words—if he did not convince me to remain in this house, is that not so?"

His lordship squinted at her, trying to remember. "I might have done. Well, Miss Douglas, *did* he convince you to remain?"

"I should say not! I will not be intimidated by such vile threats."

He eyed her in annoyance. "Is that what you broke into my sleep to tell me?"

"Well, yes."

"I *warned* her—" Varney tried again.

His lordship waved the valet aside. "Seems to me, ma'am, that you're making a quite unnecessary to-do over this. Why didn't you just leave?"

"I have every intention of doing so. But not until you

give me your word that Mr. Parks will not be discharged because of it."

"My, my," he said, cocking his head, "I had no idea you felt such loyalty to my butler. After all, you've been here only a few days."

"You are not being honest, my lord. You knew perfectly well that I would object to your threat. You wouldn't have made it if you believed I would ignore it."

"Touché, ma'am. Your point. But I did not anticipate your bursting into my bedroom to make it."

"What *did* you anticipate I would do?"

"That you would relent and remain here as you promised my mother."

Jane crossed her arms over her chest. "I have no intention of relenting."

"You, ma'am, are the most stubborn young woman I've ever encountered." He looked at her intently. "Are you truly adamant about leaving, no matter what I might do?"

"Yes, I am."

He sighed. "Very well, go. Take your leave. Depart."

"Does that mean I have your word about Mr. Parks?"

He shrugged in defeat. "Yes, of course," he said, adding in a lowered voice, "I didn't really intend to discharge him."

Jane wasn't sure she should believe him. "You certainly convinced him that you would."

His lordship turned away and threw his legs over the side of the bed. "I had to," he admitted as he rose, "if he was to be frightened enough to convince you."

"Oh, I *see*." She expelled a small breath, surprised to

realize that Lord Kettering would go to such lengths to keep her.

"It was a gamble," he said, waving aside poor Varney, who was following him about, trying to help him into a long Chinese-silk robe. "I lost. But I've been trained to be a good loser. So I bid you goodbye, Miss Douglas. Godspeed."

"Thank you, my lord," she said, all the anger she'd built up completely dissipated. "Goodbye, then."

She started to the door, while he pattered over in bare feet to one of the tall windows, the tail of his nightshirt flapping behind him. The sight of the iced foliage and the steady downpour shocked him. "I say, Miss Douglas," he called after her, "what arrangements have you made for travel?"

With her hand already on the doorknob, she paused. "Arrangements?" She peered at him as he stood outlined by the gray light from the window, his tousled hair, loose nightshirt, and bare feet making him seem appealingly boyish. "I intend to catch the stage," she said, hoping he would not notice the catch in her voice.

"It's sleeting out there. Dreadful day! Tell Parks to put my carriage at your disposal."

This was another surprise. And a most welcome one. "*Thank* you, my lord, that is most kind."

"Not at all. I have no need of it today, and it will have returned from Cheshire by tomorrow."

She gaped at him. This was an even greater surprise. "Cheshire? You cannot mean for the carriage to take me all the way! I need it only to the nearest coaching inn."

He turned from the window. "You will use my coach to take you home," he barked, pulling the robe from his valet's hand and shrugging into it. "*All the way* home! And I'd be much obliged if you'd *not dispute my every word!*"

"Yes, my lord," she murmured and left the room. She retraced her steps, but very slowly. *Will I ever understand him?* she asked herself. Was the man who had handled her so outrageously the day before the same one who had just offered her his carriage? All the way to Cheshire? Who had never intended to discharge Mr. Parks but had only used the threat to keep her here? Who, in the gloomy light of the window, had looked so gentle and vulnerable—and so confoundedly handsome, too—that she'd had to fight the urge to brush back the hair from his forehead and caress his cheek?

Mr. Parks was still sitting on the bottom step when she came down. He looked up at her, his chins quivering. "Well?" he asked tensely. "What passed upstairs? Are we both to be thrown out in the cold?"

"No, no," she assured him. "Everything is fine. His lordship never intended to sack you. It was only a ruse."

Parks got to his feet, his face lighting up in relief. "Truly? Only a ruse?" He grasped her hand and shook it excitedly. "You are a wonder, Miss Jane, and that's a fact! I don't know how to thank you!"

"But really, Mr. Parks, there's no need," she insisted. "You have nothing to thank me for. You were never in any danger."

"Perhaps, and perhaps not," he said, beaming at her, "but the way you went charging up those stairs, well, I won't ever forget—"

A sound on the stairs made them turn. It was Varney, running down. "His lordship sent me to tell you, Mr.

Parks, that Miss Douglas is to have the carriage," he announced breathlessly. "Ye're to tell Hodgkins, at the stables, that it's to take 'er to Cheshire. He'll know which horses to use."

Jane was astounded at this additional sign of thoughtfulness. Not only had he offered the ride; he'd acted to make the offer a reality. Even Lady Martha, who was generally kind, had never been thoughtful enough to offer a carriage for her in bad weather, much less to instruct her stableman to make sure it was done.

"I'll go at once," Mr. Parks was saying.

Jane grasped his arm. "No, Mr. Parks," she said, "don't bother." She took a deep breath and turned to the valet. "Mr. Varney," she said, "will you please go back upstairs and tell his lordship that I've changed my mind? I shall not be leaving after all. I, too, can be a good loser."

THIRTEEN

Suddenly the atmosphere in the household changed for Jane. There was a warmth in the servants' attitude toward her that had not been there before. Footmen who'd never even acknowledged her presence now gave her respectful greetings every time she passed them in the corridors. Parks exchanged conspiratorial grins whenever he met her eye. Mrs. Hawkins, the housekeeper, sent Meggie to inquire about her favorite foods. Extra blankets and towels appeared in her bedroom. Meggie came up at dawn every morning to start her fire, despite Jane's remonstrances. Jane felt more than welcome—she felt pampered. And all this was probably caused by Mr. Parks spreading the word that she'd saved his post, which of course she hadn't done at all.

Unfortunately, her satisfaction with this change in the atmosphere was short-lived. As soon as she'd examined the ledger books, she knew that a great deal of unpleasantness lay ahead. The good feelings between her and the staff would probably come to an abrupt end.

There were three ledgers: one for the household expenses, one for the stable costs, and one for the viscount's personal expenditures. Each one revealed that there were serious problems in the way money was spent.

Jane decided to attack the household problems first. On a quiet afternoon, when his lordship was attending a sale at Tattersall's and was not expected back before nightfall, she asked Mr. Parks to join her in the library. "Please close the door," she asked as soon as he appeared.

His eyebrows rose. "Is something amiss, Miss Jane?"

She motioned to a chair beside her worktable. "A great deal, I fear, Mr. Parks," she said flatly. She paused until he'd seated himself. Then, without mincing words, she made the necessary accusation. "It appears to me that you and Mrs. Hawkins have been stealing from his lordship for a very long time."

"What?" He reddened, stared, and half rose from the chair. "Did I hear you aright, ma'am?"

"You heard. And don't ma'am me, Mr. Parks. It will do you no good to toadeat me. These charges for meats, flour, sugar and other staples, all the kitchen and household expenses, and these enormous liquor bills are consistently higher than they should be."

The butler's chins quivered, but he stuck out his jaw stubbornly. "I don't know what you're talking about, miss."

"Don't you? Then look at this. You paid to Berry Brothers, Wine Merchants, nineteen pounds, seven shillings for one dozen bottles of port wine. One would expect the cost to be, at most, twelve guineas. And a dozen bottles every fortnight? I've never seen his lordship drink. If he does, it isn't here at home. Who does all that drinking, I wonder?"

Mr. Parks gulped. Jane watched with considerable distress as his face paled. She was taking no pleasure in this interview. In the stress of the moment, neither one of them heard the latch of the library door turn.

Jane went on, trying to disregard the pain she felt in making these accusations. "And this payment for bread for the week. Thirty-six loaves. That would be almost two loaves a day for each person on the staff. Am I expected to accept such an inflated number? And the cost—twenty-nine shillings thrupence. Isn't that a bit exorbitant?"

"This is London, Miss Jane, not Cheshire," the butler said coldly. "Prices are higher here."

"I expected you to say that, so I took a walk to the bakery this morning and purchased a loaf. It cost me sixpence. That would make the cost of thirty-six loaves about eighteen shillings, a good deal less than twenty-nine."

"Per'aps the bak'ry overcharges us," he muttered, now on the defensive.

"The butcher shop, too? Look here. Eight pounds of pork, more than ten shillings. Strange, when the cost is no more than eight pence a pound. And in addition, you have bills in the same week for mutton, beef, salmon, and sole. Interesting, is it not, when his lordship hardly ever dines at home?"

"The staff has to eat, too."

"I know that, Mr. Parks. But not like kings."

"I s'pose you'd like us to eat nothing but bread and cheese," he whined in desperation.

"What I'd like—rather, what I'd *expect* in any proper household—is for you to order no more than what the staff needs for an ample diet, and not to take advantage of your position to charge an extortionate price for it."

He drew himself up in histrionic offense. "You're accusing me of *cheating*, then?"

She clenched her fists to remain firm. "I am. Both you and the housekeeper."

Mr. Parks, the embodiment of offended majesty, rose to his feet. "Easy for you to make accusations, miss," he declared, his voice and chins quivering with self-justifying passion. "You ain't worried about your future, bein' in her ladyship's good graces like you are. She'll prob'ly take proper care of you. An' more'n likely, some day soon you'll marry some chap that's in trade an' have yourself a cushy old age. But Mrs. Hawkins and me, well, we have to think of what's to happen to us later, don't we? Who's goin' to keep us from starvin' in the gutter when we're too old to be in service? We has to take care of ourselves."

Jane was not without sympathy. Servants had difficult lives in this far-from-perfect world. But she couldn't find it in herself to justify these signs of corruption. "Lady Martha supports several of her elderly servants," she pointed out. "Certainly the Viscount will do the same."

"Nothing so certain about that," the butler countered. "His lordship ain't like his mother. He don't give us any thought that I can see. Is it a such a terrible crime, then, for us to put a little bit of blunt by for a rainy day?"

Jane shook her head. "From what I see here in this

book, it's a great deal more than a little bit. I calculate you've put by enough 'blunt' to keep you in silk for years."

The color faded from the butler's lips, and his cheeks turned ashen. Although his guilt was clearly evident, he nevertheless tried to maintain an air of truculent resistance with the feeble, last-ditch excuse of miscreants everywhere: "It don't hurt nobody."

She stood up and faced him, eye to eye. "It isn't *honest*, Mr. Parks."

He blinked at her for a moment before he lowered his head and turned away in defeat. "I s'pose you'll tell his lordship," he said glumly, walking to the fireplace. "It's the honest thing to do."

She made no answer.

"He'll sack me for sure." The thought made his knees give way, and he had to clutch the mantelpiece for support. "Funny, ain't it?" he said, glancing at her over his shoulder. "Just the other day you fought like the devil to save my post for me. And now you're causing me to lose it."

"I just *discovered* the crime, Mr. Parks. I didn't *commit* it."

"No, you didn't. That's true." He leaned his forehead against the mantel and heaved a great sigh. "You're right. Right as rain. I may as well face it—the blame's all mine."

She sank down on her chair. "I don't want you to be sacked, Mr. Parks. What I want is for this dishonesty to stop."

His head came round at once. "You mean—?"

"I mean that you should begin a new ledger book. A

clean slate. All purchases should be moderately made and honestly recorded."

Color came slowly back to his lips and hope sprang into his eyes. "Are you saying you *won't* tell his lordship?"

"If I have your word—and Mrs. Hawkins's, too—that there will be no more of this. Not one trumped-up charge. Not one mendacious bill. Not one false, perjurious penny on these pages."

He ran across the room to her chair and dropped on his knees. "I swear it, Miss Jane! On the soul of my sainted mother in heaven!" He clutched her hand and pressed it to his lips. "Bless you, miss, bless you!"

She pulled her hand away. "Please get up, Mr. Parks. There's no need for such excessive gratitude."

"Yes, there is," he insisted in a choked voice, getting unsteadily to his feet. "That you trust me enough for this second chance is cause enough for gratitude."

"I'm taking your sworn word, Mr. Parks, but not completely on trust. You may be sure I shall keep a wary eye on the ledger while I remain here, and whoever takes my place will be instructed to do the same. So watch your step. And you'd best warn Mrs. Hawkins, too."

Outside the library door Luke chose this moment to back silently away. He didn't want to be discovered eavesdropping, but he was glad he'd done it. In the last few minutes, he'd learned a great deal—about his butler, his "man of business," and himself. What he'd learned about himself was painful: his staff thought him selfish and unfeeling. What he learned about the butler was useful: he'd be less naive about the accounts in the future. But what he'd learned about Jane Douglas was astounding. This mere slip of a girl had acted as sleuth, prose-cutor, and judge. She'd detected an ongoing fraud, she'd drawn a confession of guilt from the perpetrator, and she'd passed down a sentence. It was not a very punitive sentence; he himself would have been harsher. Parks was right to suppose that he would have been sacked. But perhaps Miss Douglas's decision was wiser. She'd been kind and forgiving. As a result, the household would continue to function as smoothly as before, but there would be no more stealing. And it was all done quietly, without creating a stir and without involving him in an awkward foofaraw. "You were right, Mama," he mur-mured aloud as he climbed the stairs, "your Jane *is* a rare gem."

FOURTEEN

Luke dressed with his usual care, although his plans for the evening were not particularly exciting. He was promised to Lady Shelford for her monthly soiree, but he didn't expect to enjoy it. Lady Shelford had a habit of forcing him to dance attendance on young ladies of her own choosing, and her choices were usually not his. He'd warned his friend, Ferdie Shelford, that he intended to cut out of his mother's fete early. He wanted time to indulge in a little gambling at the club before he went to pay a late-night call on Dolly.

As he made his way up the crowded stairway of Lady Shelford's brightly lit town house, exchanging warm greetings with friends as he passed, Luke expected his spirits to rise. He usually enjoyed tossing pleasantries about with friends. Tonight, however, a strange feeling of ennui enveloped him. He hoped it would soon pass. He did not like this feeling one bit.

At the top of the stairs Lady Shelford stood greeting guests. She gave a glad cry at the sight of him. "Luke, my dearest boy, I've been speaking of you. Come and meet my favorite niece, who's visiting from Lincolnshire. Charlotte, my love, this is Luke Hammond, Lord Kettering, whom I told you of. Luke, make your leg to Miss Charlotte Gardine, my sister's daughter."

"A pleasure, Miss Gardine," Luke said, bowing. It actually was a pleasure, for Miss Gardine was more appealing than he'd expected. She was tall, slim-waisted, with a pretty mouth, clear blue eyes, and an air of serene confidence. Their first exchange of conversation was a pleasure, too, for in response to Luke's questions about her home in Lincolnshire and her first impressions of London, she neither giggled nor simpered. He was almost cheered. Perhaps the evening would turn out to be more enjoyable than he'd anticipated.

He fully expected a return to good spirits. When his hostess required him to partner Miss Gardine to dinner, he was perfectly content to do so. But that was where disillusionment slipped in—Miss Charlotte Gardine's true colors began to show.

During the first course, Miss Gardine introduced the subject of horses, and, before he knew it, she was hinting that, when Luke came round to take her riding the next morning, she would be quite ready. He gaped at her, for he'd made no such offer.

During the second course she suggested that they would undoubtedly see much of each other during the month of her stay. What had he said to lead her to that assumption?

And when the ladies rose to leave the gentlemen to their port, she made it quite clear that, when he rejoined the ladies, she expected him to stand up with her for at least three dances. Surely she knew that a man who danced three times with a girl was signaling definite designs on her. How could Charlotte Gardine believe he had designs on her, when he'd already said he would not be staying for the dancing?

Her presumptuous expectations surprised and irked him. Her air of confident serenity now seemed more like self-satisfied hauteur. Just because he'd offered her his arm for dinner was no reason for the young woman to conclude that he was interested in courtship.

When the men were left to themselves, Luke took a place beside Ferdie Shelford. Ferdie was a bookish fellow whose thick spectacles had made him a laughingstock at school but who had since earned the respect of his peers. Although not sufficiently proficient at sports to be considered a Corinthian, he was welcomed among them for his remarkable memory for sporting statistics. If one wanted to know who scored highest at the Cricket match at Harrow in '07, or the time achieved by the winner of the footrace at the Conduit Club, one had only to ask Ferdie. Luke liked him, not only for those things but for his exceedingly generous nature. Although the presumptuous Charlotte was his cousin, Luke felt sure he could speak frankly to Ferdie. He pulled his chair close to the fellow, leaned over, and whispered, "I say, Ferdie, whatever gave this cousin of yours, Charlotte, the notion that I'm wooing her?"

"Good God, did she take that notion?" Ferdie rolled his eyes heavenward. "I wish I could explain it. A bit smug, our Charlotte, I'm afraid. Mama says she's quite a belle in Lincolnshire. Perhaps that's made her expect every man she meets to dangle at her shoestrings."

"Well, I've no wish to dangle," Luke said. "In this case, Ferdie, old man, I think the better part of valor is to execute a strategic retreat. I'm off to the club. Make my excuses to your mother, will you?"

He was down the stairs and on his way to the club before the gentlemen at Lady Shelford's table had returned to the ladies. Although it was not yet ten, there was already a game of hazard under the way, with a crowd surrounding the players. He was welcomed with familiar greetings and soon had the dice in his hand.

He threw a seven, and several of his supporters among the observers bet that he would "nick it." But he threw a four. A quick calculation of the odds that Jane had taught him indicated that his chances of throwing the matching four were two to one. He bet a hundred, and several of the observers joined in the bet. He did manage to throw a four, and won. There was a loud cheer. "Luke's synonymous with luck tonight!" someone shouted.

Luke laughed. "Don't count on it. Whenever Lady Luck gives me a kiss, I always wonder what blow she's saving up to strike me with later."

He was right. At his next turn he lost all he'd made. As he watched the winners take his money, he suddenly wondered why he was spending his time this way. Before this, losing had always driven him to keep trying to make up his losses, but not tonight. Tonight, inexplicably, he felt bored and restless. He wanted to get away.

As soon as possible he excused himself and left. He hoped that an evening in Dolly's arms would help him lose this disheartening feeling of aimlessness.

Dolly welcomed him with the same glad smile he'd

been receiving from friends all evening, but his unaccountable mood prevented him from responding with equal enthusiasm. Yet he could not blame Dolly for his discontent. She'd done everything she could to please. She looked enticing, dressed in a flowing dressing gown of a soft, sheer fabric, her hair hanging loose and curled oh-so-slightly round her face, and her red, full-lipped mouth pursed for kissing. She'd set a table with a number of things she knew he liked: a platter of little apricot soufflés, gooseberries with truffles and Bavarian cheese. A bottle of his favorite wine stood cooling in a silver bucket. Everything was arranged to perfection. Yet, again, all he wanted to do was to get away.

He responded to her welcoming embrace, and he smilingly admired the new draperies and pieces of furniture that she'd acquired in her redecoration. But before long, he announced with regret that he was unable to stay. None of her protestations—even the exaggeratedly tearful ones—induced him to change his mind.

As he made his way home, he mulled over his strange behavior. Something was definitely different about him. His usual pursuits seemed pointless, his usual amusements unamusing. What, he wondered in alarm, was happening to him?

FIFTEEN

࿔☙⚜❧࿔

All during the following day Jane could not shake off her feeling of depression. The business with Mr. Parks had revolted her. That such kindly-seeming people as Mr. Parks and Mrs. Hawkins could be guilty of corruption darkened her view of human nature. And, what was more troubling, she wasn't sure of her own motives. Why had she agreed to keep the information from the Viscount? Did she do it in sympathy for the servants' plight or to keep from having to face their resentment? Was she kind or merely cowardly?

Worst of all was her feeling of loneliness. Without a single friend, she was imprisoned in this vast house and forced to play the repressive role of custodian to the Viscount's fortune. That's what she was, a Constable of Finance. What sort of role was that for a young, vital woman?

Except for the library, there was no place here for enjoyment, no outlet for her spirits to lift from the doldrums. Even the act of eating was depressing. Lady Mar-

tha had generously decreed that she was to take her
meals with the "family," but there was no family here.
Her ladyship herself was gone, leaving only the Viscount to dine with. She would have enjoyed his company—at least there would be some conversation over
the soup—but his lordship's habits of eating were peculiar. He breakfasted much later than she, took luncheon on the fly, and never dined at home. So, day after
day, she was forced to sit alone at the round table of the
morning room, her food served by a footman who
treated her with too much awe. It made her feel like a
leper.

That evening, too disheartened to subject herself to
another solitary dinner, she decided not to go down to
dine at all. Instead, she lit a candle, sat down at her
dressing table, removed the restricting tucker from round
her neck, took down her hair, and, thus relaxed, began
to read a book of poems by Cowper that she'd brought
up from the library. However, when she found herself
dripping pathetic tears over simplistic lines like

What peaceful hours I once enjoyed!
How sweet their memory still!
But they have left an aching void
The world can never fill

she shut the book in annoyance. She was a sensible
woman, not the sort to indulge in foolish self-pity. More-
over, she was suddenly very hungry. She got up, took a
quick look in her little mirror, and, deciding that she
needn't bother to pin back her hair when there was no-

body to see it, picked up her candle and went down to dine.

The morning room was dark. She set her candle on the table, wondering if she'd been completely forgotten by the staff. But only a moment after she'd seated herself, Parks appeared in the doorway and cleared his throat. When she glanced up at him curiously, he threw her a warning look. Before she could interpret his meaning, he stepped aside to permit the Viscount himself to enter. "Tell Mrs. Hawkins I'll take my dinner here," his lordship said to the butler before turning to Jane. "That is, if you don't mind my joining you, Miss Douglas."

"Of course I don't," she responded, startled. She'd never before known him to be at home at this hour. "But shouldn't you prefer taking your dinner properly in the small dining room?"

"The small dining room seats eight. I'd much prefer the intimacy of this room. I don't think it *im*proper, do you?"

"No, of course not," she said quickly.

He took a seat and looked round at Parks. "Good God, fellow, it's as dark as Hades in here. Do you always make Miss Douglas dine in such gloom? Have Joseph bring in a candelabrum."

"Yes, my lord," Parks said, hovering over him. "Is there anything in particular you'd like for dinner? We have pearled barley soup and trout provençale for the first course. And Mrs. Hawkins can prepare some poultry fillets *à la marechale* in a trice. Or, if you wouldn't mind waiting a bit, sautéed pheasant with truffles."

"What is Miss Douglas having?"

"Mutton pâté à l'Anglaise, isn't it, miss?" Parks asked her.

"Why, er, yes," Jane answered awkwardly. The question, and her answer, made her feel like a conspirator in a deception; she'd never before been asked what she wished to eat. Her meals always consisted of whatever the housekeeper chose to serve.

"Mutton paté will be fine," his lordship said.

"And some wine, my lord?" Parks asked, throwing Jane a glinting look.

"Why isn't there a bottle on the table?" Luke asked. "Aren't you having any wine, Miss Douglas?"

"Miss Douglas doesn't usually take spirits, my lord," the butler said.

"Perhaps she will this evening. Bring up some port, will you, Parks?"

Parks nodded, threw another there-I-told-you-so glance at Jane (a glance that his lordship, though amused by it, pretended not to see), and took his leave.

"Do you always take your meals here?" his lordship asked when they were alone. "I thought Mama said you were to eat at the family table."

"Do you mean in the small dining room?" She threw him a quick grin. "Where there's seating for eight?"

"Touché, ma'am. It *is* much cozier here."

She had a question for him, too. "Is there some special reason you are not dining at your club tonight?"

"No special reason," he replied. "I'm bored with the club dinners. Always roast beef and kidney pie. Besides, I've been wishing to speak to you."

"To me?" This was a greater surprise than his presence. "What about?"

"What do you think? About the accounts, of course."

"The accounts? But didn't you say—and quite firmly, too—that you had no interest in them?"

"I changed my mind."

"I'm delighted to hear it. I would very much like to speak to you about them. About the stable accounts in particular."

"Go ahead, then. I'm all ears."

"You are stabling nine horses at great expense, my lord. And I—"

"Eight, I'm afraid," he said with a sigh. "I . . . er . . . lost one."

"But you went this very day to Tattersall's, where I understand horses are sold, so I must assume you are now in possession of another one."

"Your assumption is incorrect," he said, his cheerful demeanor gone. "I did not buy another one. I was outbid."

"If you expect condolences, my lord, you shall not get them. I fail to see why you have need of so many horses."

"My stable, ma'am," he declared with unmistakable implacability, "is the one area where I do not intend to practice economy. I will brook no interference there."

"But, my lord," she objected, braving his displeasure, "how can you defend the possession of so many horses? It seems to me that five—four for the coach and one for riding—would be more than adequate—"

"It seems to *me*, ma'am, that your opinion is less than adequate. What can a mere slip of a girl, one who's been buried in ledgers and accounts, know about horses?"

"I've not always been buried in ledgers and accounts.

I once had a horse of my own. I was thought to be a rather fine horsewoman, too, if I may say so."

"Were you indeed?" He leaned toward her, peering at her through the dim candlelight. "You, ma'am, are a constant astonishment to me."

"I don't see what is so astonishing about my having had—"

But she didn't finish, for the footman, Joseph, came in at that moment with a brightly burning candelabrum. He was followed in by Parks, who carried the wine, and another footman carrying a large tray with a soup tureen and several covered dishes on it. While the manservants all busily served the soup and portioned out the trout, Luke studied the face of the girl opposite him. She was quite lovely, he realized in some surprise. He hadn't taken particular notice before. He saw now, in the light of eight candles, that her bright eyes were not brown but a striking greenish-gray and that an appealing dimple appeared in her left cheek at the merest twitch of her lips. Her hair, which had always been primly pinned in a coil at the nape of her neck, now hung about her face in careless waves. He could see now that it was a glowing auburn rather than the faded brown it had seemed before. And with her neck and shoulders bared, she gleamed with inner warmth. Tonight she was not in any detail the prim, Friday-faced bluestocking he'd once judged her to be.

When Parks and the footmen had served the food, his lordship waved them all out of the room. "So you're a fine horsewoman, eh?" he asked, pouring a glass of port for her.

"I was," she said. "It's been many years since I last sat a horse."

"Oh? Why is that? Did you take a fall or have an accident?"

"Really, my lord, isn't that a rather naive question? I'm your mother's secretary. A servant. Servants do not keep horses."

"No, of course they don't. Foolish of me. But in your case, this was not always so?"

"My father, while he lived, kept his family in comfortable circumstances." She held her wineglass up to the candlelight, staring into the red liquid as if it contained scenes of her happier past. "I had a lovely, gentle hack for my very own."

"I see. Your father did not leave his family well provided for, I take it."

"My father had a nobleman's taste. He lived beyond his means and died a pauper." She threw a little smile across the table at him. "Perhaps that should be a lesson to you."

"A cautionary tale, eh?" He returned her smile with a mock glower. "If you're suggesting that my having a stable of eight horses is living beyond my means," he retorted, "you don't know the full extent of my fortune."

"Even a *great* fortune can be dissipated by immoderate spending, my lord," she said primly.

He snorted. "Spoken like a veritable parson. A cliché for the sermon of the week." He cocked an eyebrow at her. "What a little prig you pretend to be, Miss Douglas."

The word *prig* cut her to the quick. "A prig I may be, but—"

"I did not call you a prig. I said you *pretend* to prig-gishness."

"There's no pretense in what I said. I believe every word, even if it is a priggish cliché."

The second course was served, but Jane could not eat. The thought that his lordship might really consider her a prig was terribly disturbing. Was she truly a prig? Or was it her assignment—being the constable of his finances—that made her seem so in his eyes? She glanced over at him. He was looking at her with an expression she could not fathom, but it was not dislike. There was a warmth in his eyes she'd not seen there before. A man would not look at a woman that way if he thought her a prig, would he?

She felt her color rise. She had to escape from his gaze at once or he would see her agitation. She dropped her eyes from his and got up from her chair. "I beg you to excuse me, my lord. I'm . . . rather tired."

He rose, also. "But you've barely touched your mutton paté, and it's quite delicious."

"The soup was enough for me. I'm no longer hungry. Please don't disturb yourself on my account."

"Very well, ma'am, go along," he said, feeling disappointed. He crossed the room and held the door for her. "Good night, Miss Douglas."

"Good night, my lord."

She took only a step over the threshold before his voice stopped her. "Would you care to try riding again?" he asked.

She stopped short. "What?"

"I have a sweet little mare who'd be quite perfect for

you. Spirited but not wild. You may take her out whenever you wish."

"*I?* Take one of your horses *riding?*" The offer was astonishing.

"Yes, why not?"

"But I . . . Surely it can't be proper for me to . . . for you to . . ."

"I see nothing improper about it. I sometimes think, ma'am, that your ideas of propriety are too . . . too—"

"Priggish?" she offered, that little dimple appearing in her cheek.

"Deucedly so. Good God, woman, don't you *want* to go riding?"

"Of course, but—"

"But what?"

"What will people think? The staff—?"

"But me no *buts*, ma'am. If I have no objection to your making use of my stable, why should anyone else?"

She could not believe she'd understood him. "You're not suggesting that I go riding with *you*, are you?"

"Not with me. I don't ride with females. That would be much too sedate for me. I'll have one of the grooms accompany you. My stableman, Hodgkins, will arrange it all. He can surely procure a sidesaddle for you. When do you think you'd like to go?"

She shook her head. "It is very kind of you to offer, my lord. Very kind. I thank you most sincerely, but . . . I couldn't."

"More *buts*? Why couldn't you?"

"It's not . . . I'm not . . . well, you see, my lord, I don't even possess a riding costume!"

"Oh. I never thought of that." He looked nonplussed,

but only for a moment. "Wait! Mama used to ride in the park in her younger days. There must be something stowed away in her chests or cupboards that you can use. I'll have Mrs. Hawkins see to it."

She stared at him agape. The prospect of sitting a horse again was as thrilling as it was unexpected. She could hardly speak. "B-b-but, my lord—" she stammered.

"Enough!" He waved her off. "No more objections. My mind's made up. You'll go riding tomorrow sometime before noon. The Ladies Mile in Hyde Park should be suitable. I see many young women riding there. And when I see you tomorrow at . . . well, let us say at tea . . ." He suddenly leaned down and squinted into her eyes. "You do take tea, don't you?"

"Well, only a small pot at my desk."

"You'll take a real tea tomorrow, right here in this room."

"T-Tea, my lord? With *you?*"

"Yes, with me. Why the surprise? I've been known to take tea."

"Yes, my lord, I suppose you have," she said with a sudden twinkle, "although I've never witnessed it."

"You may take my word, Miss Saucy Tongue. And when you join me at tea tomorrow, I shall expect a full report on the entire riding experience."

"A report?"

"Yes, a report on how you liked the mare . . . if she was too spirited for you, for example. And on how you found the bridle path. And if the saddle was satisfactory, that sort of thing. But no more questions now. My dinner will be cold, and all your fault. Take yourself off to bed."

SIXTEEN

When she woke next morning, Jane warned herself not to expect too much. In the first place, his lordship might already have forgotten his offer to let her ride his mare. In the second place, Mrs. Hawkins might not have been able to find any suitable riding dress for the purpose. And in the third place, it might be raining.

But a peep through the curtains showed a sunny sky. And, just as the clock in the hallway struck seven, Mrs. Hawkins and Meggie entered her bedroom, both of them breathless and both carrying an assortment of clothing. His lordship had not forgotten, and Mrs. Hawkins hadn't failed her. All her doubts had been allayed. Before noon that day, it seemed, she would be riding a horse, just as the Viscount had promised.

With the help of a needle and some well-placed pins, Mrs. Hawkins soon had her fitted out with a full-skirted black gown, a high-necked white tucker, and a tight-waisted riding coat. "Per'aps a little full in the bosom," the housekeeper said, eyeing her critically, "but otherwise it could've been made for ye."

Meggie held out a tall, narrow-brimmed riding hat and, reaching up, placed it on Jane's head, cocking it at a stylish angle over one eye. "There!" She stepped back to see the effect. "Oh, miss," she cried, awed, "you do look a real lady!"

The housekeeper clapped her hands together. "Yes, indeed, Miss Jane, you look in fine feather! I couldn't be more pleased."

When they'd gone, Jane studied as much of herself as she could in her little mirror. The rakish angle of the hat was too daring, she felt, and she adjusted it to sit more squarely on her head, but otherwise the costume seemed perfectly acceptable. She could hardly wait to get to the stable. She hurried to the door, but there she paused. Then, turning back to the mirror, she cocked the hat at the angle at which Meggie had originally set it. "Let me be rakish," she said aloud, grinning at herself in the glass, "just this once."

Two hours later Luke and his friend Taffy, after having tired themselves out with a good long gallop along Hyde Park's sandy bridle path, were trotting at their leisure when Taffy cried out, "My word, Luke, ain't that your mare over there? I think your stableman's let some blasted female ride her!"

"It's all right, Taffy. I know all about it."

Taffy's eyebrows rose. "You do?" He peered at the distant rider intently until she disappeared round a curve in the path. "She looks an out-and-outer!" he exclaimed. "Who the devil is she?"

Luke laughed. "You'd never guess. That, my dear Taffy, is my new man of business."

Taffy blinked at him stupidly. "It's a *girl*," he said.

"I'm quite aware of that. Mama brought her to me from Cheshire to get my finances in order. Claimed the girl's a wonder. And, do you know, Taffy, I really think she is."

Later that day Taffy was joined at luncheon at the club by his friend Ferdie Shelford. Ferdie looked agog behind his spectacles. "Who was that delicious game pullet riding one of Luke Hammond's horses in the park this morning?" he asked as soon as he'd seated himself.

Taffy grinned. "She's no game pullet, Ferdie," he said conspiratorially. "You'll never credit it, but she's Luke's man of business."

Ferdie Shelford gaped. "What are you saying? *Man* of business? That lovely creature?"

Taffy nodded. "Seems she's talented in financial matters. Luke says she's a wonder."

After Taffy left him, Ferdie wandered over to where George Poole was drinking his luncheon. "Did you notice the lovely young woman riding Luke's mare this morning?" he asked.

George's face brightened. "I'll say! A great gun if ever I saw one." His interest was piqued enough to cause him to put down his glass. "Don't tell me you know who she is?"

"You won't believe it," Ferdie said, preening with the

pride of being the possessor of secret information, "but she's his man of business!"

George Poole's heavy eyebrows rose. "That's ridiculous," he sneered. "I *don't* believe it."

Ferdie responded in an awed whisper. "I know. I wouldn't have believed it, either, except that I have it from Taffy Fitzgerald. He says that Luke says she's a wonder."

George Poole could hardly wait to be off. Excited at being in possession of so choice an item of gossip, he gulped down his drink, made his excuses to Ferdie, and ran off. There was one person in particular who would be interested in his news—his friend Sir Rodney Moncton. He found Monk downing a tankard of ale in the lounge at Brooke's. "Monk, old fellow, you won't believe what I learned about Luke Hammond," George said in an eager undervoice, pulling up a chair. "He has a new man of business."

Monk merely shrugged. "I thought as much. He had to be getting some new advice to have paid off his debt to me so promptly. The fellow's been behaving like a pudding-heart of late. Won't even sit down at the tables these days."

"Stubble it for a moment, will you, Monk? You're not taking my point." George, his eyes shining gleefully, pulled his chair closer. "It's who the adviser *is* that's the point."

"What difference does it make who he is?" Monk asked, waving the matter off with a flick of his wrist.

"The difference," George said with dramatic emphasis, "is that the *he* is a *she*."

Monk glared at him. "What are you babbling about, George? Are you squabbled?"

"Sober as a judge, s' help me. Do you want to hear this or don't you?"

"Very well, then, speak up!"

"Luke's man of business," George announced in triumph, "is a girl!"

"What?" For a moment Monk stared at his friend blankly, but soon his expression changed to disbelief. "A *female* giving him financial advice?"

George chortled. "Isn't that a howler?"

"I should say!" Monk smiled, a slow, smirking smile that he promptly hid by taking a swig from his tankard. "How did you learn this, George?"

"I saw her riding Luke's mare in the park. Lovely-looking filly she is."

"I take it you don't mean the horse."

"No, you gudgeon, the girl. So pretty, in fact, that I can hardly believe she's as clever as Taffy Fitzgerald claims."

"So . . . the girl is as clever as she's pretty, eh? How very interesting." Monk, still smiling wickedly, heaved himself from his chair. "I think, George, if you'll excuse me, I'll take myself off. There's someone I know who'd very much like to hear about this."

George Poole was, in fact, a bit squiffy, but he was not so cast away that he failed to recognize a certain malevolent look in Monk's eyes. He peered at his friend in suspicion. "I say, Monk, you don't mean to tell—?"

Monk cut him short with a gesture. "Never mind what I mean, old fellow. But I do thank you. You've turned this into the best day I've had in weeks."

• • •

In less than half an hour Monk was being admitted to a charming, newly redecorated flat on Curzon Street. The uniformed housemaid led him to the sitting room. "Sir Rodney Moncton," she announced loudly to a closed door.

"Go away, Monk," came a voice from behind the door. "I can't see anyone now. My face is covered with cucumber lotion."

"I've seen you with a green face before now," he said, taking a stand close to the door. "It won't be a shock to me. You'd better come out if you want to hear my news."

"News?"

"Absolutely fascinating news."

The door opened and a lady, swathed in a voluminous, filmy dressing gown, her face masked to the eyes in a pale green paste, emerged. "Monk, you makebait," she cooed and held out her hand, "what a time to drop in. It's midafternoon."

"Dolly, my love!" He took her hand to his lips. "Beautiful even now!"

Her smile could be distinguished despite the thick green ointment. "Jackanapes! What are you doing here?"

"I knew you'd want to hear this news at once. I think you'll find it *most* amusing."

SEVENTEEN

The afternoon seemed endless to Jane. She kept listening for the clock to strike four. She was to take tea with the Viscount this afternoon, and four o'clock was an appropriate hour. Surely he would send for her by that time.

She was reluctant to admit to herself how eager she was for this encounter. She did not like to believe she was behaving foolishly. But her pulse was racing in anticipation, as if she'd been invited to a ball. In fact, she was behaving quite as if she *were* going to a ball. She'd put on her best dress, the Moravian-worked muslin gown she kept for holidays. Of course, it was far from a ball gown. It was dark blue and looked, she feared, rather severe and spinsterish, but she'd softened it with her most precious article of clothing—a delicate tucker of Alençon lace that her father had brought back to her from France years ago. What's more, she'd taken pains to dress her hair less primly than usual, pulling free some tendrils to curl round her face. And all for *tea!*

She knew she was behaving like a silly, dewy-eyed schoolgirl—good heavens, like her sister, Adela!—but she couldn't seem to help herself. Ever since the dinner last night, her inner eye could see nothing but Luke Hammond's face, the high forehead partially covered by the unruly lock that always fell over it, the strong nose and chin, the lips that turned up at one corner in sardonic humor except in those moments when he'd smiled warmly across the table at her, the candlelight reflecting in his eyes.

Time dragged on. To quell this inordinate feeling of impatience, she tried to concentrate on the accounts. She'd just taken out the books, however, when Mr. Parks entered with the news that she had a caller.

"Me?" She shook her head. "Who could be calling on me?"

"It's a friend of his lordship's," Parks said conspiratorially. "Here's his card."

The card read Ferdinand Shelford, Esquire. Jane had never heard the name. "You must have misunderstood, Mr. Parks. He must wish to see his lordship."

"He asked particularly for you. You may as well see him, Miss Jane. No use causing offense."

The gentleman who presented himself a short time later was unremarkable, except for a foppishly high collar and the thickest pair of spectacles Jane had ever seen. "How do y' do, ma'am," he said, making a bow.

"How do you do?" Jane, feeling awkward, got to her feet. "Mr. Shelford, is it?"

"Yes, I'm Ferdie Shelford. I . . . er . . . saw you riding in the park today."

She could not imagine what this could be about. "Oh?" she asked.

"You ride very well," he said, shifting his weight nervously from one leg to the other and twisting the brim of the high hat he held in his hand. "Very well."

"Thank you," was all she could think to reply.

"I was wondering, Miss Douglas—"

She interrupted. "You know my name?"

He smiled. "Oh, yes, indeed. Everyone does."

She was startled. "Everyone?"

"Lord Kettering's man of business, y'see. You have everyone buzzing."

She flushed in annoyance. "I suppose a female business adviser would set tongues wagging," she said irritably. "But I interrupted you, sir. You said you were wondering—?"

"Yes. I was wondering if you might . . . if you would consider going riding with me."

She gaped at him. Was this fellow actually trying to pursue her? A member of his friend's staff? A woman to whom he'd never been introduced, with whom he'd never exchanged a word? She had a sudden impulse to giggle. "You cannot mean it, Mr. Shelford," she said, swallowing the giggle down. "I thank you, of course, but it would not be appropriate for his lordship's business adviser to accept social invitations from his friends."

"Oh, I can make it right with Luke, I assure you," he said eagerly.

"No, I'm sorry. Even if his lordship should approve, I could not. I could never consider something so improper."

Poor Mr. Shelford looked crestfallen. "Are you sure?"

"Quite sure."

"Oh," he said, turning his hat brim round and round but making no effort to depart.

"But I do thank you for asking me," she said in what she hoped was a dismissive tone.

"No need to thank me," he muttered glumly, his eyes averted.

She waited for him to go, but he remained fixed. "Was there something else—?" she asked in desperation.

"I'm good at numbers, too," he said, looking up with sudden hope. "They say my memory for facts and figures is quite remarkable."

"Do they?"

He nodded. "We have something in common, you see?"

"Perhaps we do, Mr. Shelford, but that doesn't change anything. I thank you again for your kind invitation, but please excuse me now. I have a great deal of work to do."

Mr. Shelford bowed himself out at last. Jane returned to her table, smiling to herself. Mr. Ferdinand Shelford, Esquire, seemed to be a sweet-natured fellow, and she didn't wish to make fun of him, but his suggestion that they could be mutually attracted by a fondness for figures almost made her laugh out loud.

She turned her attention back to the accounts and was soon absorbed in the work. Within a few moments, her caller was forgotten, for, in her examination of the Viscount's personal expenses, she ran headlong into a new difficulty.

She had not examined his personal account before, but

now that the household accounts were settled, and his lordship had declared the stable accounts out-of-bounds, only his personal expenses remained to be audited. It didn't take long for her to realize that something was very wrong with them.

Most of the withdrawals listed in the ledger were properly attributed: twenty-nine pounds six to Hoby, the bootmaker; one hundred and twelve guineas to Weston, clothier; two pounds ten for a silver pocketknife, and so on. But the largest amounts—six hundred pounds in one case—were not attributed at all. The withdrawal amount was listed, but the recipient was not. Jane did not know what to make of it.

The grandfather clock in the foyer struck two. Jane sighed. There was still plenty of time to work. She rang the bellpull for the butler. When he arrived, she asked him to shut the library door. Since she only did that when she did not want to be overheard, he braced himself for trouble.

"Look at this, Mr. Parks," she said, motioning him to the chair beside her worktable. "His lordship's accounts. Six hundred pounds here, four hundred here, all followed by blanks. And here—two notations in succession for over one hundred guineas. Where does all this money go?"

The butler looked uncomfortable. "I couldn't say, Miss Jane. You'll have to ask his lordship hisself."

"You know *something,* Mr. Parks. I can see it in your—"

The library door burst open. Joseph, the footman, hurried in. His eyes were widened in a kind of titillated excitement. "You'd better come, Mr. Parks," he said breathlessly. "That lady's in the foyer, lookin' like thunder."

"Lady?" Parks asked. "What lady?"

Joseph glanced at Jane uneasily and then gave the butler a meaningful look. "Ye know whut lady."

"Oh!" Parks got up quickly. "Very well, Joseph, I'll come. Excuse me, Miss Jane, it's urgent that I—"

But the library door burst open again. "How long do you expect to keep me standing in the foyer like some blasted shopkeeper?" a female voice demanded.

Jane, startled, turned to the door. Standing in the doorway was a shapely young woman draped in the most stylish costume that Jane had ever seen. From the hood of her fur-trimmed pelisse of plum-colored velvet (which had fallen over her shoulders like a cape) to the silver sandals on her feet, the woman was a living fashion plate. A diamond pin in her carefully curled pale-blond hair held a number of plumes, a diamond ring gave sparkle to the glove on her right hand, and the round-gown that peeped from the opening of the pelisse was of exquisite Persian silk dyed a shimmering amethyst. It took a moment before Jane was able to tear her eyes from all these adornments to take in the face.

It was a lovely face—oval-shaped, almond-eyed, clear-skinned and perfectly featured. If Jane had the impression that the eyelashes held too much blacking and the cheeks were too heavily rouged, it was probably because she herself was too provincial to appreciate the manner in which the sophisticated ladies of the *ton* touched up their faces.

Mr. Parks was bowing to her. "I beg pardon, Miss Naismith, I did not hear you come in. If you'd be good enough to follow me to the sitting room, I shall have some refreshment brought to you at once."

"Just one moment." The woman had caught sight of Jane, and her eyebrows rose. She brushed Parks aside and stepped inside. "And who is this, pray?" she asked, her eyes raking over Jane from head to toe.

Jane got to her feet. "My name is Jane Douglas," she said, making a little curtsy.

"The latest addition to our staff," the butler added.

"Indeed?" Her head cocked, Dolly Naismith circled Jane, appraising her with shrew eyes. "And what do you *do* on the staff, Jane Douglas?"

Jane stiffened under this rude scrutiny. "I suggest you ask his lordship," she said.

"Oh?" The voice was icy. "Is it some sort of secret?"

"Not at all," Parks put in quickly, wishing to avoid provoking a display of Miss Naismith's notorious temper. "It's only that Miss Douglas is really employed by Lady Martha, not by his lordship. As her secretary, you see. Lady Martha only lent her to his lordship temporarily, to straighten his accounts."

"How interesting," Miss Naismith said. "To straighten his accounts. Quite an unusual position for a female, is it not?"

"I don't see why it should be," Jane said, feeling defensive and not knowing why. "One needs only to know how to add."

Parks threw Jane a quelling look. But he needn't have worried, for Miss Naismith gave Jane one more appraising glance and, apparently deciding she'd seen enough, abruptly turned away. "Very well, Parks, lead on," she said, throwing one side of her pelisse over her arm and sweeping to the door.

But the door opened before she reached it. The Viscount strolled in, came face to face with his paramour and stopped short. "Dolly!"

"Luke, you gamecock!" she cried, beaming and extending her arms to him. "You've been neglecting me so long, I had to come to you." The tone in which these words were spoken, Jane noted, was very different from what it had been earlier. To his lordship Miss Naismith positively cooed.

Despite his embarrassment, Luke submitted to her embrace. Over his paramour's shoulder he threw a quick shamefaced glance at Jane. "I hope you haven't been waiting long," he muttered awkwardly in Dolly's ear.

"No, no, my dear, only a few moments," she said as he took her arm and urged her from the room. "And I spent them very pleasantly, being entertained by your dowdy little accounts manager."

Parks and Joseph followed the pair out, but Jane stood frozen to the spot. Dowdy, indeed! Her fingers trembled, and her blood bubbled furiously in her veins. But her turmoil was not caused by the insult but by the sudden comprehension of the situation that had been a mystery to her only a moment before. So *this* was the "guest" his lordship was expecting the night she and Lady Martha arrived! He'd had an assignation with that . . . that vulgar light-skirt! She knew *now* what those unidentified expenditures in the account book were for!

To think she'd been taken in by him—a mistake she would not make again. What difference did it make that he'd been kind to her, that he'd given her a book, offered

her his carriage, let her ride his mare? He was as repel-
lent as she'd first thought—a wastrel, a gambler, and a
lecher! She was ashamed she'd ever thought otherwise.

The clock struck four. She lowered herself into her
chair and let her tears fall. She was disillusioned, disheartened, devastated. And, what was more, she wasn't
even going to have her promised *tea!*

EIGHTEEN

Two men, dressed stylishly in tight, tailed coats, buckled breeches, and high beaver hats, walked slowly away from the Fives Court and proceeded along St. Martin's Street. They were the only two figures emerging from the arena; the shouts, cheers, and catcalls emanating from behind them indicated that the boxing bouts were still continuing inside.

The flickering light from the streetlamps elongated the shadows they cast on the pavement. The taller man was swinging a cane, but not with the insouciance that would indicate high spirits. Any stranger viewing the pair would have seen at once that they were out of sorts. There was no bounce or energy in their stride.

After walking a few moments in silence, the shorter of the pair sighed loudly. "Perhaps we shouldn't've left early," Taffy Fitzgerald said. "There are still a couple of good bouts scheduled."

"I'd had enough," his companion, Luke Hammond,

said glumly. "But you didn't have to leave with me, you know."

Taffy didn't bother to respond. When they went any-where together, he always left when Luke did. A friend was a friend. It didn't need saying.

They continued on in silence until Taffy spoke up again. "You must admit it was a damned good bout. It's too bad Cribb lost—I'm as disappointed as you. But I don't see why you're quite so down in the mouth about it."

"Why don't you see? Didn't you lose on Cribb, too?"

"Yes, a couple of ponies." Losing fifty pounds on what was touted as a "sure thing" was not something to elevate one's spirits, that was true. "Can't say it don't ruffle me," he admitted, "when the odds had Cribb at five to one. Who'd have thought Belcher'd give him such a beating? Belcher's a bruiser but not nearly up to Tom Cribb's left hook."

"Well, if you're ruffled, why shouldn't I be?" Luke muttered. "I lost ten times what you did."

"A monkey, eh? I don't deny five hundred's a far from trivial loss, but it ain't the first time."

"No, but this time it feels worse, somehow. Do you know what I want to do now, Taffy? I want to find a tavern and get soused. Completely, totally, knee-walking woggled."

"So do I," Taffy agreed. "The Red Lion ain't far. On Mount Street, just a short way past Tilbury's stables."

They turned a corner and continued walking. From time to time Taffy glanced up at his friend quizzically. Finally he screwed up enough courage to speak his mind. "You know, Luke, falling into the dismals over a bad bet ain't like you. You never seemed to mind losing when you were restricted by an allowance. Yet now, when the money is in your control, you're in a pucker."

"The money's not in my control, you gudgeon. Not fully. Not until the end of the month."

"But you said, didn't you, that you don't have to ask your mama anymore? You can just write a cheque."

"True enough," Luke said. "It's easier now to pay my debts. But I feel foolish, tossing away five hundred. If I go on this way, I won't pass the probation."

"Oh, I see. Then it *was* foolish, I suppose. Why'd you do it, Luke?"

Luke frowned in self-disgust. "I thought, with the odds at five to one, it wouldn't pay to bet less than five hundred. Winning less than a hundred would hardly be satisfying."

Taffy nodded in agreement. "That's what the old Luke would've said. You always were a reckless gambler, but you never blinked at the outcome."

"The 'old' Luke?" He looked down at his friend with a worried frown. "I say, Taffy, do you think I'm changing?"

"Yes, I do," Taffy said, studying Luke's face closely. "You're different, somehow."

"You mean the old Luke wouldn't have fallen into the dismals over the outcome."

"No, he wouldn't. He might have disliked having to ask his mother for additional funds, but a loss like this wouldn't have blue-deviled him."

"You're right. It wouldn't." Disconcerted, Luke struck out at a lamppost with his cane. "Dash it all, what's come over me? Am I getting old?"

"I wouldn't say that. . . ."

"Wouldn't you? Well, *something* is wrong with me. I've even changed about Dolly."

"What do you mean? Changed how?"

Luke shrugged. "Hard to explain. Remember how we always agreed that she was the most beautiful creature of all the *demimondaines*?"

"Yes, of course. And so she is."

"She no longer seems so to me. In my eyes these days she appears—oh, I don't know—too . . . too . . . gaudy. I've been thinking for a while now of what would be the best way to disentangle myself."

"That shouldn't be a problem," Taffy said. "There's a long list of fellows more'n eager to take your place. With Monk on top of the list. I'd be on it, myself, if I could afford her."

"Would you, Taffy?" Luke studied him in some surprise. "I'd have thought you more the marrying sort."

"I am. But the females I like all seem to have eyes for more—how shall I say?—more Herculean types. I'm always too short for 'em."

Luke snorted. "Nonsense. You're as well-built and preposessing as a girl would wish."

"Then how is it that the young ladies of our acquaintance have eyes only for you?"

"That's not true. It's only that you don't speak up when we're in female company."

Taffy made a face. "Never mind all that. We were speaking of you. Are you truly feeling ensnared by the divine Dolly?"

"Yes, it's all too true. I no longer find her divine." He

threw his friend a troubled glance. "But what does that say about me? Am I getting old?"

"Perhaps," Taffy answered thoughtfully, "but I have another theory."

"Oh, you do, do you?" Luke surveyed his friend, a glint of amusement in his eyes. "You are full of theories lately. What is it this time?"

"It's your pretty little 'man of business.' She's exerting a bad influence on you."

"Miss Douglas?" Luke gave a snorting laugh. "A bad influence? You must be mad!"

"I don't think so. She's been with you a fortnight, now, is that right?"

"Not quite. About a week and a half, I suppose. Why do you ask?"

"I ask because, in that time, you've sat down to cards not more than twice, you've skipped at least three nights at the club, you didn't buy that spirited gray stallion at Tattersall's the other day although you said yourself you hate driving your curricle with a mismatched pair, you didn't accept Poole's challenge for a coaching race, and now you tell me you want to rid yourself of Dolly, all of which would not have been true a fortnight ago."

Luke, his brows knit, gazed down at him speculatively. "So you *are* saying I've changed."

"Yes. And I'm not the only one saying it." He took a deep breath before going on. It needed courage; Luke might turn on him in fury. But if he was to be a true friend, it was his duty to proceed. "Everyone at the club has noticed what your new business adviser has done to you. They've been laughing about it for days!'

"Laughing, eh?"

Taffy dropped his eyes to the ground. "Afraid so."

But Luke did not get angry. He merely looked baffled. "Do you know, Taffy, I believe you may have hit on something," he said slowly. "I didn't understand, myself, why I dropped out of the bidding for that prime bit of blood at Tatt's. And I wondered, later, why I didn't take Poole up on that challenge." He blinked at his friend in sudden astonishment. "By God, I think you're right! Miss Douglas *is* a bad influence!"

NINETEEN

～❦～

Jane was packing her portmanteau again. She trembled
with unexpressed rage as she tossed her meager possessions helter-skelter into the bag. She could not bear the
thought of remaining in this household another day, a
household where the master brazenly entertained his paramour right on the premises, where the staff engaged in
petty thievery, and where someone who was honest and
straightforward was made to feel like a prude. She
wanted to go home! Home was where she could forget
the emotional turmoil that Luke Hammond had stirred
up in her, where she could restore her sense of herself,
where she could regain some perspective on the real values of life.

The task of packing did not take long. The last item
to pack was her precious Caxton Malory. She was about
to slip it into the folds of her good Sunday dress when
someone came knocking at her door. She stiffened. Who
would want her at this late hour? The knock surely pre-
saged trouble.

She opened the door. The butler stood in the dark corridor, his candle throwing an eerie light on his face. "Mr. Parks!" she exclaimed in surprise.

"Sorry to disturb you so late, Miss Jane," he said, "but you've a visitor downstairs."

"A visitor? Who—?"

"She says she's your sister."

"My *sister?*" Jane's breath caught in her chest. She gaped at the butler for a moment and then drew in a breath. "Oh, good heavens," she cried, darting past him and dashing down the hallway, "something's happened to Mama!"

"I don't think so, Miss Jane," Parks said, hurrying after her with his candle, trying to light her way. "The young lady seemed perfectly cheerful."

But Jane, flying down the stairs, had so far outdistanced him that she did not hear. Only the faint light from the candles in the wall sconces prevented her from falling headlong down the main stairway.

She burst into the small sitting room. The young woman seated on the sofa, still wearing her bonnet and cape, was indeed her siser. "*Adela!* What's *wrong?*" Jane cried from the doorway.

Adela jumped up. "Jane, there you are! At last!" And she rushed across the room and enveloped Jane in a fervent embrace.

"Adela, please," her worried sister pleaded, "why are you here? Tell me at once."

Adela stepped back and, for the first time, took note of Jane's agitation.

"Goodness, Jane, you needn't fall into apoplexy," she

said with a grin. "Nothing's amiss. Lady Martha arranged for me to visit London, that's all."

Jane put a hand to her heaving breast. "Mama is well, then?"

"As well as she ever is."

Expelling a deep breath, Jane sank down on the nearest chair. "Thank goodness!" She shut her eyes in relief. As her alarm subsided, however, other questions made their way into her consciousness. She looked up at her sister curiously. "Let me understand all this," she said, motioning Adela to resume her seat. "Are you saying that her ladyship suggested this visit?"

"Yes, isn't it the most thrilling pass?" The girl perched on the arm of the sofa and leaned toward her sister eagerly. "She came to visit us—at your request, she said—and sat with Mama for a whole hour. Then she invited me for luncheon at the castle, and she asked me all about myself. One thing led to another, and I told her that going to London was my dearest wish in all the world. Well, she clapped her hands together at that, and she got the notion to send me here—as company for you, she said—and here I am!"

Instead of returning her sister's happy smile, Jane could only glare at her. "How *could* you, Adela!" she exclaimed. "How could you agree to such a scheme? How could you think only of your own pleasure, and leave Mama all alone?"

Adela drew herself back in immediate offense. "Really, Jane, must you always find fault with me? Mama is *not* alone. Lady Martha sent over one of the maids from the castle. She's housed in my room until we come home. All the while we're here, Mama will have, in addition to Mrs. Appleby and the half-day girl, her own live-in maid. So there!"

"Oh."

After that feeble expression of contrition, Jane fell silent. She was ashamed of her unkind accusation, but too many other problems were looming up in her mind to think about an apology. Why on earth, she wondered, had Lady Martha sent the girl? Her ladyship had meant it as a generous gesture, that much was certain. But the timing was all wrong. Dreadfully wrong.

There was no way, of course, that Lady Martha could have suspected that her precious Jane was going to leave this place. *Dash it all, your ladyship,* she cried to herself, *I'm going home! Tomorrow!*

But there was nothing to be gained by falling into— what had Adela called it?—an apoplexy. She had to think rationally, to find a way to deal with this troublesome situation. And troublesome it was. Poor Adela had come all this way for nothing. *How dreadful she'll feel*, Jane told herself guiltily, *when she learns that my bag is packed and that I intend to leave this house first thing in the morning.*

"Just think, Jane," Adela was saying, jumping up from the sofa in excitement, "a whole fortnight in town! Tomorrow I'll be able to walk to the Pantheon Bazaar! And cross London Bridge! And oh, how I long to stroll down Old Bond Street and see the shops! Mama asked me to find a shop called Berry Brothers and buy their tea. She says it's her favorite, and she's missed having it all these years. And do you know the very best thing? Geraldine's given me a note of introduction to her aunt who lives in Mayfair and is very well to pass. She says that her aunt will surely invite me to dinner, and perhaps even to a *party!*" She threw out her arms and twirled about in ecstatic delight. "It's going to be the most *wonderful* fortnight of my entire *life!*"

Jane watched her sister with troubled eyes. How could she tell this bedazzled girl that her dream-bubble was about to burst . . . that there would be no Pantheon Bazaar, no London Bridge, no party in Mayfair? She'd break Adela's heart.

There was, of course, another solution. For Adela's sake, she could remain at her post in this house for another few days. She could bear it, she supposed. Not for a fortnight, of course—that would be too much to ask of herself—but for two or three days. It was not a solution she liked, but . . .

With a sigh of defeat, she got to her feet. "I *am* glad to see you, Adela, despite my ungracious greeting," she said, putting her arm about her sister's shoulders. "We'll talk about plans in the morning. Right now, you'll surely wish to get some sleep."

"Yes," Adela said, leaning her head on her sister's shoulder, "the journey was tiring."

As they left the sitting room, Jane asked, "Where is your luggage? And, by the way, I hope you won't mind sharing my bedroom."

Parks was lingering in the foyer. He'd been upset by Jane's earlier alarm. Now, observing the affectionate way the two sisters were entwined, he felt relieved. "Joseph has the young lady's boxes," he said with a smile, "and, Miss Jane, we can surely find another room for your sister."

Adela was looking about her, wide-eyed. Overcome

with awe at the magnificent surroundings, she whispered to her sister with unwonted shyness, "I'd prefer to stay with you, Jane, if you don't mind. We've shared a bed before."

Jane nodded and led her to the staircase. Then, releasing her hold on the girl, she turned to the butler. "Will you ask Joseph to bring her things up to my room, please? And I'd be obliged to you, Mr. Parks, if you'd show my sister the way."

"My pleasure, Miss Jane," he said, taking up a candle and heading up the stairs.

"But aren't you coming, Jane?" the girl asked.

"I'd better remain here and wait for his lordship. It wouldn't be right to install someone on his premises without his permission."

"Oh, heavens," Adela gasped, "do you think he might not wish for me to—?"

"No, no, miss, don't concern yourself about that," Parks assured the girl as he led her up the stairs. "Lord Kettering is very hospitable."

Jane sat down on the stairs to wait for his lordship. She hoped she wouldn't have to wait very long. She knew he'd gone to the boxing matches—she'd overheard the footmen talking about all the famous boxers who were fighting that night. But since it was already past eleven, she suspected that the bouts would all have ended by this time. He'd surely be home soon.

But an hour passed without his arrival. The candles guttered in the sconces. The foyer and stairway grew dark. Bone-weary, Jane rested her head against the banister. Before the clock struck one she was fast asleep.

Luke came in quietly. No one could have told by his

appearance or his manner that he was badly foxed. He felt his way in the dark to the table where a candle and a flint were always waiting for him, and he lit the candle with only the faintest tremor in his fingers. It took three tries, but when the wick caught fire, he picked it up and walked—almost steadily—toward the stairway. At the sight of the sleeping figure on the stairs, he stopped short. "Miss Douglas!" he exclaimed. "Wha' on earth—?"

Her eyes flew open. "Oh! Your lordship!" She scrambled to her feet. "I've been waiting for you."

"Tha's kind of you," he said, squinting at her. "Wha' for?"

From where she stood on the second stair, Jane could look down on him. His hair was disheveled and his neckcloth slightly askew, but there was otherwise no sign of disorder. His eyes glittered a bit strangely, but that might be caused by the candlelight. She rather liked the gleam. It made him seem boyish and vulnerable, and she wished, as she had so often before, that she could put out her hand and smooth back his hair. She clenched her fingers tightly, to fight off the effect of his nearness. "I only wished to inform you that your mother has sent my sister to stay with me. I hope you will not find it an imposition."

"Sister? You have a sister?" He lifted the candle higher to get a better look at her. "Are you sayin' there are two of you?"

The question puzzled her. "Yes, my lord. Is there something strange about my having a sister?"

"Good God, *two* of you? An' both under m' roof? 'S too much."

She didn't understand him. "Too much? What do you mean?"

"I mean too much. Too much . . . prudence. Too much smugness." He waved his arm in the air in a wildly exaggerated arc. "Too much so—sober-riety."

She was so badly stung by his words that she failed to recognize his inebriated state. "I assure you, my lord," she said tightly, "that my sister is neither prudish nor smug. She is not at all"—she gulped back a sudden clench in her throat—"not at all like me."

"Thank goo'ness f'r that. One bad influence 's enough."

She blinked. "What did you say?"

He tried to enunciate more clearly. "I said . . . one bad in-flu-ence is e-nough."

"Bad influence? *M-me?*"

"Yes, you! Who else?"

She was stunned. "In what way am I—?"

"Who kep' me from buyin' that sweet little gray at Tatt's, eh? Who's to blame for my absence at the gaming tables? Who's makin' me feel ashamed, right now, of admittin' to losin' a monkey tonight?"

She didn't understand. "A monkey? Did you have a monkey . . . for a pet? I never saw one here—"

"No, no, not a' *animal*," he said impatiently. "A monkey. Five hundred pounds."

"Good God!" She gaped at him, appalled. "Are you saying you lost another *five hundred pounds* tonight?"

"I did. An' you needn't look at me with tha' . . . tha' *look!* That's just the point."

"What's the point?" she asked bewilderedly.

"You're the point! *You!* You, who've made me a

laughingstock afore half the worl'!" He lifted his arm to point to her, but the effort made him stumble. "Who else bu' you?" he managed as he righted himself.

This time she could not miss recognizing his condition. "Viscount Kettering," she exclaimed, "I believe you're *drunk!*"

"Yes, ma'am, I am. Verti-gi-nous. Bewottled. Cupshotten. Raddled and ploughed. But not so crocked tha' I don' know whut I'm sayin'. An' I'm sayin' tha' *you*, ma'am, are a *bad influence.*"

Though she knew he was not in a state to be reasoned with, she could not help herself. "My influence evidently wasn't strong enough to keep you from losing a monkey tonight," she declared, drawing herself up to her full height, "but if it was indeed my influence that kept you from gambling and profligacy for a *few* days, I don't see how it can be called bad."

"You don' *see?*" He tottered to the stairway and, although worked up into a drunken fury, carefully placed his candle on the flat-topped newel post to free his hands. Then, with his teeth tightly gritted, he climbed up the one step below her and grasped her shoulders in a painful grip. "You don' see how you spoiled my pleasure in my usual ac-activ'ties . . . an' how you've ruined my rep-reputation?"

They were nose to nose, eye to eye. He seemed to be drinking in the details of her face, hungrily, angrily . . . and yet his eyes showed hurt. *How can he be hurt,* she asked herself bewilderedly, *when it's he who's saying all these cruel things to me?*

And he hadn't finished yet. "You don' see that you've taken a devil-may-care, audacious, reckless gamecock," he accused, "an' turned 'im into a spineless jellyfish?"

Frightened though she was, she had to laugh. "A spineless jellyfish? *You?*"

"Yes, I! Even now I feel unmanned." He pulled her closer, so close she could feel his heart pounding. "A fortnight ago I wouldn't have hesitated to . . . to . . ."

Her heart, too, began to pound. "To wh-what, my lord?"

"To do *this*." Abruptly, in one quick movement, he lifted her off her feet, crushed her to him, and kissed her with an unexpected and breathtaking ardor.

She wanted to resist him. She wanted to beat him with her fists. She wanted to slap his arrogant, cocksure, unregenerate face. But she could not. She'd never dreamed that being held in a man's arms and feeling his lips pressed on hers would stir her like this. Something within her melted, bubbled, churned with yearning. Without any direction from her brain, her arms crept up to his neck and clutched him tightly. There was no thought in her mind at all, only sensation . . . an excitement of her blood, a tingly warmth that spread itself throughout her body to the very tips of her fingers and toes, an overwhelming desire to be closer and closer and never to let go.

But soon, too soon, he did let her go. He lifted his head and stared at her as if he'd never seen her before. For some moments they both were shocked into immobility. At last Jane, although still breathless, broke the silence. "I do not believe," she said in an awkward attempt to make light of the incident, "that *that* was the act of a spineless jellyfish."

He dropped his eyes from hers. "I'm sorry," he muttered thickly. "I'm . . . quite drunk."

"Yes, my lord. I'm sure you are."

"I would not otherwise have . . . in my own house . . . to someone in my employ . . ."

"I understand."

He put a hand to his forehead. "My brain's utterly befuddled. I barely remember what I've said or done. I hope you will forget it, also."

"I will try," she said, but she knew she would not. Girls did not always remember their first kiss, she supposed, but there was no doubt about this one. This one would be remembered. This one had left a mark on her—an indelible mark.

He went up another step and then paused. "I seem to recall your saying something about . . . about your sister?"

"Yes. I was asking your permission to—"

"To have her stay? Of course. You needn't have asked." He sounded suddenly sober, and very depressed. "She is quite welcome. If there's any problem," he said as he turned to continue his climb, "we can deal with it in the morning."

"Yes, my lord. Here, don't forget your candle." She held it up to him, wondering at the same moment where she might find another after he'd taken this one away.

"No, you take it," he said. "I can find my way."

"Thank you," she said in surprise. But the words in her mind were not grateful. *Damn you, Luke Hammond,* she thought as she watched him climb wearily upstairs, *another act of thoughtfulness? How do you dare to be kind, when I'm trying so hard to hate you?*

She sank down on the stair and pressed her hands against her mouth. She could still feel him there. In fact, her entire body still tingled with excitement. *Good God,* she thought with an ironic laugh, *I'm in a state!* This would not do. She had to find some way to soothe her agitation before going up to her room. But she didn't know how. In the past, good sense and reason had always come to her aid. But when it came to dealing with her feelings toward Luke Hammond, they failed her. Was this what love was—a state of unreason? Was love a temporary loss of sanity? And was what she felt for Luke love? If so, it was not what she'd expected. Love, she'd always believed, was bred from two people who shared values, whose characters were harmonious, and who felt a mutual affection. How could she love someone who was, in every detail, the opposite of what she imagined a lover should be?

But, in truth, she didn't want that imaginary lover anymore. It was Luke she wanted. And, judging from the passion of his kiss, he must want her, too. Could that be possible? Could Luke care for her?

She knew the answer before the question had fully framed itself in her mind: he could not. He thought of her as a sobersides—a smug prude who'd robbed him of his audacious manliness. Those acts that she believed were signs of improvement in his character seemed to him nothing more than weaknesses. How could a man possibly fall in love with someone who was undermining the very qualities he admired in himself?

Had she really done that—belittled and disparaged those very traits that made him manly and charming? Perhaps she had. The mere possibility that he might be right was a blow to her soul. Wincing in inner pain, she pressed her hands to her mouth. "Oh, God," she murmured as the tears began to trickle down her cheeks and through her fingers, "can it be true? Can I really be a bad influence?"

TWENTY

Luke closed the door of his bedroom and leaned against it, feeling ill in body and soul. It was dark in the room, and he had no candle. He could shout for his valet, he supposed, but it was not his habit to demand that Varney wait up for him. He'd told the fellow years ago, when Varney had persisted in hanging about, sleepy-eyed, into the wee hours, that he was not to wait up past ten. "I'm perfectly capable of undressing myself," he'd said then. Well, he did not feel capable now.

Nevertheless, he would not call out. He would manage. He squirmed out of his coat and dropped it on the floor. Then, feeling his way carefully across the room, he found his bed and sat down heavily. He managed to remove his neckcloth and one boot before he gave up. With a groan, he threw himself back against the pillows and fell into a stertorous sleep.

When the clock on his mantel struck five, the sound woke him. *Strange,* he thought, *those musical bongs never disturbed me before.* He tried to recapture sleep, but his head throbbed, and his britches felt dreadfully constricting. And he still wore a boot. He tried to rise, so that he could take the offending items off, but the effort required to lift his head was too great. It made him dizzy. *Curse me for a bobbing block,* he swore to himself, *if I ever take another swig of that Red Lion rum!*

He lay back against the pillows and stared into the darkness. There was something lurking at the back of his mind making him uneasy. What was it? He tried to reconstruct what had passed last night. Vague impressions floated into his consciousness: the Cribb-Belcher bout on which he'd lost a monkey . . . a talk with Taffy about the disturbing changes that were occurring in his nature of late . . . drinking whole flagons of cheap rum at the Red Lion when he knew he should have taken only claret. The memories were hazy and disjointed, but he knew there was more. He tried to think carefully. Whatever it was must have occurred when he came home.

Yes! He *remembered!* He'd come home and encountered Miss Douglas on the stairs. Jane Douglas, his man of business. Jane of the silky hair and speaking eyes. Jane, whose translucent skin revealed every flush of her emotions, whose glance of disapproval could cut him like a swordthrust, and whose mouth—

He sat up abruptly. That mouth! He remembered it clearly now! He remembered how those full, rosy lips had gleamed in the candlelight. He'd been tantalized by them, by the luscious trembling of them, and by the little pulse that beat at the base of her lovely throat. The desire to put his own lips against that throbbing pulse had been so strong it clenched his innards. But he'd not given in to it, he remembered that. Not until he'd gone up the first step and discovered those lips so close to his own, and then—Good God!—he'd *kissed* her.

He winced in shame. How could he have done it? How *could* he, after he'd assured her more than once that he was not the sort to lay hands on the women of his household staff? She was probably furious with him, and he couldn't blame her. He was furious with himself.

He fell back upon the pillows and threw an arm over his face. Little hammers beat on his brain, and something behind his eyes throbbed painfully. Nevertheless, despite the aches in his head and the weariness of his entire body, he could feel that kiss again. He could recall in the tiniest detail those trembling lips pressed against his, the incredible softness and pliability of her body in his arms at first, and then how she'd stiffened as the smoldering tension inside her seemed to flame up and spread to every part of her and made her cling to him so tightly that, for a moment, he believed they couldn't be wrenched apart. This had not been the kiss of a bluestocking or a prude. The mere recollection of it sent a wave of heat through his entire body and made him ache for her with an intensity that startled him.

What was the matter with him? Why did his perception of the girl change so radically? How could a woman who had first appeared to be a snobbish and managing prig suddenly become a paragon in his eyes? Her smile, which he'd at first found coldly ironic, was now warmly charming; her barbs, which once seemed biting, he now found sweetly witty; and her cleverness, which once made her seem conceited and unwomanly, he now found admirable and modestly displayed. What did it mean? Was he in love with her? Had love blinded him to her faults? Was Cupid with his carelessly aimed arrows making a mock of him? Could he possibly be in love with this overbearing creature who seemed bent on destroying the man he was and turning him into a quivering pinchpenny?

He sat up in bed, his teeth clenched. The answers to all these questions was the same: no, no, and NO! He would not surrender his manhood to Miss Jane Douglas, no matter how powerful her allure. If it cost him his financial independence, he would not surrender. He would show her—as well as all the fellows who'd been laughing at him—that he was every bit as devil-may-care as he'd always been. He threw his legs over the side of the bed and got unsteadily to his feet. He had something to do, at once.

The clock struck six. The daylight was seeping in just enough to help him make his way—limping on the single boot—to his writing table. There he lit his argon lamp, pulled a sheet of paper from a drawer, prepared a nib, dipped pen in ink, and wrote:

Dear Taffy:
   I haven't changed as much as you think. I know I said I didn't care to engage George Poole in a coaching race, but I want to retract. I'm quite prepared to race him as soon as the matter can be arranged. Will you pass the word to him at once? I shall be at home, waiting for you to come.
Yours, Luke.

The door opened as he was sealing the letter. Varney, who was accustomed to looking in on his lordship first thing in the morning, had never before found him awake at this hour. "Your lordship's risen very early," he remarked, trying to hide his surprise at the Viscount's appearance.

The mere sound of the fellow's voice set Luke's head throbbing. "Hush, Varney, for the love of God, hush!" he said, wincing. "There's no need for you to hang about. I'll be returning to bed in a moment."

But when the valet saw the evening coat—a particularly fine one, that he'd so carefully brushed the evening before—heartlessly discarded on the floor, he could not contain himself. "I say, my lord," he exclaimed in indignation, "have you slept in your clothes?"

"Afraid so," Luke answered, getting up, "but there's no need to get on your high ropes. I'll take them off now. Here, give this letter to Joseph and have him deliver it to Mr. Fitzgerald." He threw his valet a weak smile. "Don't look so disapproving, man. I'll put on my nightshirt before I return to bed, I promise."

TWENTY-ONE

When Jane awoke the next morning she did not need to look out her window to discover that rain was pouring down in buckets. She could hear it splattering on the panes. She sighed. Adela's first morning in town would prove a disappointment.

She got out of bed reluctantly. She had not slept well. Even after having gone to bed many hours later than her usual time, she could not fall asleep. Her mind kept gnawing away at the details of the encounter with Luke like a little mouse with a piece of stale cheese. She didn't want to keep going over it. She didn't want to think about his unkind words or that disquieting kiss. In order to keep herself from dwelling on it, she forced herself to concentrate on what she'd been brought here to do—straighten his finances. She let her mind drift over various possibilities that might permit him to pay his new debt and still show a decent balance at the end of the month. All at once, she got an idea. It was such a good plan it made her sit up in bed. If she could make it work, he would not be able to say she was a bad influence. Pleased with herself, she was able to fall asleep at last.

That was her goal for the day—to try to implement her plan. She got out of bed with what energy she could muster and began to dress. The sound of her ablutions woke her sister. Adela sat up eagerly. "Good morning, Jane," she chirped. "Shall I get dressed, too? I can't wait to start the day. We're to go to Covent Garden, are we not?"

"Not today, I'm afraid," Jane said with gentle sympathy. "Just listen to that rain."

"Oh!" Adela's face fell. "But perhaps there is something else we might—?"

Jane sat down at the edge of the bed and smoothed her sister's tousled hair. "I can't go anywhere with you today, my love," she explained. "There's some work I must do for his lordship that can't wait."

"But when you came to bed last night, you told me that Lord Kettering had no more work for you. That you were ready to leave for home." She threw her sister an accusing glance. "You said you were staying three days more only for my sake."

"That's true. But in the night I thought of something I ought to do for him before I go. Something important."

"Important enough to ruin even the few days you've given me?" Adela asked in a voice that trembled on the brink of self-pitying hysteria.

"Yes, important enough even for that. But may I suggest to you, as you did to me yesterday, that you need not fall into apoplexy. When the rain stops, I shall ask Mrs. Hawkins to let Meggie escort you to Covent Gardens. And if I'm not interrupted in my work today, I may complete it in time to take you about town myself tomorrow. So, you see, all is not lost."

Adela took a deep, relieved breath, but her pout remained. "But what am I to do in the meantime?"

"In the meantime, why don't you go back to sleep? Then go down for a late breakfast. I'll tell Joseph to watch for you. Perhaps by that time the rain will have stopped."

But the rain did not stop. Adela, with youthful optimism, had dressed herself in her new walking gown. Made of delft blue cambric, it was the loveliest gown she'd ever worn. Her mother had engaged the finest seamstress in the village to fashion it especially for this occasion (paid for with funds Jane had scraped together and left with them, instructing her mother that they were to be used for "dire emergencies only"). But Adela soon realized there was little hope of showing off the gown on the streets of London today. It was after eleven, and the rain had not abated.

She went down to the morning room, where the footman, Joseph, set a sumptuous breakfast before her, but as soon as he left the room, she pushed it aside. She couldn't eat. She took a cup of tea, went to the window, and watched the unremitting downpour with an expression on her face of utter despair.

So abject was her misery that she didn't hear the voices in the corridor outside the morning room. Taffy Fitzgerald had arrived and was handing his rain-soaked overcoat to the butler. "Tell Luke I'm here, will you, Parks?" he requested. "I'll wait in the morning room. I assume, since Luke hasn't come down yet, that the breakfast things haven't been removed?"

"No, Mr. Fitzgerald, they haven't. Do go in and have something. Joseph is quite ready to serve you."

As he crossed the threshold of the morning room, Taffy was preoccupied with wondering what sort of breakfast fare his queasy stomach could accommodate. One quick glance into the room, however, and the problem ceased to exist. He stopped in his tracks. A girl stood at the window, a teacup in hand, staring out at the rain. He blinked at her in disbelief. Still feeling the effects of the previous night's debauch, he was not sure she was real. She was, to his bleary eyes, a delft-blue-clad vision. Her light hair fell in profuse curls round her shoulders, her profile, with its retroussé nose and full upper lip, was charming, and her form was slim and lithe. He couldn't see her eyes, but he knew they'd be lovely. Now, however, those eyes were fixed on the view, a view so depressing to the girl that she didn't even know he was there. He had to say something to make her aware of his presence, but he didn't know what words to use. He cleared his throat. "G-good morning," he said hesitantly.

She wheeled about. "Oh!" she cried, and the cup fell from her startled fingers. She looked down and, to her horror, saw that the cup had cracked. Worse, a large, ugly tea stain was spreading itself out on the carpet. "Oh, dear!" she cried again and, pulling out a handkerchief from the bosom of her gown, knelt down, and made a helpless attempt to stanch the spread.

Her fright made Taffy brave. He knelt down beside her and stopped her hand. "No need to spoil your handkerchief," he said comfortingly. "It's nothing. Joseph will take care of this."

She looked at him, her eyes wide. "Will he?"

Taffy smiled to himself. He was quite right about her eyes; they were a melting, opalescent gray. "Of course he will," he assured the girl, "as soon as he returns from wherever he's gone."

He took hold of her elbows and helped her up. When they stood erect, he discovered something about her that was even more admirable than the rest—she was shorter than he! The headache and churning stomach that had been plaguing him all morning disappeared at once. His smile broadened. "How do you do, miss?" he said, bowing. "I hope I don't intrude."

"Oh, n-no, no," Adela stammered. "I was j-just . . . that is, I—"

"I startled you. I'm sorry. I'm his lordship's friend, Theophilus Fitzgerald, but everyone calls me Taffy. May I know your name?"

"H-how d-do you do?" Adela blushed as she dropped a curtsy. "I'm Adela Douglas."

"Douglas?" The name surprised him. "Related to his lordship's Miss Jane Douglas?"

"Her sister. Lady Martha invited me to stay here in town with Jane for a fort . . . for a few days. It's my very first visit to London."

"Really?" Taffy asked, beaming. "How very delight-ful."

"Yes, but"—her eyes flicked to the window—"it would be more so if it weren't raining so dreadfully."

"Don't let the rain distress you," he said, taking her arm and turning her away from the gloomy prospect outside. "There are all sorts of sights that can be enjoyed in the rain. I daresay Luke will let his stableman take you about in the curricle."

"Oh, I don't think I dare ask—"

"Nonsense. Luke is the soul of generosity." He paused, wondering suddenly if he dared suggest his own escort. He shot a quick, appraising look at her. She was looking down at the floor with a slight, shy smile. There was nothing daunting in that smile. Yes, he *would* dare. "Of course, I'd be honored if you'd permit *me* to squire you about, Miss Adela." The words tumbled out of him in a rush. "My curricle ain't the equal of Luke's, but it's a very passable trap."

She lifted her head and threw him a glance of pure ecstacy. "I'd like that above anything," she breathed.

Her glance and her response both conspired to put him in a state of bliss. "Tomorrow?" he suggested promptly. "I could take you driving tomorrow."

Though utterly delighted at the offer, she hesitated. She had nothing proper to wear for a drive. *If I had but one day to prepare,* she thought, *I could contrive.* "I must do some shopping tomorrow," she said shyly, "but the day after . . . if you could—?"

"I most certainly could!"

There was no doubting his enthusiasm. They beamed at each other happily. Taffy had never before found a girl so easy to talk to. He had to keep this enchanting conversation going. He looked over at the table. "Oh, but I see you haven't eaten!" he exclaimed, crossing the room and pulling out her chair.

"Well, you see, I wasn't very hungry," she murmured.

"Please join me, Miss Adela. I'm quite famished, and I hate to eat alone."

Adela gave a shy nod of acquiescence, but, inside her, nothing was shy. She had met the man of her dreams. Her heart was leaping about in her chest like a caged puppy, and the blood was dancing in her veins. It was amazing, she thought as she slid gracefully onto the seat he held for her, how beautiful the weather had become.

TWENTY-TWO

If Luke had been in a condition to notice, when he came into the morning room half an hour later, he would have seen that his friend and the strange girl at the table had their heads very close together and were utterly absorbed in their whispered conversation. "Smelling of April and May, the pair of them," he would have said. But he didn't take notice. His head was still pounding from his overindulgence in rum, and his determination to return to his profligate ways was so compelling that it overwhelmed all other interests. "There you are, Taffy," he said in abrupt greeting. "Are the arrangements—?" But the sight of the unfamiliar face staring up at him stilled his tongue.

Taffy jumped up. "Ah, Luke! I don't believe you've yet met your guest. May I present Miss Adela Douglas? Miss Adela, this is Lord Kettering."

Adela rose and made a low bow. "Your lordship."

"So, you're the sister I've heard about." Luke gave

her a piercing look. "Jane was quite right; you are *not* like her. Fortunate for you."

Since the barb was not at her expense, and since she didn't quite understand it anyway, Adela took no offense. "May I be permitted to thank you, my lord, for your kindness in—"

"Yes, yes," he interrupted, waving off the sentiment, "I hope you've been made comfortable. But I beg leave to deprive you of your breakfast companion, ma'am. Mr. Fitzgerald and I have some pressing business to discuss."

"Yes, of course," Adela said hurriedly, casting an almost imperceptible look of disappointment in Taffy's direction. "I'm quite finished. I'll go at once."

"No, stay," Luke ordered, grasping Taffy's arm firmly and pulling him to the door. "Take your time over your tea. Taffy and I'll find ourselves another room."

Taffy pulled himself loose. "You won't forget that you're to go riding with me, will you?" he asked the girl. "Day after tomorrow?"

Her cheeks reddened with pleasure. "No, I won't forget."

"Two o'clock?"

She nodded. "Yes, two. I'll be ready."

Only then did Taffy allow himself to be pulled out. But this final exchange caught Luke's attention at last. "I say, old man," he said, peering down at his friend with a sudden grin, "did I hear aright? Did you actually find the courage to arrange to come calling on a girl?"

Taffy eyes gleamed, but he didn't otherwise reveal his inner exuberance. "Well, you see," he said with a modest shrug, "I'm taller than she."

Luke gave a shout of laughter and clapped his hand on his friend's shoulder. "Very deedy, old fellow, very deedy. That was well done!"

The good spirits lasted until they closeted themselves in the small sitting room. Then Taffy's face became sober. "I wish you wouldn't agree to this race, Luke. I don't like the sound of it."

"What do you mean? What can be amiss? I've done coach races four-in-hand dozens of times."

"But Monk's made up some special rules this time. He says that if you drive your own team, you're bound to win. Neither his nor Poole's horses can equal yours."

"He's right about that. Well, what does he suggest? That I give myself a two-mile handicap?"

"Worse. He says that the real challenge would be to use the horses the professional coachmen drive."

"Does he mean that we should drive a professional stage, horses and all?"

"That's just what he means."

"Unusual, I admit," Luke said thoughtfully, "but not impossible. I raced Hell-fired Dick's stage once, remember? And I beat his best time by two full minutes."

"Yes, but there's something smoky about this match. Monk wants to use two fully loaded coaches, with the horses that customarily draw them."

"Hmm." Luke rubbed his chin. "Not having my own horses is a challenge, I admit. But the horses will be strange to Poole, too. I can outdrive Poole under any circumstances."

"There's more. They want to race this afternoon, rain or shine. At best, the roads will be thick with mud. And there's an even worse stipulation. The bet must be two monkeys."

"A *thousand pounds?* Is the fellow looney? From what I know of Poole's finances, he's scarcely in a position to drop so large a roll of blunt."

Taffy nodded glumly. "That's what worries me. I think he has some secret reason to believe he'll win. It seems to me, Luke, that you should exercise some caution here. Turn the match down."

The word *caution* was not one that could please Luke at this moment. "Damnation, Taffy," he burst out, "I don't want to exercise caution! I don't want to be turned into the spineless jellyfish that she . . . that some people would like me to become. You yourself were saying, just yesterday, that I've changed. Well, I don't want to change. I want to be the same reckless ne'er-do-well I always was."

"Even if it means you'll lose this match? Even if it means you won't achieve your independence at the end of the month?"

"Even so! Dash it, what good is having my independence if it turns me into a mollycoddle?"

Taffy shook his head in disapproval. "Is it being a mollycoddle to take precautions? To refrain from rushing into situations that are fraught with risks?" he argued.

"I never worried about risks before. Why should I start now?"

"But you weren't a tom-doddle before, either. You'd never let yourself be taken for a chump."

That gave Luke pause. He frowned at his friend with

eyebrows knit. "Do you think I'll be taken for a chump in this match?"

"I don't know." Taffy walked slowly over to the fireplace and gazed down into the flames. "There's just something about this entire scheme that sets up my bristles."

Luke paced about the room, debating with himself. After three turns, he paused. "Two coaches, both working stagecoaches, is that right? You and I will inspect each one, and then Poole and I will draw for the privilege of choosing first. If we insist on those stipulations, I don't see how they can trick me."

Taffy sighed. "Neither do I. But still—"

"If it were Monk doing the driving, I'd be suspicious, too," Luke said slowly, "but I'm racing Poole. Poole's not the sort to palm an ace." He strode over to the fireplace and looked down into Taffy's face, silently seeking his understanding. "I'm going to do it, Taffy. Say you'll second me in this."

"Damnit, man, you know you can count on me. I just wish you'd reconsider."

Luke shook his head and turned away. "Don't you see? I *need* to do it, to feel like a man again. Go and tell Monk to make the arrangements."

TWENTY-THREE

❧

Although the sun was darting in and out of the dissipating clouds by the time Taffy and Luke arrived at Islington for the race, the improving weather was not enough to make Taffy feel cheerful. The ground was still muddy, the two coaches waiting in the courtyard of the White Hart Inn were ancient, clumsy, and sagging at the rear, and the circumstances of this peculiar race still seemed murky. It was only when he saw George Poole emerge from the inn doorway that his spirit lifted. "Look, Luke," he chortled, "Poole's arm is in a sling."

"I slipped on a cobblestone dashing through the rain this morning," Poole explained, "and wrenched my shoulder."

For Taffy, this was the best of news. "Good!" he cried impulsively. "Then the race is off."

The tip of Poole's nose quivered in offense. "*Good?* Thank you so much, Mr. Fitzgerald. I'm so glad my injury pleases you!"

"I didn't mean that, you codshead. I only meant that

I'm relieved that we won't have to race today. I've felt from the first that this ain't a good day for it."

Poole turned to Luke with raised brows. "You ain't saying you're backing off, are you, Luke? I've never known a little mud to stop you."

"But you don't intend to go on with this, do you, George?" Luke asked. "You can't drive a stage with an injured shoulder."

"No, of course not. But we cannot simply cancel the race. Not after all the trouble we took to arrange for the carriages and the teams and all. So Monk's agreed to take my place. He's waiting inside. Come on in."

Luke and Taffy exchanged looks. Then Luke shrugged and followed Poole into the inn. Taffy had no choice but to do likewise.

Monk was seated at a table in the crowded taproom with a mug of ale in front of him. He lifted it and waved it in greeting. "The sun's breaking through," he said with a broad smile. "At least we won't be soaked through."

"Sun or no sun," Taffy said angrily, "the match is off. We agreed to it only on condition that Poole was driving."

Monk's smile changed to a sneer. "What's the matter, Luke? Afraid of the prospect of some *real* competition?"

Luke's fist tightened. The urge to plant the fellow a facer was hard to control. He had no doubt that this substitution was prearranged; there was probably nothing at all wrong with George Poole's shoulder.

The situation was peculiar, to say the least. He wondered why Monk had gone to such devious lengths to arrange this match. Did that make-bait really think him too cowardly to face a stronger competitor than Poole?

Never in his life before had he been taken for a coward. Had his reputation sunk so badly in such a short time? It was a humiliating thought. But there was no need to concern himself; he could change things simply by a win today. And he had no doubt he could outrace Sir Rodney Moncton under any circumstances, on any day of the week. "I *welcome* some real competition, Monk, old man," he said, pulling up a chair and sitting down opposite his rival. "Just tell me the rules."

Taffy came up behind him. "Excuse me, Luke, but may I have a word with you outside?"

Luke nodded, and the two left the room. As soon as they were out of hearing, Taffy turned on his friend. "What on *earth* are you about, Luke? Didn't you say, just this morning, that you would *not race Monk?*"

"I know." Luke sighed. "I'm being played for a chump."

"Yes, you are. George's shoulder is no more injured than mine is."

"You're right about that. What I don't understand is why Monk went through this rigamarole just to cozen me into accepting the match."

"I understand it. If he was the opponent, he was afraid you'd turn him down. And so you should."

Luke knit his brow thoughtfully. "If I did so, the implication to the world would be that I was willing to take a chance on a weaker opponent but was afraid to take on the stronger one."

"No one would believe that of you. They would simply assume that you were too cautious to engage in so risky an enterprise."

"Damnation," Luke burst out angrily, "there's that

word again! I tell you, Taffy, I will *not* be cautious. I refuse to turn myself into a nose-twitching rabbit, frightened at the slightest risk!"

"But Luke, you *can't*—"

"Why can't I? Do you truly believe Monk can outrace me?" He glared at Taffy belligerently. "Are you implying that I've beaten him before merely because I had better horseflesh under me?"

"You know I don't believe that," Taffy argued earnestly. "I know you can outrace him. But not if he has some sort of ace up his sleeve."

"You think he's planning to make an ass of me again, eh?" His air of belligerence died. "You're probably right."

Taffy expelled a breath of relief. "Then let's go in and *call this off.*"

"No. I can't call it off. But what we *can* do is keep our eyes open for the ace. Forewarned is forearmed."

They returned to the taproom, Luke full of determination and Taffy full of misgivings. Monk and Poole immediately began to outline the rules. "The object," Poole said excitedly, "is to simulate a real stagecoach ride. We've rented the two coaches and their teams for three guineas each from those two stage drivers sitting there at the window."

"One is taking a load to Oxford. He agreed to put off the departure until this evening," Monk put in, "and the other is setting off for Birmingham in the morning."

"In order for this to be an authentic stagecoach race, we've persuaded eight of their passengers to ride with us," Poole continued. "We'll let them draw lots to determine which coach they'll board. We'll reward them with a few shillings after the race."

"All expenses to be assumed by the winner, of course," Monk said.

"Of course," Taffy said dryly.

Poole continued to outline the rules. The coaches were to be loaded with four passengers each, with each rider allowed no more than two pieces of baggage, eight pieces on each coach, tied onto the rear platform. The two stages would start together from the courtyard, drive up the Great North Road ten miles to a posting stage called the Bull's Head Inn, where the teams would be changed. Then they'd immediately race back to the starting point. "Agreed?" Poole asked.

Taffy and Luke exchanged looks. Taffy opened his mouth to speak, but Luke put up a hand to restrain him. "Any passengers to be seated outside on the box?"

Monk shrugged. "I'd prefer that they be seated inside, to prevent unnecessary distractions."

"Yes, that's acceptable," Luke said. "And we draw cards to see who is first to choose his team, is that agreed?"

"Of course," Monk said. "Shall we shake hands?"

"In one moment," Luke said, rising. "First I'd like to talk to Taffy again."

The two men walked outside. Taffy guessed what Luke was going to say. "It's the changing of the horses at the posting stage, isn't it?" he asked worriedly. "That's the ace."

"Yes, I think so. It's a good ploy. In the hurry to change the horses, how could I possibly notice if one of the four was a flat-sided screw?"

"Even if a horse looks fine and has an elegant shuffle, he might very well be tied in below the knee when running," Taffy muttered.

Luke paced about the yard, considering the situation. After a moment his expression brightened. "Look, Taffy, perhaps we can outsmart them in this," he said. "If you rent a decent hack, you can make it to the Bull's Head in better time than we. You can look over the second teams and make certain we're not being tricked."

Taffy nodded eagerly. "Good idea, by jove!" he cried. "If I discover a deplorable slug, I'll make the ostlers put in another." He slapped Luke on the shoulder. "I'll be on my way at once and ride like the devil. Good luck!"

Luke returned to the taproom and the two contestants shook hands. While the ostlers loaded the passengers and baggage, Luke and Monk drew cards for first choice. Luke won. They went to the stables, and Luke looked over the two four-horse teams carefully. There was not much difference between them that he could see—the horses were all tired and overworked. Since neither team seemed more promising than the other, he chose the team whose left leader nuzzled his shoulder. It was as good a reason to choose as any other.

They were now ready to go.

The two coaches started out evenly. The passengers, hanging out the windows, shouted encouragement every time he drew out ahead. The passengers in the other coach did likewise. Luke, up on the box, tried to block out their shouts. He was not happy with this match. It was not pleasant driving these tired horses, and the coach itself was clumsy and lacking in spring. He was not accustomed to driving so sluggish a vehicle. His experiences driving coaches-and-four at the Four-in-Hand Club had not prepared him for this. This stage was so heavy it seeemed to drag at the rear.

The road was wide enough for the two carriages to move along side-by-side, but at one point Monk edged his coach into the center, forcing Luke's front right wheel off the road into a muddy gully. For a moment Luke feared he'd be stuck. Monk pulled ahead. Monk's passengers, aware of his unsportsmanlike trick, for once did not cheer.

Gently, Luke coaxed his horses to dance to the left, rocking the coach, and the wheel came free. Realizing that Monk might use that base maneuver again, he picked up speed until he managed to pass Monk's coach. Then keeping his team to the center, he did not permit Monk to pass him again.

They were making remarkably good time. A fast stagecoach could make tweve miles an hour, but Luke, glancing at his pocket-watch at the half-way point, anticipated reaching the posting stage in under forty minutes. Luke arrived there only a few seconds ahead of his opponent. The ostlers came running. Two groups of boys untied the first teams and two others quickly harnessed the second. Luke sighed with relief as he caught sight of Taffy. Monk, who was using the pause to take a quick swig of ale, looked surprised to see Taffy there, but he showed no sign of alarm. Luke interpreted Monk's untroubled expression to mean he'd not done anything tricky with the new teams. He now could easily anticipate what Taffy was going to tell him. "I know," he said when he saw Taffy's discouraged face, "they're *all* slugs. This *wasn't* the ace."

"There must be something else, then, Luke," Taffy muttered, casting a look of loathing at the complacent Monk. "Keep your eyes open."

"Don't worry, I will. Hurry on back to the White Hart. I may need you at the finish."

Having come in first, Luke started the return run first. He tried to keep ahead, but Monk managed to catch up. They rode neck-and-neck for several miles, Luke keeping a wary eye out for Monk to swing into him, but Monk made no effort to do so. This convinced Luke, if he needed more convincing, that Monk had something else up his sleeve. He studied Monk's carriage as it lumbered along beside his. It seemed to him that the other coach had a bit more spring than his, but it was certainly far from what one could call well-sprung and would probably not make much difference to the outcome. The condition of the coach, he decided finally, was probably not the ace either.

When Islington came in sight, and Luke was preparing to spur the horses to the final sprint, Monk's carriage made a sudden lurch to the center of the road. To avoid a collision, Luke had to give ground. With Monk ahead and keeping to the center, there was no hope for Luke to win unless he could pass. And he could only pass by going slightly over the edge of the road. If he could find a dry patch, where the wheels would not be obstructed by mud, he might manage it.

Maneuvering to the side, he watched for his opportunity. At the first dry-looking stretch, he whipped the horses to their greatest speed and circled the obstructing carriage. For a moment it seemed that he would make it. As his carriage trundled past the other, his passengers sent up a triumphant shout. But just as he was turning back onto the road, to his surprise, the right rear wheel sank into the dirt and stuck. The carriage rocked alarmingly to a stop, the horses reared up, and Monk's coach wheeled by. It was only moments to the finish line. The race was lost.

Luke tried to rock the wheel loose as he'd done earlier, but it was stuck fast. Since the race was obviously over, the passengers climbed down to offer help. It took several minutes of back-breaking effort—all the passengers pushing and the horses pulling—to get it free. When they eventually limped into the courtyard, Monk, Poole and Taffy were waiting. "Good race, old man," Monk said with ill-concealed triumph. "And don't worry about the blunt. You can pay me whenever it's convenient."

Monk and his cohort turned and strolled cheerfully toward the inn, shouting an invitation to the passengers of both coaches to the taproom for a drink on the winner. "It's a bloody shame," Luke heard one of his passengers mutter to another. "That chap whut won didn' play fair."

The remark did little to lift Luke's spirits. As the ostlers led the horses to the stable, Luke stood staring at the carriage that had cost him a fortune in money and pride. Monk had bested him, and there had been no ace to help him do it . . . at least no ace that Luke could discover. He'd apparently won by his own skill. The maneuver to run him off the road was a scurvy act, but not illegal. Thus there was no one Luke could blame for his loss but himself.

Taffy stood beside him but, sensing how Luke must be feeling, wisely remained silent. The setting sun threw long shadows across the yard, providing an all-too-appropriate aura of funereal gloom.

At last Luke recovered his equilibrium enough to describe to Taffy what had happened. "I don't want to seem to be avoiding responsibility for losing this damned match," he said when he'd finished, "but I don't see how that deuced wheel sank so deeply into the ground. At the speed I was going, it should have glided over the soft spot."

Taffy walked over to the coach and examined the wheel. He could see nothing amiss. Just then a couple of ostlers appeared and began to untie the baggage. "Why are you doing that?" Taffy asked one of the boys. "Aren't the passengers going out again in a few hours?"

"This isn't their baggage," the boy said. "It's just some boxes and bundles Sir Rodney told us to load."

Taffy's eyebrows rose. "You don't say!" He threw a speaking look at his friend. "These all belong to Sir Rodney, then?"

"Don't know, sir. They was a'ready sittin' here in a pile when Sir Rodney tol' us to load 'em. Damn heavy they are, too. Took the pair of us to load each one. An' we needed more help with those two." He pointed to two lumpy bundles wrapped in burlap and stacked just above the right wheel.

Luke, eyes intently fixed on the bundles, came up and joined them. "Would you be good enough to unload those two? We'll help, if you can't manage them yourselves."

"But, m'lord," the boy said hesitantly, "I don' know if Sir Rodney'd like us to—"

"We'll take the responsibility," Taffy said, holding out a gold sovereign to each of them.

The boys' eyes popped at the sight of the yellowboys. Gold coins were a rarity for them. Without further ado they untied the two bundles that Luke had indicated. Taffy and Luke had to help them lift the bundles from the luggage platform and set them on the ground. When the task was completed, they sent the ostlers about their business and Taffy, taking out a pocketknife, cut off the ropes. The two men knelt down and stripped away the burlap wrapping. What they uncovered made them gasp. The burlap had disguised two large iron *anvils*.

Luke snorted bitterly. "No wonder the wheel sank."

"It makes no difference, you know," said a voice behind them. They turned to discover Monk, watching them.

"No difference?" Taffy cried in fury. "It's a damned cheat!"

"You, Rodney Moncton," Luke said in a voice of ice, "are nothing more than a damnable blackleg."

Monk sneered. "Calling me names, Lord Kettering, does not change the outcome. I won."

"By overloading Luke's coach?" Taffy shouted. "Do you call that a *win?* I call it outright chicanery!"

"No, it isn't," Monk said smoothly. "We agreed that there would be no more than eight parcels per coach. We did not stipulate what those parcels would contain."

"Is that so?" the little fellow raged. "I'll bring the matter up before the FHC, and we'll see what they have to say. They'll drum you out!"

"There's nothing the Four-in-Hands can blame me for," Monk said with a smug smile. "We laid out the terms, and you agreed to them. It's all quite legitimate."

"*Legitimate?*" Taffy was red-faced in fury. "It's a blasted *fraud!*"

"Never mind, Taffy," Luke said quietly, taking his friend's arm. "The man's right. We agreed to the terms. Let's go home." And he pulled the resisting Taffy toward his curricle.

"Hang it, Luke," Taffy cried when they were out of Monk's hearing, "you ought to call the fellow out!"

"What? And have everyone believe I'm forcing a duel to wriggle out of paying my debt?"

"Who cares what everyone believes? The muckworm deserves a bullet in his chest. Or, better yet, to be run through. You know you can best him with either the pistol or the foils."

Luke gave a small, ironic laugh. "He'd probably find a way to cheat me even then." He shook his head morosely. "It can't be done, Taffy. There are no real grounds for a duel. It seems Monk's thought of everything." With a deep, discouraged sigh, he climbed up into the curricle and picked up the reins. "I have to admit it," he muttered, "the man's made a chump of me again."

TWENTY-FOUR

It was dark when he arrived home. Parks was already carrying a lighted candle when he met him at the door. If the butler was surprised at his lordship's disheveled appearance, he made no sign. "Miss Jane's asking for you to step into the library, my lord," he said. "She says there's something important she'd like to show you."

"Some other time, Parks," Luke said wearily, heading for the stairs.

"But 'twill only take a few moments, she says."

Luke did not turn round. "I said, not now," he muttered and began to climb.

But Jane had been listening for him. She came into the foyer and ran to the bottom of the stairs. "My lord, please wait. I have something to show you."

Luke turned but did not descend. "What is it?"

She took one look at his rumpled clothes, muddy boots, and tormented expression, and her chest clenched. "Has something happened to you, my lord?"

Parks, who knew that such a question was inappropriate in a member of the staff, gave her a warning cough.

But Jane did not heed it. "Something's amiss, isn't it?" she insisted.

Parks coughed again. Luke glared at both of them. "I don't see, Miss Douglas, why the question should concern you. And as for you, Parks, take yourself off."

"Yes, my lord," Parks said, and he quickly disappeared.

"Now, Miss Douglas, what is it? And be brief, woman. I'm in no condition to listen to a protracted sermon."

"It's far from a sermon, my lord," she said, stepping forward eagerly and holding out a sheet of paper. "It's a plan. A financial schedule for the rest of your probation. I've worked out a scheme by which you can pay off last night's debt, continue to live in your accustomed style, and still meet your mother's requirements at the end of the month. All you need do, you see, is borrow the amount I've indicated here and invest it short term in the funds—"

His lordship's sudden, strange snort of laughter silenced her. "You've worked out a plan, have you?" he asked mockingly.

"Yes, my lord, I have." She looked up at him with an encouraging smile. "You'll be able to pay the five hundred without having to be—what was your phrase?—a spineless jellyfish. Here, won't you come down and take a look at the details?"

"Forget it, Miss Douglas."

Her face fell. "Forget it?"

He turned and proceeded up the stairs. "It's no use,

ma'am. No use at all. It's too little and too late."

"B-But, my lord," she cried, her thoat tightening, "at least take a look. I worked on it all day. It's perfect, down to the last penny! Don't you want to see—?"

But he was gone.

She stared up at the empty stairway. "It *does* have use!" she cried to the unhearing walls. "Don't you see? I did this to prove to you that you needn't change! I never wanted you to become a weak and petty pinch-penny."

The paper trembled in her hand. She sank down on the lowest step, the tears beginning once more to roll down her cheeks. She had hoped her latest effort would win a word of praise from him. "I only want to sh-show you," she said brokenly, "that I n-needn't always b-be a b-bad influence. That the last thing I'd ever wish to do would b-be to . . . to undermine your m-manhood!' "

But nobody was listening.

TWENTY-FIVE

I suppose, Jane thought as she lay abed trying to discover a reason for the Viscount's rejection of her plan, *that I am a bran-faced bore to him.* His Constable of Finance. A bookish scold who carped and nagged and was little better than a nuisance. It didn't matter that she was a female. She would probably have been regarded as just as insipid, inconsequential, and annoying if she'd been a male.

Of course, if she'd been a man, he would not have kissed her. But the kiss was probably insignificant. After all, the man had been drunk.

She wished she could get up right this moment, pack her things, and leave. But she'd promised Adela a few days. How could she go back on her word? For Adela's sake, she would remain fixed here a bit longer. And in that time, perhaps she could manage to interest his lordship in her plan. If she could, then this disastrous fortnight might not have been passed completely in vain.

The Viscount himself was passing an equally miserable night. When morning came, he still lay tossing in his bed, berating himself for being an ass. His mind dwelt painfully on yesterday's events, reviewing every decision he'd made and judging each one as foolish in the extreme. Three were outstanding:

1) He'd agreed to participate in the too-high-stake stagecoach race with Poole after having already decided against it.

2) He'd ignored Taffy's advice about reneging when he learned that it was Monk who'd be racing him.

3) He'd told himself that he could recognize any dishonest trick Monk might try.

In each case, he'd sensed at the time that he was not making the wise decision. Why had he chosen the foolish one? Only to prove that he'd not changed . . . that he was still the bold, reckless, devil-may-care fellow he'd once been. A Corinthian—the model gentleman-sportsman for boys to envy and emulate. Was that his goal in life—to be admired by callow youths?

What was the matter with him? Why had he felt impelled to accept Monk's challenge? Did it matter that some other fools would take him for a coward? He was like a schoolboy, forcing himself to "step over that line" because another boy had dared him to. Good God, he was thirty-one years old! He could not act the reckless youth all his days. Wasn't it time to grow out of such childish behavior?

He'd declared to Miss Douglas that she was turning him into a spineless jellyfish, but that had been a ridiculous accusation. She was merely trying to help him reach his full majority . . . to teach him to handle his responsibilities like a sensible man. His accusation had evidently disturbed her; he remembered how troubled she'd looked last night when she'd stood at the bottom of the stairs holding out that paper—her plan to salvage his fanancial muddle "without," she'd said, "turning you into a spinless jellyfish." How lovely she'd looked, gazing up at him with those worried eyes! What would she have felt if she'd known that he'd *trebled* his debt? He knew—and dreaded—the answer. She would despise him.

The self-recriminations continued for hours, but when he realized the morning was half gone, he admitted Varney and forced himself to face the day. He was disconsolately eating a solitary breakfast when Parks came in to inform him that Miss Naismith was calling. The words had scarcely left the butler's tongue when Dolly flounced into the room. "I didn't believe Parks when he said you were at breakfast, you slug-a-bed," she greeted cheerily, waving a gloved hand at him. "It's almost noon!"

Luke pulled himself to his feet. "Well, Dolly," he said with a forced smile, "I've known *you* to breakfast at noon. Sit down and join me."

She did so as Luke signaled Parks to withdraw. Luke took his seat, watching as the shapely young woman slid out of her fur pelisse and let it drape elegantly over the back of her chair. "To what do I owe the delight of this visit?" he asked.

"I don't suppose you remember, my love," she said archly, "but you are promised to me tonight for the Cyprians' Ball. I came by to remind you. Tonight Amor reigns supreme."

Luke winced. He would have said, a moment before,

that his spirits could not have been lower, but they now dropped to a new bottom. The last place he wanted to be tonight was the Cyprians' Ball. The annual affair had never been pleasing to him. It was a night for the *demimond* to display itself. Every courtesan, every demirep, every one of the "Fashionable Impures" (identified by a silly sobriquet, like the White Doe or the Brazen Aphrodite) turned out in all her finery, with her plumes waving, her jewels (real or paste) sparkling in the light of a thousand candles, her best silver slippers gleaming, and her most luxurious gown slipping from her shoulders. And every gentleman in London—married or single, town-bred or rustic, youthful or doddering, sporting or bookish—panted to participate in the orgy.

Luke himself had wanted to attend when he was young. He'd gone once, quite eagerly, the year after he'd finished school. He'd found it disappointing even then. The garish affair had seemed too noisy, too dissolute. The wild dancing, the loud music, and the shrieking laughter had not appealed to him. He'd not attended again until last year, when he'd escorted Dolly at her request. He had not enjoyed the affair any better in her company. "The deuced ball's tonight?" he asked, a piercing headache stabbing him just over his right eye.

"Yes, my dear, tonight. You must be the only gentleman in London who does not know. Absolutely everyone is speaking of it. Lord Edgeworth—who, by the way, always rides his bay alongside my carriage when I drive through the park, hoping for a smile from me, the dear boy—well, he's already begged me for the first gavotte."

"I don't remember promising to escort you," Luke

said, pressing his fingers against his aching brow.

Dolly's cheerful expression did not change. "Of course you did, my love. And even if you didn't say it in so many words, your escort is something I took for granted."

He squared his shoulders and faced her. "I wish, Dolly, that you would excuse me. I am in no condition to attend any ball tonight, especially a squeeze like that one."

Her smile lost a small degree of its brightness. "Are you saying you wish me to release you from your duty tonight?"

"Yes, I am."

"Luke Hammond, you bounder," she cried in mock offense, "you don't expect me to go alone, I hope."

"No, I don't. I'm sure you have many gentlemen only too eager for the privilege. Lord Edgeworth, 'the dear boy,' for one."

Dolly, not smiling now, studied him carefully. "Is this your way, Luke, of informing me that matters are no longer *en rapport* between us?"

He eyed her uneasily. "You can't pretend they are, can you, Dolly? I haven't visited you for . . . for . . ."

"For almost a fortnight. Yes, I noticed. I admit I've been pretending to myself that things are not as they appear, but now I must recognize the sad truth."

"Come now, my dear," he said, "please don't play the tragic heroine. This is not the first time you've changed alliances. You've undoubtedly already chosen my replacement—someone in that entourage that follows your carriage when you drive out every afternoon. Lord Edgeworth, perhaps?"

She sighed and rose. "No, this is not the first time I've changed alliances," she admitted, reaching for her pelisse. "But that does not mean I am not put out with you."

Luke got up and went round the table. "Why be put out, when it's happened before?" he asked, draping the fur garment about her neck.

She frowned at him over her shoulder. "Because, my dear, it is I who usually initiates the change. I do not like to be the one who's rejected." With a sudden premonition that this rejection might not be the last, she shuddered and pulled the pelisse closely about her. "Perhaps it means I am losing my charm," she said with unaccustomed candor.

The tiny note of vulnerability touched him. "Nonsense," he assured her. "You are not known as the *Venus Perpetuum* for nothing. A Goddess Forever."

Her expression brightened at once. "Is *that* what I'm called, the *Venus Perpetuum?*"

"So I hear. Better even than the notorious Garbon woman, wouldn't you say? She's called the *Venus Caritas*, Goddess of the High Price."

Dolly patted the coil of hair that hung over one shoulder with satisfaction. "When Harriette Garbon hears my new name, she'll be livid," she crowed, preening like a peacock as she went to the door.

"Dolly," Luke called after her, "I hope you know that, if you are ever in need, you can come to me."

She dismissed the offer with a flippant wave. "You needn't concern yourself about that," she said as she started down the hall. "My protectors have all been generous. I'm very well situated in the funds."

• • •

Dolly's flippancy did not last long. By the time she was admitted into Sir Rodney Moncton's rooms a short while later, her mood had changed. The realization had burst on her that, for the first time in a dazzling career as a *demimondaine*, she was a woman scorned. She strode into Monk's drawing room and ordered his man to bring him to her at once. As soon as Monk appeared, pulling together the edges of a Chinese-silk robe over his massive frame, she wheeled on him. "I'd like to scratch his eyes out!" she snapped without preamble. "That cock-of-the-game discarded me!"

"You are speaking of Luke, no doubt," Monk said, shrugging. Dolly having been his paramour for two years and an intimate *confidante* ever since, he was quite accustomed to her outbursts. "Don't take personal offense, my dear. The fellow probably can no longer afford you."

"What?" The remark surprised her and caused her to suspend her display of temper. "Whatever are you saying? Luke Hammond, impoverished?"

"Temporarily, anyway. He just lost a double monkey. And to me, my dear, to me!"

"Did he really?" Dolly sat down on her host's divan and looked up at him through narrowed eyes. "By what chicanery did you manage to accomplish that?"

He slid down on the divan beside her. "There was no chicanery involved," he murmured, slipping her fur from her shoulders and kissing the nape of her neck. "It was a perfectly legitimate win."

She paid no heed to his advances. "Be that as it may,"

she said thoughtfully, "I don't think that his being temporarily in Dun Territory was the reason for his crying off. I think he's fixed his affections elsewhere."

"Balderdash! If he were paying his addresses to someone, we would have heard."

"Not if she were living in his own house," Dolly pointed out.

Monk sat up. "In his own house? Good God, you can't mean the chit his mother installed to help him with his finances?"

"That's exactly whom I mean. He's been a different man since the day she arrived."

Monk's eyes widened interestedly. "My, my. George said she was pretty, but she must be an out-and-outer to have superceded you."

"That's just what I find so irksome!" Dolly exclaimed, jumping to her feet and striding about the room. "She's nothing more than an insipid little bookworm!"

"I'll lay odds she is," Monk said with heavy sarcasm. "An insipid little bookworm is just the sort to capture a fellow of Luke's ilk."

Dolly raised her brows in offense. "Believe me or not, as you wish. But I don't know what that filly has that won him away from the *Venus Perpetuum.*"

"The *Venus Perpetuum?* Who's that?" Monk asked in sincere ignorance.

"You haven't heard that title applied to me?"

"No. Who told you? Luke?" He gave a loud snort of amusement. "Damned clever of the fellow."

Every muscle of Dolly's body tightened. "Are you

saying he *made it up?* Confound it, I *will* scratch his eyes out!"

He pulled her down beside him. "Never mind," he said, taking her in his arms, "you'll always be the *Venus Perpetuum* to me."

TWENTY-SIX

❦

Adela had also lain awake during the night. She needed to solve the most serious problem she'd ever faced: how to acquire a proper costume for her drive with Taffy. She didn't really need a new gown (she could wear her blue gown again, even though Taffy had seen it already), but her bonnet was dreadful, her cloak was shabby, and her only pair of gloves was rubbed badly at the knuckles. How was she to acquire these necessities without sufficient funds? She had a little pocket money, but even if she used all of it, that would hardly be enough. She could ask Jane, of course, but Jane would not understand. There seemed to be no way in which she could acquire all she needed with the resources available. It was indeed a vexing problem, and sleep overcame her before a solution presented itself.

The next morning she convinced Jane that a trip to the Pantheon Bazaar was her dearest wish. Jane, who had hopes of finding a second opportunity to accost his lordship sometime during the day and force him to look at the figures she'd drawn up, was only too happy to let her sister go out. Little Meggie would make an adequate escort. "You will surely wish to make a purchase of some kind," she said to Adela as the girl readied herself for her outing. "You have some pin money, don't you?"

"Not really," Adela lied, looking downcast. "Only a few shillings. I had *so* wished to buy a new bonnet."

Jane gave the girl five shillings from her precious hoard. "That should be enough for a bonnet. Try not to choose one too frivolous to wear at church."

Adela was overjoyed. She confided to Meggie that she now had enough for a bonnet and gloves. Of course, there was still the problem of a new pelisse. "Don't worry about that," Meggie whispered as they eagerly left on their expedition. "You can borrow one of her ladyship's. Lady Martha's left all sorts of clothing lying about in the cupboards."

Jane, with her sister thus disposed of, turned her thoughts to her mission. She walked back and forth from the library to the foyer all morning, hoping to catch sight of the Viscount. It was past noon when she learned from Joseph that his lordship was finally downstairs and having his breakfast. She took up her notations and made for the morning room. She was just about to open the door when a shout from Mr. Parks stayed her hand. "Miss Jane, wait!" the butler called. "Don't go in there!" He hurried up to her, chins aquiver. "He's got company," he said in a hissing whisper.

"Company?"

"Sssh!" He pulled her away from the door. "It's *her!* Miss Naismith. You don't want to go in there when he's got Miss Naismith with him."

Jane tried not to show her chagrin. "No, I certainly don't," she said, clenching her fists. "Let me know when he's free, will you, Mr. Parks? I'll be in the library."

Several hours went by, hours in which Jane paced about the library, trying to contain her turbulent emotions. How was it, she kept asking herself, that she herself was held in such low regard that she couldn't claim his lordship's attention for five minutes, while that overdressed, overendowed hussy commanded his attention for all these hours? It was infuriating!

Teatime came, yet Jane heard nothing from the butler. At last she left the library and went looking for him. "Oh, sorry, Miss Jane," the butler said, "I forgot to call you. His lordship left the house hours ago."

Jane wanted to stamp her foot, to scream, to throw the nearest *objet d'art* onto the marble floor and smash it into a thousand pieces. But she was, she reminded herself, a creature of reason. Screaming and stamping and throwing things were not the acts of a person of sense. So she controlled herself and asked, in a voice that shook only slightly, if someone might bring her some tea in the small sitting room. She hoped the soothing qualities of the brew would ease her unwonted inner turmoil.

She was pouring herself a second cup when Parks entered with a puzzled expression on his face. "There's a Sir Rodney Moncton calling on his lordship, Miss Jane, but when I said he wasn't at home, the gentleman asked for you."

"For me? But I don't know any gentlemen in town."

"But I know you," came a deep masculine voice from the doorway.

Jane looked up to discover a well-dressed gentleman in a wine-red coat, a fellow so huge he filled the doorway. He was not handsome, but his appearance was made memorable by the startling streaks of white in his dark hair. "You must be mistaken, sir," she said. "I'd certainly remember if we had met before."

He came into the room and bowed to her. "We haven't met, but I've heard much of you."

"You must be thinking of someone else," Jane said, putting down her cup. "I'm but newly come to town and have not been much about."

"But your reputation is widespread," the man insisted. "We all know of the young lady who can do complicated sums without pencil and paper."

Jane's brows rose. "That is surely a puny talent with which to make a reputation," she said dryly.

"You must not belittle that talent, ma'am," he said, approaching her chair. "It is certainly an admirable one, and when combined with such beauty as I now see before me, it becomes quite remarkable."

She cocked her head and regarded him with some amusement. "You do not know me, sir. If you did, you'd realize that I am not susceptible to fulsome compliments."

"And if you knew me, ma'am, you'd realize that I am not one to offer you Spanish coin. May I sit down?"

Jane, at a loss, threw Parks a questioning glance. He answered with merely a shrug, as if to say that the visitor was hers to deal with, not his. Making a quick decision, she got up from her chair. "Of course, sir," she said, dropping a little curtsy, "but you must excuse me. You are waiting for his lordship. Please sit down and make yourself comfortable."

His large frame blocked her way, but she slipped by him and made for the door. He caught her arm, however, and pulled her back in a manner that brought her close to him, much too close for her comfort. She turned away, but he held her arm fast. "I would not for the world disturb your taking tea," he said softly into her ear, standing right behind her.

"Not at all," she said, throwing Parks a wordless request for assistance. "I've quite finished."

Parks took a step into the room and, to remind Moncton of his presence, coughed discreetly. Monk looked at the butler in annoyance. "You may go, Parks," he said shortly.

"I beg pardon, Sir Rodney," the butler said, "but Miss Douglas and I have some business in the library."

"Yes," Jane said quickly. "Urgent business. Please excuse us."

He did not let go of her. "Give me a moment, ma'am. Only a moment. I have a request to make of you. It concerns your employer."

She did not refuse, but she looked down coldly at the place on her arm where his hand still remained. He quickly removed it. "Very well," she said, "I can spare a moment, I suppose."

"It's a private matter," Monk said with a meaningful glare at Parks.

"I'll wait outside," Parks said pointedly. "Right outside."

Jane returned to her seat. "You may as well sit down, sir. What is it you wish to ask me?"

He took a chair facing her. "How well do you know Luke Hammond, ma'am?"

"I don't know what you mean," she said carefully. "I know him as well as might be expected for someone who's been in his employ for less than a fortnight. Why?"

"Before I make my request, you see, I must be sure you understand the reason. The subject is in Luke's interest but rather . . . er . . . sensitive."

Jane could not deny she wanted to hear more, but she was not at all sure she should encourage the continuation of this conversation. Though his words were straightforward enough, Sir Rodney Moncton had a sly, insinuating way of speaking them. Something about him made her ill-at-ease. "Are you a good friend of his lordship?" she asked.

"Yes, indeed. The very best. We've known each other since boyhood."

"And you have his best interests at heart?"

"That's exactly why I'm here. And that's why I asked you how well you know him. I must be sure that you, too, have his best interests at heart."

"I think I do. As his business agent, his interests must be mine as well," she said.

"Then let me ask you, ma'am, to speak to him in my behalf. Knowing him as I do, I know he would not take it kindly coming from me."

"I cannot agree to such a request, sir, until I know what it is you're asking me to say to him."

"It's simply this," Monk said. "His conscience is such that he is uncomfortable owing a large debt to anyone. I simply want to assure him that he need not concern himself about the debt to me. I am in no hurry to be paid. Tell him he may take all the time he requires. No one shall know but the three of us that it is still not paid."

Jane stiffened. "A large debt, you say?"

"I'm afraid so, yes."

"How large? Forgive me for asking, but I am concerned with his finances."

"You may ask, of course. I know you will not let the information go further. It amounts to one thousand pounds."

She gasped. "One *thousand?*"

"It was foolish of me to have permitted him to go so far. It was only a coaching race, after all. But he insisted. He would not hear of a lesser amount. It would not be exciting enough, he said, unless the stakes were high."

"I see." Jane's voice was calm but she seethed inside. It seemed clear at last that Luke Hammond was incorrigible. Every shameful trait she'd suspected him to possess he possessed to a worse degree than she'd imagined. Not only was he a wastrel, a gambler and a lecher, but he reveled in those qualities. It was hopeless. Her advice to Lady Martha had been mistaken. The fellow was too foolishly reckless to be permitted to get his hands on his fortune one day sooner than the law permitted. He ought to be whipped . . . jailed . . . hanged!

But it was no business of Sir Rodney's to see the extent of her distress. She rose from her chair, the only sign of her perturbation being a slight tremor of her fingers. "Thank you, Sir Rodney, for your consideration in this matter," she said tightly. "I fear, however, that I cannot speak for you. It is not my place. You'd do better to remain here and speak to him yourself."

She started toward the door, but he rose and blocked her way. "Thank you for listening, anyway," he said, taking her hand. "I think Luke is a fortunate man to have you in his employ." And he lifted her hand to his lips.

"Good day to you, sir," she said, trying to remove her hand from his.

"Miss Douglas? One last thing. My aunt, Lady Delsey, is holding a fete tomorrow evening. I was wondering if you would consider attending it with me."

"I, sir?" She felt herself coloring. Never before had a gentleman invited her to an evening festivity. Under ordinary circumstances, she would have found it flattering that a gentleman of Sir Rodney's sort would find her interesting in that way. But at this moment, all she could think about was Luke Hammond . . . that the damnable fellow, in throwing away another thousand pounds, had made all her efforts to help him useless. All she wanted now was to be rid of this intruder, to be alone so that she could relieve her agitation with a good cry. She tried again to remove her hand from Moncton's grasp. "Thank you, but I don't believe such an invitation is appropriate for someone in my position," she said.

He reached for her other hand and smiled down at her. "It is not only appropriate," he said, "but I'd be honored—"

The door burst open. "Monk, what on earth do you—?" Luke asked from the doorway. Then he saw Jane. "Good *lord!*" he gasped, stopping short.

For Jane, Luke's sudden appearance at just this moment was the last straw. Fury, embarrassment, hurt, and frustration all welled up in her at once. Trembling noticeably, her eyes filling with the tears she'd tried so hard to hold back, she wrenched her hands from Sir Rodney's hold and stalked across the room to where Luke stood, in shocked immobility, in the doorway. "I wash my hands of you, my lord," she said in a trembling undervoice as she brushed by him. "I shall be leaving this house first thing in the morning!"

"Jane?" Bewildered first by the scene he'd just interrupted and now by the intensity in her voice, Luke ran after her. "I mean, Miss Douglas, wait!" He caught her arm just as she reached the stairway. "Damn it, what's wrong? What happened?"

She looked up at him, her cheeks wet and her lips white. "How c-could you have done it?" she asked. "After all your mother and I have tried to do for you! How *could* you throw it all away?"

"What are you talking about?" he asked, grasping her shoulders urgently.

"You know very well. One thousand pounds!"

Wincing painfully, he dropped his hold. "How did you—?" But he didn't need an answer. *"Monk!"* he shouted, wheeling about.

Monk, having followed them out of the sitting room, took a step forward. "Yes, I was the informant," he said, his slight smile revealing the pleasure he was deriving from this scene.

Luke approached him, his eyes burning. "Oh, you were, were you?" he asked through clenched teeth. "Then permit me to thank you!" And he made a fist and swung it furiously to Monk's jaw. Monk dropped to the floor like a stone.

"Luke!" Jane cried, running across to the fallen Moncton. Parks, who'd been an interested but unperturbed observer, followed her.

"Damned makebait," Luke muttered, rubbing his knuckles. "I've wanted to do that for years."

"Not only are you a gambler and a wastrel," Jane said in agitation, kneeling beside Monk and trying to bring him back to consciousness by slapping his cheeks, "but a brute as well."

"How can I be a brute when he's two inches taller and more than two stone heavier than I?" Luke snapped. "And he deserved worse."

"How can you say that?" Jane asked. "He meant only to offer you kindness."

Luke snorted. "I'll wager a monkey he did," he said with heavy irony. "What business of his was it to come and report my loss to you?"

"What difference does it make? I would have discovered so large a loss sooner or later," she said, lifting Monk's head on her lap. "Mr. Parks, will you get me a bottle of sal volatile?"

Parks hurried off.

"You needn't bother about him," Luke said to her. "I didn't seriously harm him. He has a glass jaw. He'll wake in a moment."

"I hope you're right," Jane said, staring at Monk's lifeless face.

"You seem unduly concerned about him, ma'am," Luke said coldly.

"I would be concerned about anyone who was brutally mauled before my eyes."

Parks returned with the smelling salts, knelt down,

and held it under Monk's nose. Monk stirred and groaned.

"There, you see?" Luke said. "Not so badly mauled after all." He turned his back on them and stalked off to the stairway. "As soon as he's awake, Parks, and as soon as Miss Douglas can bear to part with him, throw the deuced muckworm out of the house."

TWENTY-SEVEN

Adela purposely avoided her sister when she returned from her shopping expedition. Fortunately, Jane seemed too preoccupied to question her sister about her purchases, so Adela did not have to explain why she'd bought a frivolous bonnet with flowers and three large plumes that fell tantalizingly over one eye. She hid her parcels under the bed (along with a brocaded pelisse she and Meggie discovered in Lady Martha's dressing room) and, after retiring early, fell into a blissful sleep.

When she woke the next morning, however, Adela was horrified to see that her sister was packing. "What are you *doing?*" she cried.

Jane did not look up from her work. "We are going home this morning, Adela. I'm sorry."

"But we *can't!*" The girl bounded out of bed in alarm. "Please, Jane! You can't *do* this to me!"

Jane looked at her with sympathy. "I'm afraid I must."

"No, please, not today! Surely you don't have to leave *today!*"

"I do have to, Adela. There is no reason for me to remain here any longer."

Adela's underlip trembled. "I don't understand. Just yesterday you said you had such important work to do. Couldn't you continue to do it just a bit more?"

Jane lowered her eyes. "There is nothing more I can do for his lordship." She tried to keep her voice steady so that her sister would not recognize how much pain was hidden in those words. "I can no longer postpone my departure."

But Adela was too preoccupied with her own concerns to notice her sister's pain. Growing desperate, she grasped Jane's arms in an effort to prevent her from proceeding with her packing. "Just this one day, Jane," she pleaded urgently. "I won't ask for any more. Just this one day."

The note of hysteria in her sister's voice surprised Jane. "I know how great a disappointment this must be," she said, gently urging her sister to sit down on the bed. "Other than the bazaar, you haven't seen anything at all of the sights of London or—"

"Oh, who cares for the sights," Adela said impatiently. "That's not—"

"The shops, then. Or the visit to Geraldine's aunt in Mayfair." Jane sat down beside her sister and stroked her hair. "But perhaps an opportunity may arise for you to come to London again. Her ladyship has promised me a rise in salary. If we can manage to save a bit, perhaps in a year or two—"

"In a *year or two!*" With a bitter sob Adela thrust her sister's hand away. "By then it will be too late!"

"Too late?" The words were bewildering to Jane. "What will be too late?"

"He'll be betrothed—or wedded!" And Adela burst into tears.

"*Who'll* be wedded?" her confused sister asked. "What are you talking about, Adela?"

"Mr. F-Fitzgerald! He's c-coming this afternoon to take me riding in his c-c-curricle!"

"Mr. Fitzgerald? Are you referring to his lordship's friend Taffy?"

"Yes, T-Taffy!"

Jane stiffened. "Good heavens, Adela, is all this rhodomontade merely over a ride in a curricle?"

"You don't *understand!*" Adela's shoulders shook with weeping. "I . . . we . . . he *l-likes* me."

Jane peered at her sister as if she'd taken leave of her senses. "Well, I suppose he does like you if he's offered to take you up for a drive. But what has that to say to anything?"

"Don't you see?" Adela drew in a trembling breath and, stanching the flow of tears with the back of her hand, attempted to explain. "He is the sweetest f-fellow, really—the very sweetest in the *world!*—b-but he's a bit shy with young l-ladies. He's never t-taken a young lady riding b-before. He told me so. So, you see, the fact that he asked m-me must mean that he l-likes me a great deal—"

The full impact of her sister's purpose burst on Jane at last. The silly, impetuous girl was imagining herself in love! "Adela! What are you *thinking?*" she demanded, unable to hide her disappoval. "You couldn't have met the man more than once. Do you imagine the fellow is going to ask for your *hand?* It's only an afternoon drive in a curricle, after all, not an invitation to meet his mother."

Adela let out a despairing wail and threw herself down on the bed. "What good would it be if it *were* an invitation to meet his mother? You probably wouldn't let me go to that, either!" And she buried her head in the pillow and wept piteously.

Jane, not unsympathetic to anyone so lovelorn, leaned over her and patted her shoulder. "Hush, dearest, please don't take on so. It's foolish to make such to-do over a gentleman you've met on only one occasion."

Adela turned and looked up at her sister with wet, tragic eyes. "Once was enough to make me l-love him!"

"I've never set much store by the claim that one can love at first sight," Jane said, but she didn't pursue the subject. She had a sudden recollection of her feelings at her first sight of Luke Hammond. If that hadn't been love at first sight, it was close enough. But it did no good to weep over it; Jane knew *that* very well. The best course for her sister, as it was for herself, would be to leave this place. "Try to be reasonable, dearest," she said as kindly as she could. "Write him a note explaining why you had to leave, and I'll have Joseph take it round to him."

"A *note?*" Adela threw her sister a look of loathing. "That is *cruel!*" she cried, burying her face into her pillow again. "Cruel to him and cruel to me!"

Jane's body sagged. It *was* cruel, she supposed. She studied her sister as she lay sobbing into the pillows, feeling suddenly stricken with guilt. She'd given her sister no joy on this visit, a visit that the girl had anticipated with so much excitement. How could she refuse to permit her sister to have this one last bit of pleasure? On the other hand, if her sister really cared for Mr. Fitzgerald, wouldn't the pain of separation be even greater after the second meeting?

She had no answer. "Do you think, Adela, that if I postponed our departure until you returned from your curricle ride, anything would be gained?" she asked helplessly. "You would still have to part with him in the end."

Adela sat up, a gleam of hope springing up in her eyes. "I could at least avoid having to say goodbye in a note! I could see him once more. Oh, Jane, dearest, *may* I?"

Jane, surrendering her good sense to the lure of a smile from her sister's eyes, held out her arms. "Yes, dearest, I suppose you may."

She accepted Adela's fervent embrace, but she remained unsure that she'd done the girl a favor. At best, Adela's tears were only postponed.

Taffy noticed, as he helped Adela into the carriage, that her eyes were red-rimmed. He said nothing about it until they reached the park. Once there he gave his pair their head and turned his attention to the girl. "You seem a bit blue-deviled, Miss Douglas. Is something amiss?"

She shook her head. "We were using our first names by the time we said adieu the other day," she said shyly.

"Yes, we were. I'm glad you remembered that." He smiled at her. "We did become friends very quickly, did we not?"

"Yes, we did." She tried to hold back the tears that

clogged her throat. "It's too b-bad it will end quickly, too."

"End?" He looked at her in alarm. "Why?"

Her tears began to spill. "My s-sister says we must l-leave today."

His face fell. "But she *can't!* We haven't even had time to—! Dash it, Adela, you said you were fixed in town for a few days at least!"

"I know." She dabbed at her eyes. "But Jane says that his lordship has no further need of her, so we can no longer remain. She says you must have me back by four."

"By four? That's two hours!"

Adela nodded sadly. "She says we must have a couple of hours of daylight travel to put some miles behind us before we stop for the night."

"This is *dreadful* news!" Taffy exclaimed. "I counted on having time to . . ." He cast her a look of longing. "How can we possibly come to an understanding in two hours?"

She blinked up at him, tears sparkling on her lashes. "An . . . understanding?"

"You know what I mean." He stared at his horses' heads for a moment. Then, in an abrupt movement, he turned and seized her hands. "Adela, I know this will sound absurd, for I've known you such a very short time. Of course, I never intended to tell you so soon, but the situation is desperate."

Adela couldn't breathe. "Tell me—?"

"I think I—" He hesitated, and then, just as abruptly, dropped her hands and turned away. "Damnation, girl," he muttered in despair, "it's too soon for such a declaration to be believed!"

"I'll believe you," she said softly.

That was encouragement enough. Gulping down the tightness in his throat, he turned and grasped her hands again. "It's true, you know, no matter how bubbleheaded I sound," he burst out, "but I've fallen top-over-tail in love with you."

"Oh, Taffy!" She gazed at him with eyes alight. "Me, too."

The horses ambled along the road untended, while the two passengers indulged in the rapturous expressions of mutual delight that newly awakened love requires. With her head nestled in his shoulder, and his arm tucked tightly about her waist, they were blissfully unaware of their surroundings or the passage of time. It was only when Adela suddenly noted that the sun was setting that the urgency of reality brought them down from the clouds. "Oh, heavens, it must be late!" she cried, sitting up in alarm. "Jane will be furious with me."

Taffy reluctantly picked up the reins. "I cannot bear to part with you," he said.

"Nor I." Adela sighed helplessly.

"I wish I were the sort to spirit you off to Gretna."

The idea of an elopement to Scotland was not displeasing to Adela. "Why aren't you the sort?" she asked.

"I wouldn't care to soil a lady's reputation."

"Oh," Adela said, disappointed. "Then, I suppose, there's nothing you can do but take me back to my sister and . . . and say g-goodbye."

They sat in silent misery as he guided the curricle out

of the park. Poor Adela felt the tears rise up in her throat again. "My sister was right," she mutterred glumly, half to herself. "She warned me not to expect too much. 'It's only an afternoon's drive' she said, 'not an invitation to meet his mother.' "

"What did she mean by that?" Taffy asked.

"I think she meant that a ride in the park is not the same as an offer."

"No, I don't suppose it—" His eyes suddenly widened, and he jerked his horses to a halt. "Good God! Why not?"

Adela turned a questioning look on him, but before she could ask anything, he grasped her shoulders. "Why not come and meet my mother?" he asked excitedly, the words tumbling out of him. "She lives in Devon and would surely be delighted to have you visit for a fortnight. I'd stay, too, of course, so we wouldn't have to say goodbye at all."

She peered at him in wonderment. "Do you mean to go off to Devon now?"

"Right this moment!"

"Like an . . . an elopement?"

"Well, in a way. But much more respectable. By the end of the visit, you see, we would have had sufficient time to be well-enough acquainted to become quite properly betrothed."

She gaped at him, afraid to let herself believe that this delightful plan was actually a possibility. "But . . . I must get my things, must I not? And . . . tell my sister—?"

"Mama can supply whatever you need. As for your sister, let's not give her the opportunity to dissuade you.

Once we get to Devon, you can send her a letter explaining everything. Please, Adela, say you will!"

"Oh, Taffy," the girl breathed ecstatically, throwing her arms about his neck, "yes, yes, *yes!*"

TWENTY-EIGHT

⌒⋄⌒

While Adela was off on her outing with Mr. Fitzgerald, Jane remained in her room. She paced about the small space, trying to reorganize her plans for their departure to Cheshire. If she and Adela could have left early this morning, as she'd originally planned, the matter would have been simple: they would have stolen out before anyone knew, carried their baggage to the nearest coaching inn, and departed. Now that they would be leaving in the late afternoon, however, an unobserved departure was less likely. But an unobserved departure was still Jane's goal. She didn't want to have to explain to anyone—and especially not to his lordship—why she was leaving. The circumstance she wanted most desperately to avoid was coming face-to-face with him as they were tiptoeing out the door. If only she could learn what his schedule was for this afternoon, she could make her plans accordingly. Possibly she could extract that information from Mr. Parks.

She went downstairs to look for the butler. She found

him belowstairs in his little office, doing his weekly accounts. At her entrance he looked up at her with a blink of alarm. "I hope you haven't come to see me about a problem with my accounts, Miss Jane," he said, his chins quivering as he rose to his feet. "I've been right straight with them, I swear I have, and I'm keeping them just as you wished me to."

"No, I have no problem with the accounts at all," Jane assured him. "I'm very pleased with your books now. I came to ask you about his lordship. Do you expect him to be available at any time this afternoon?"

Mr. Parks shook his head. "I'm sorry, but he's gone away. I hope you don't need him for some important matter."

"No, it's . . . er . . . not urgent. Will he be gone all afternoon?"

"All day, I'm afraid. He's gone to see his old governess, Miss Simmons. She lives in Ramsgate, in a tidy little cottage his lordship provided for her. Every year on her birthday he spends the day with her. Very fond of her he is."

"Oh, I see." Jane was taken aback. She had a sudden recollection of the letter she'd found, the childish little note he'd written to "Simmy." *Blast you, Luke Hammond,* she thought, *why is it you always do something lovable right after doing something dreadful?*

"Per'aps you can catch him tomorrow," the butler suggested with a touch of sympathy, "when he comes down to breakfast."

"Thank you, Mr. Parks, perhaps I can."

She returned to her room with her emotions churning. She could not explain, with her logical mind, how she could feel both love and revulsion for the same man. But what did it matter now? She was putting all this behind her. She should be feeling relief—relief that she would be able to depart secretly, just as she wished. His lordship would surely not return from Ramsgate before nightfall. By that time she and Adela would be well on their way to Cheshire. This confusing, disturbing, heartbreaking period of her life was coming to an end. It was almost four. In a little while she and Adela would be gone.

But four o'clock came and went without Adela's appearance. Jane's portmanteau and Adela's boxes stood packed and ready, Jane was wearing her bonnet and cloak, but there was no sign of Adela. As the hour progressed toward five, Jane's perturbation grew. *That girl is taking advantage of my kind gesture*, she said to herself in fury, tossing off her outer garments and throwing herself on her bed. *What can she be doing in all this time?*

By the time the clock struck seven, her anger had turned to panic. Some dire accident must have befallen her sister, she was certain. She went downstairs and found Joseph. "Do you know the address of his lordship's friend, Mr. Taffy Fitzgerald?" she asked.

"Yes, Miss Jane," the footman said, eyeing her curiously. "On Harley Street."

"Would you go round to his house for me, please? It's most urgent. Ask if he's returned from his drive. If he has, request that he bring my sister back at once. I'll explain to Mr. Parks."

The footman nodded and went off. Jane, realizing that a departure that day was now impossible, had nothing left to do but wait. Though she had no appetite, she went to the morning room for dinner. It was a way to pass the time.

She'd been seated no more than five minutes when, to her surprise, the Viscount came in. "Good evening, Miss Douglas," he said, taking his seat.

She hadn't expected to see him ever again. She had hoped to be gone by this time. She didn't want to speak to him. But circumstances seemed to be subverting her at every turn. "Good evening," she said reluctantly, averting her eyes.

"I realize that I'm in your black books," he said, "but I hope you will not object to my dining here."

"It is your house, my lord," she said, rising. "I'll take my dinner downstairs."

"Don't leave, Miss Douglas," he said, jumping to his feet. "If my presence is so repugnant, then I'll be the one to go. I'll take my dinner on a tray in my bedroom."

She couldn't help giving a sardonic little laugh. "A tray in your bedroom, indeed! As if Mr. Parks would even permit—"

"Then let us sit down like two civilized people." And he came round and held out the chair for her.

"Very well, if I must," she said and slid into it.

There was a long silence. Parks came in carrying the wine and the first course. He looked at each of them for a moment, served the food without a word, and withdrew.

"I was thinking, ma'am," Luke said as he poured out two glasses of wine, "that you must be wondering how to occupy your time for the rest of the month of your stay here, now that it is obvious I've failed my probation."

Jane didn't know what to say. She did not want to inform his lordship of her departure beforehand. She wanted simply to disappear without argumentation. "I am never at a loss as to how to occupy my time," she said evasively.

"I suppose that's true, great reader that you are. My father's library can provide many diversions. But I wish, ma'am, that you'll keep up your attempts to educate me in finances. Even if I won't be master of my inheritance at the end of the month, I shall be someday. Therefore, I can still benefit from your advice. You can continue to reorganize the books and show me ways to reduce expenditures. It's never too early to learn, isn't that so?"

"Good heavens, my lord," she said in mock amazement, "I can hardly credit my ears. Can this be Lucian Hammond, Viscount Kettering speaking? The same Lucian Hammond who declared that attention to finance was turning him into a spineless jellyfish? The same Lucian Hammond who found me, not two days ago, to be a bad influence?"

"Very well, ma'am, have your fun. Attack me with my own words. I deserve it." He held his glass up to the light of the candle and peered ruefully at the ruby glow of the wine. "I don't suppose you believe that I can change."

"Not for a moment," she said flatly.

Parks came in with the second course. While he served, they sat in silence, but as soon as he left, Luke resumed his questioning. "Why don't you believe it? People can change."

"Only if they want to," she said.

"You don't believe I want to?"

"No, I don't. I think you like yourself the way you are."

"Then why do you suppose I am saying all this to you? Am I not, figuratively at least, groveling at your feet?"

"I think, my lord, that you're doing what you always do when you're caught like a child with his fingers in the cookie jar—using your boyish charm to avoid reproof. But I've told you before that, although your boyish charm is considerable, I am not susceptible to it." And, to underline her words, she got up to leave.

He rose quickly and blocked her way. "*Is* it considerable?" he asked, looking down at her with a glint in his eyes she found disturbing.

"What?"

"My boyish charm." He lifted her chin and made her look at him. "Is it considerable . . . to you?"

Her heart jumped up to her throat. The glint in his eyes flared up into flame, and one corner of his mouth turned up ever so slightly into an off-center smile. It was the look of a man who was very sure of himself. "Is it, ma'am?" he asked again, his voice low and husky.

She gulped. Her voice seemed to be gone. His smile broadening, he lowered his head, and one of his arms came round her. As his face came closer to hers, and she felt the tingle of excitement begin to bubble inside her, she wondered how many times he'd begun a seduction in just this way. He seemed so practiced, so confident, so sure of her response. She, however, was not at all sure what her response would be. She wanted to feel his lips on hers again, but she did not want to be seduced. Not so easily. Not by him. "If you're going to kiss me, my lord," she said, shutting her eyes and lifting her head toward his, "do get it over with. But I warn you, it will not make me any more susceptible than before."

A laugh burst out of him. "No?" he asked, tightening his hold. "You, Jane Douglas, are the most provoking, devilish creature it's ever been my misfortune to know. How can I kiss you when you tell me to 'get it over with'?"

She opened her eyes. His face was so close that the slightest movement would have brought their lips together. "In that case, you may as well release me," she said, but the tremor in her voice belied her words.

"I suppose I should," he said, but he promptly made that slight movement and kissed her, intensely, hungrily. The passion of it awoke in her a surge of pure joy. It seemed to her as natural as breathing to respond. They clung together, and for a while she forgot who she was, where she was, and why she was leaving. The room spun round, the candle-flames whirled about in the air, and the ground evaporated beneath her. Her whole body seemed made up of little sparkles of excitement. It was only when he let her go that the walls righted themselves and the ground solidified under her feet.

Both his arms were around her now. She could feel them trembling. He was staring down at her in astonishment. "Oh, *God*, Jane!" he muttered.

She was as astounded as he by the powerful effect of that embrace. But now that it was over, thoughts came streaming back into her mind, logical, reasoning thoughts that she'd evidently banished from her mind the moment he'd touched her. Suddenly her head was full of reminders . . . reminders of who she was, who he was, what she'd planned to do, and why. This was Luke Hammond, gambler, wastrel, and lecher. Just yesterday he'd tossed away a thousand pounds. Just yesterday he'd closeted himself in the morning room with his paramour for hours. How could she have kissed him—and in such a way!—after all that?

She drew a shaking hand across her mouth as if to wipe away a stain. "I suppose that proves that, given provocation, I can be as degenerate as you."

"Degenerate?" The word seemed to strike him like a blow. "Jane!" he exclaimed, appalled. "You *can't* believe—!" He dropped his hold on her and shook his head in disbelief. "I know you think me a wastrel, but that hardly makes me a degenerate."

"It can't matter to you what I think," she said.

"Obviously, it does."

The look of hurt in his eyes astounded and touched her, but her reasoning mind warned her not to continue this conversation. The kiss, she knew, had little significance to him, but it was devastating to her. Her emotions were dangerously close to the surface. "Please, my lord, no more," she begged. "I'm too discomposed to speak logically."

He made a gesture with his hand as if he wanted to hold her there, but then he expelled a breath of defeat. "Very well, ma'am. Go if you must. We'll talk tomorrow."

But there won't be a tomorrow, she thought. To prevent breaking down before his eyes, she said a quick

"Good night, my lord" and ran from the room.

At the bottom of the stairs she met Joseph. "Mr. Fitzgerald ain't home," the footman whispered conspiratorially. "I asked 'is man. 'E's gone to Devon."

Jane put a hand to her throbbing temples. "I don't
understand," she said, trying to concentrate. "How could
he have gone away? Where's Adela?"

Joseph lowered his eyes uneasily. "The fellow thinks
that a young lady wuz with 'im."

"What? Are you saying they ran off together? An
elopement?"

The footman shrugged. "If I wuz to elope, Miss Jane,
it wouldn't be to Devon. It'd be to Scotland."

"Of course," Jane agreed. "Gretna. Then, why—?"

"Dunno. But Mr. Fitzgerald's man did say that 'is
mother lives in Devon."

"His mother?" Jane's eyes widened. "Good God! He's
taken her to his mother!" She sank down on the stair.
"What on earth am I to do now?"

TWENTY-NINE

Degenerate? Is that what she thinks of me?

Luke stood at the morning room window, peering out at the moonlit garden with unseeing eyes. That one word had pierced him like the unexpected slash of a knife blade from a cutthroat on a dark road *I, degenerate?* he asked himself repeatedly. A degenerate was someone guilty of severe moral decline. How could she think it of him?

He was a wastrel, that much was true. But there was no *moral* infraction in his gambling; it was his own wealth he was dissipating, not someone else's. He was no worse than most of the men in his class in that regard . . . in fact, he was rather typical. And typical, too, in his attention to dress and in his enjoyment of sport. His interests might be considered trivial by someone as serious-minded as Jane Douglas, but they were not immoral. In fact, most of his peers would say that his standard of behavior was quite high. He was affectionate toward his mother, kind to his servants, loyal to his friends. He was, he believed, a pretty good fellow, all things considered. Where was the degeneracy?

The fact that he'd kissed her (twice!), after declaring that he wasn't the sort to accost a female living in his own home, was probably a lapse, but certainly not degenerate. He'd been impelled to kiss her, not from lust, but from a deep, overwhelming attraction that seemed almost . . . well, pure. It was a very different thing from the sort of urge that he'd felt when he kissed Dolly—

Dolly! That was it—Jane had seen Dolly yesterday! *That* was why she'd called him degenerate. In Jane's eyes that connection was undoubtedly reprehensible. The realization gave Luke a sense of relief. The problem was not that he was degenerate but that Jane was unsophisticated. Clever as she was, in these matters she was a naif, a rustic, an innocent. She didn't understand that most men in his circle had such connections. In truth, almost every fellow he knew had a fancy piece. Jane could hardly consider most male members of the *ton* degenerate, could she?

He gave a mirthless laugh. *Yes*, he said to himself, *she probably could.*

But it didn't matter. Now that he understood her, he could make it right. He could explain. He could tell her that he'd ended his liaison with Dolly. He could make her see that Luke Hammond was not such a bad fellow after all.

He strode out of the morning room and down the hall to the foyer, hoping to catch her. But the only person in view was Parks. "Have you seen Miss Douglas?" he asked the butler.

"I believe she's retired, my lord," Parks said, lowering his eyes.

"Retired? It's not yet eight o'clock."

"Yes, my lord, I know. But she . . ." He lifted his head and looked the Viscount in the eye, but he couldn't hide the quiver of his chin. ". . . she told me she's retiring early."

Luke knew his butler well enough to recognize that the quiver was a symptom of the man's inner discomfort. "Come now, Parks, don't be evasive. I can see that you're hiding something."

"I, my lord?" Parks was the picture of offended innocence. "Hiding something?"

"Yes, damn it! I can tell when—"

A knocking at the door interrupted him. Parks breathed a sigh of relief. "Shall I see to the door, my lord?" he asked.

Luke threw up his hands. "Yes, go on. It's probably Taffy, wishing to accompany me to the club."

But it wasn't Taffy. To his surprise, the caller at the door was Ferdie Shelford. The fellow was dressed in the most formal of evening wear, complete with top hat, cape and cane. "Good evening, sir," Parks said to him with proper formality. "Did you wish to see his lordship?"

"Ferdie!" Luke said, coming up behind the butler. "Come in. What on earth brings you here dressed to the nines?"

"To tell the truth, Luke," Ferdie said hesitantly, stepping over the threshold, "I didn't come to see you."

"No? Then who—?"

Ferdie colored in embarrassment. "Well, you see, I . . ."

"You've come to call on Miss Douglas, isn't that so?" Parks said, his tone excessively innocent.

Luke was too startled to notice his butler's mischief-making interjection. "Miss Douglas?" he asked, gaping. "You can't mean it. *Jane* Douglas?"

"What's wrong with my calling on Miss Douglas?" Ferdie demanded defensively.

"I regret that she unavailable," Parks said, throwing a gloating glance at his employer. "She's retired."

"Oh, blast!" said the disappointed Ferdie. "I wanted to ask her to accompany me to the opera."

Luke gawked at him in disbelief. "You wanted to take my Jane to the opera?"

"What do you mean, *your* Jane?" Ferdie asked.

"Well, I only—" Luke put a hand to his forehead in confusion. Had he really said *my* Jane? "It was a slip of the tongue," he muttered in hasty apology. "I only meant the Jane Douglas who works for me." But *was* that what he meant? Had he begun to think of Jane as *his?*

"There's nothing wrong in my escorting her to the opera, is there?" Ferdie persisted.

Luke was nonplussed. "No, I suppose not. I just . . . didn't know you even knew her."

Ferdie put up his chin belligerently. "I've met her."

"You have? When was that?" Luke wanted to know.

"Well, I don't exactly remember," Ferdie mumbled, "but I don't see—"

"It was last week, I believe, my lord," Parks put in, barely able to hide his amusement. "The day Miss Douglas went riding."

Luke eyed the butler with one eyebrow cocked. "Providing entertainment for you, are we, Parks?"

Parks's lips twitched. "I beg pardon, my lord. If you have no further need of me, I shall withdraw."

"An excellent suggestion," the Viscount said dryly.

No one spoke until the butler disappeared into the back hallway. Then Luke turned to his friend. "I hope you'll forgive my curiosity, Ferdie, but I'm puzzled. You've never been noted for pursuing the ladies. Then what in blazes induced you to call on Miss Douglas in the first place?"

Ferdie was perfectly willing to explain. "I saw her riding, you see. She seemed very lovely."

"Yes, she is," Luke agreed. "Very lovely. But you've met lovely ladies before and didn't pursue them."

"I wouldn't have pursued Miss Douglas, either, but then I learned from Taffy about her mathematical mind."

"It was her mathematical *mind* that captured you?"

Ferdie threw Luke a sheepish glance. "Well, you see, I thought, since I have a talent for numbers, too, that she . . . that we might have something in common."

"And did she agree?" Luke asked with intent interest.

"I don't think so. She said she didn't believe it proper for her to accept social engagements with your friends."

"She said that, did she?" Luke murmured, secretly pleased.

"I assured her you wouldn't object," Ferdie went on, "but she would not be moved." His shoulders suddenly sagged, and he gave Luke a look of glum entreaty. "Tell me, Luke, since you're so much more skilled with females than I—was the girl rejecting me? Am I a fool to persist in this?"

Luke shook his head. "I'm not skilled, Ferdie. I only pretend to be skilled. The fact is that women are as much a mystery to me as to you. I don't know how to advise you."

"Then I suppose I should give it up," Ferdie said, discouraged.

"Blast it all, thinking about women can drive a man mad," Luke exclaimed in a burst of disgust. "Let's forget about her for tonight." He put his arm about the other man's shoulder. "Come on, Ferdie, old fellow, let's take ourselves off to the club, where men are men, and women are not allowed."

THIRTY

When Luke and Ferdie arrived at the club, they both felt too depressed to indulge in gaming. By some unspoken agreement, they went instead into the lounge and sank into the club's deep leather chairs. Each was preoccupied with gloomy thoughts about Jane Douglas. Ferdie was reviewing every word she'd said in their one interview, hoping that somewhere in that recollected conversation he could discover a nugget of encouragement. He did not. Luke tried composing a speech in his mind, a carefully worded defense of his manners and morals, designed to reinstate him in her good graces. He could not seem to find the proper words.

They sat for a long while, just thinking. But thoughts are not action, and action was always more to Luke's liking. "Let's go upstairs," he said to Ferdie, rising purposefully to his feet. "Nothing like a little win at hazard to lift the spirits."

"I never win at hazard," Ferdie grumbled as he followed Luke up the stairs.

As they made their way across the floor, they were hailed by an acquaintance at a round table at which six men were playing commerce. "Come on and join us," the fellow said, indicating a couple of empty chairs.

"I'll play," Ferdie said without enthusiasm and took a seat.

But Luke only waved and walked on. He was looking for Taffy, wondering what had kept his friend from calling for him this evening. He suddenly realized he hadn't seen Taffy for two days. It was unlike Taffy to keep his distance. Luke hoped nothing was wrong with him. It occurred to him that perhaps he should take himself over to Taffy's rooms right now, and check on him. He turned round to retrace his steps, but he found his way blocked by Sir Rodney Moncton. "Ah, Luke," Monk greeted. "Just the man I wanted to meet."

"Really?" Luke said coldly. "That's surprising, considering that the mark I left on your jaw still shows."

Monk fingered the dark bruise on his chin. "Oh, well, I'm not one to hold a grudge. Let bygones be bygones."

"Cut line," Luke muttered impatiently. "What is it you want of me, Monk?"

"A game of picquet. You're the only player here who can give me a good game."

"No, thanks," Luke responded, walking off. "I'm already in debt to you for a bundle. I've no wish to increase it."

Monk fell into step beside him. "Come now, old man, this isn't like you. You were never one to quail at the loss of a thousand or more. What're you afraid of, a scolding from your pretty business manager?"

Luke stopped in his tracks and fixed Monk with an

icy stare. "You seem to show an inordinate interest in my pretty business manager."

"Not any more than she shows in me," Monk boasted.

Luke snorted. "Miss Douglas interested in you? As I recall, she showed no interest at all when you called on her the other day."

"That's because you interrupted us at precisely the wrong moment. Have you forgotten how she tended to me when you floored me?"

"Don't fool yourself, old man. That was only human kindness. She won't have anything to do with you. As she told Ferdie Shelford, she's doesn't make social engagements."

"Good God, has Shelford been after her?" He laughed scornfully. "The man's a jackass."

"The man has many qualities that would appeal to a woman of sense," Luke retorted.

"You're not implying," Monk said arrogantly, "that Shelford would be serious competition for me?"

"There is no competition," Luke said, turning and striding toward the stairway. "No woman of sense would consider you at all."

Monk followed him and grasped his arm. "Do you want to bet on it?"

"What?"

"Back up your claim with the ready. Let's wager on it. A hundred guineas that I can convince Jane Douglas to run off with me to Gretna within a week."

Luke pulled his arm loose. "You're out of your mind."

"Try me and see," Monk urged.

Luke laughed. "The only way you could win such a wager would be to dose the lady with laudanum and carry her off unconscious. And knowing you, that's just what you'd do."

"No, I give you my word. She would have to go willingly. A straight, clean bet. Let's put a monkey on it."

"You'd be throwing your five hundred away. Gibraltar would float to sea before Jane Douglas would consider running off—and certainly before running off with such as you."

"A thousand, then. Just think, man! If you win, you'll be square with me."

Luke turned on his heel and walked away again. "I don't bet on certainties," he said over his shoulder.

He was halfway down the stairs when Monk caught up with him again. "All right, double or nothing," he said, breathing heavily. "Two thousand if you win."

Luke couldn't believe his ears. "You're losing your wits, old chap. Two thousand?"

"That's what I said."

Luke scrutinized the man's face closely. "And you'll play completely fair? No lies, no tricks, no coersion?"

"Word of honor," Monk said, lifting his hand in a pledge.

Accepting a challenge was too habitual with Luke. A gamester in the blood, he could not resist. And in this case, the wager was especially tempting. A win was a certainty—everything he knew of Jane proved her character to be too high-principled to ever accept such a proposal. The payout would clear his debt and give him a thousand-pound profit to show his mother. He would pass his probation after all. "All right," he said, "done! But if I discover that you've coerced her in any way, or played one of your vile tricks, I swear I'll come after you and plunge my sword right through your black heart."

The rain was pouring down as Monk left the club, but he paid it no heed. He was having misgivings about his wager. Perhaps he'd been too hasty. Although he was convinced that Jane Douglas had revealed an attraction for him that day he'd called on her, with women one could never be certain. He remembered that when he'd taken her hands, she'd blushed at his invitation, and her hands had trembled in his. And when he'd opened his eyes after Luke had knocked him senseless, and found himself cradled in her arms, his head on her breast, he was sure that he'd captured her. He'd felt, that day, that just a little more persuasion would do the trick.

He'd never had difficulty capturing the hearts of the ladies, except for Dolly, and she had no heart. He would probably have little difficulty with Jane Douglas. After all, she was just a simple country maid, with neither title nor wealth. She would no doubt be overjoyed to find herself under the protection of a man of his stamp . . . a baronet with a sizable income and a place in the highest society.

But what if he were mistaken? He hadn't intended to wager quite so much on the girl's interest. He couldn't chance a loss of that size. The thousand pounds he'd won from Luke on the stagecoach race would help to pay some of his debts, and another thousand would be a windfall, but if he lost, he'd find himself in the deepest debt of his life. He could not afford to lose. He'd sworn to play it straight, but if the girl made difficulties, he'd have to use persuasion.

With a plot developing in his mind, he changed his direction and went to Dolly's rooms. She was entertaining a gentleman in her bedroom, but when she heard Monk's key in her lock, she excused herself, slipped out of the room and closed the door. "Monk, you numskull," she whispered, "didn't I tell you I would be occupied this evening?"

"I know. I'll only be a moment. I have a favor to ask of you. I made a huge bet with Luke Hammond that I can't afford to lose. I must find a way to lure him from his home tomorrow. For the day. Can you help me? Can you send him a note that you're ill, perhaps, and keep him here?"

"No, he won't come here," Dolly said with a sigh. "I'm sure of that. And even if he did, he wouldn't stay."

"Isn't there some pretense—?"

She shook her head. "Nothing I can think of."

Sir Rodney dropped down on the sofa, discouraged. "It's absolutely necessary that he be out of the way."

The two of them were silent for a long while, their brows knit. "Wait," Dolly said in sudden inspiration, "I have it. Miss Simmons, his old governess. He's very fond of her. What if he should get a message that *she's* ill?"

"His governess, eh?" Monk speculated on the possibilities. "But when he got there and found her well, would he remain with her all day?"

"She lives in Ramsgate. By the time he got there and returned, the afternoon would be gone."

Monk's whole aspect brightened. With a grin, he leaned down, lifted Dolly in his arms, and kissed her soundly. "You are a prize, my love, a prize. I don't know how to thank you."

"I do," she said, squirming out of his hold and preparing to return to her gentleman friend. "Just be sure you give me ten percent of your winnings."

Luke headed home from the club filled with misgivings about the wager, too. As he walked home through the downpour he began to doubt his judgment. Had he let Monk make an ass of him again? Did the fellow have some filthy trick up his sleeve?

But no, he assured himself, it wouldn't matter if he did. Monk would be dealing with Jane, not with him. He, Luke, might be an ass, but Jane was too upright and clever to be taken in by one of Monk's ploys.

He had nothing at all to worry about.

THIRTY-ONE

Jane sat huddled into the corner of the Viscount's coach, feeling guilty. The fact was that she'd stolen Luke Hammond's coach-and-four.

In her need to get to Devon to find her sister, she'd made a liar of herself, of Mr. Parks, of Joseph, of Meggie, and of Hodgkins, the groom, who, as a favor to her, was at this moment sitting up on the box driving the Viscount's best team through the black night. Stealing a coach and four horses was a heinous crime, especially heinous to someone who'd never in her entire life performed a dishonest act.

Of course, she fully intended to return the stolen property before daylight. As Mr. Parks had explained to Mr. Hodgkins, his lordship would not require the coach tonight, and, since the equipage and the horses would be back in the stable by morning, he'd never know that they'd been borrowed. Hodgkins had resisted at first, but he'd eventually taken pity on her (probably because he'd never seen her so greatly agitated) and agreed to go, but he was not happy about it. If anything went wrong, it would mean the end of his employment, or worse.

It was a hastily arranged plan. Jane and Mr. Parks had devised it. Mr. Parks would inform anyone who asked for Jane that she'd retired for the night. Meanwhile, while she and Mr. Parks made arrangements with the groom, Joseph would return to Taffy Fitzgerald's rooms and learn from his man the exact location of his mother's house. Meggie would pack a small repast. The trip, they estimated, would take three hours in each direction. With another hour to extricate Adela from the Fitzgerald domicile, they should be back in London by three or four in the morning. By sunup everything would be back in place, as if nothing untoward had occurred.

Thus far, things were working out as planned. But Jane was miserable. She did not like dishonesty. She did not like driving through the night in a stolen coach. She did not like the prospect of dealing with her headstrong sister. She did not like the fact that the moon, which had lit the road for the first hour of the drive, was now obscured by clouds. This entire venture was abhorrent to her. *Dash it, Adela*, she said to herself, *the moment I clap eyes on you, I'm going to wring your blasted neck!*

By the time they arrived at the Fitzgerald estate, a cold rain was falling. As the carriage turned onto the curved drive, Jane peered out at the house. There was not a light in a window, but the two carriage lamps revealed an old castle-like stone mansion with an impressive pediment over a wide doorway. It was not as large as Kettering, but a mansion nevertheless. Jane jumped out as soon as the carriage drew up. Disregarding the rain, she ran up the steps and pounded on the door. She would be rudely wakening everyone within, but this was not a time to concern herself with the niceties.

After several moments, during which she got a good soaking, the door creaked open. An elderly man—the butler, Jane assumed—peered out at her. He was wearing a robe and nightcap and carrying a candle. "An' who might you be, wakin' the dead at such an hour?" he asked in a hoarse, sleepy voice.

"I am sorry to disturb you," Jane said firmly. "but I've come for my sister, Miss Adela Douglas. I understand she's staying here."

"We have a Miss Douglas stayin' here. But you surely ain't expectin' me to wake her now. It's past midnight!"

"I'll wake her myself, if you'll show me the w—"

"Heavens, Burgess," came a tremulous voice from within, "who's out there?"

"It's a young woman, m'lady," the butler said. "Says she's Miss Adela's sister."

Another candle came into view. It was carried by a diminutive woman in a ruffled nightdress and shawl. In the dim light Jane could see a small face with a pointed chin topped by a lace cap from which fell a long braid of gray hair. "I am her sister, ma'am. I believe your son's abducted her. I've come to get her back."

"Abducted her, indeed!" The elderly lady snorted as she came up to the door, but one look at the bedraggled creature in her doorway changed her tone. "Gracious me, it's pouring!" she exclaimed. "Come in, child, come in, before you catch your death!"

The butler moved aside, and Jane gratefully stepped over the threshold. "My driver is sitting out there on the box," she said. "May he be given some shelter, too?"

"Of course," Lady Fitzgerald said. "Burgess, get an umbrella and see to him, please. And you, Miss Douglas, come along with me. We'll go to the sitting room and be comfortable."

She led the way across the foyer. "You don't really believe my Taffy would ever abduct—" she began, but the appearance of a candle on the stairway stayed her tongue.

"What's going on, Mama?" came a masculine voice from the stairs.

"You'd better come down, dearest," Lady Fitzgerald called up. "There's a young woman here who says you've abducted her sister."

Taffy gasped and came leaping down the stairs. "Miss Douglas," he cried, "did you think you had to come to her rescue? How can you say abducted? You must know your sister came quite willingly."

"I can certainly second that, my dear," his mother said placidly. "Although I've known her only a few hours, I think I can say with perfect confidence that your sister is very happy to be here."

"I'm sure she is," Jane said, "but that is no excuse. She was removed from my care without a word to me, nor was her mother's permission sought for this . . . this excursion. I would call absconding with her in that secret way an abduction, even if Adela agreed to it."

"I can certainly second that, my dear," the elderly lady said, nodding.

"Come now, Mama," Taffy said in disgust, "you cannot second both points of view."

"I can if I wish," Lady Fitzgerald said. "Come, both

of you, into the sitting room where we can talk this over."

An hour-long debate ensued, during which Taffy pointed out that his intentions were honorable, that Adela was properly chaperoned, and that this time together at his mother's house would help the couple to become acquainted.

Taffy's mother seconded every point.

Jane pointed out that this method of becoming acquainted was irregular, that society might not look favorably upon such an arrangement, and that Adela's mother had not given permission for her daughter to visit people who, one had to admit, were relative strangers.

Taffy's mother seconded every point again.

In the end Taffy admitted that it was only right that he seek Adela's mother's permission before proceeding further. "If you agree, Miss Douglas, I won't wake Adela now," he said, "but I give you my word that I'll take her home to her mother tomorrow."

His mother seconded the plan.

Jane gave Taffy's suggestion some thought. Under the circumstances, she decided, the plan was a good one. Lady Fitzgerald was obviously not a very strong-minded woman, but she was kind and good-natured. And Taffy not only seemed to be trustworthy, but appeared to truly care for her sister. Adela would come to no harm in their care. If matters worked out between Adela and this young man, it would be a very beneficial match for the girl. "Very well, so long as your promise is sincere, I agree," she said at last. "And now, I'd best take my leave."

"So soon?" Lady Fitzgerald asked. "You must at least stay for breakfast."

"No, thank you, ma'am. I must go back. I've already stayed half an hour longer than I planned."

They accompanied her to the door. "I shall be leaving London and returning home myself tomorrow," Jane said to Taffy, "so I'll probably see you there."

"I say," Taffy said, "if you're going home tomorrow, why don't you come with Adela and me? Hodgkins can take Luke's carriage back himself."

"I wish I could"—Jane sighed—"but it wouldn't be right. I have to be sure that Hodgkins and Mr. Parks are not punished for my sins. Besides, there's my baggage to collect, and Adela's, too. Thank you for the offer, but I must decline."

Hodgkins was greatly relieved when Jane informed him that she was ready to go back. "It's just 'alf-past one," he said. "We should be 'ome before sunup."

"There won't be any sunup," Jane remarked as she climbed into the coach. "This rain doesn't show any sign of stopping."

In fact the rain became heavier as the hours passed. The roads grew muddier and muddier, and their progress slower and slower. Even in the depths of the carriage, Jane could hear Hodgkins cursing in frustration.

As they neared London, early-morning tradesmen began to clog the roads. The rain finally stopped, but the ruts that the increasing traffic made in the road grew worse. As Hodgkins had been fearing, one of the wheels became mired. The four tired horses—even with Jane and Hodgkins pushing from behind with all their might—could not summon the strength to pull the carriage free.

And then, as the two weary travelers stood at the side of the road, staring gloomily at their immobile coach, the sun came up.

THIRTY-TWO

Luke came down to breakfast before seven, hoping to find Jane at the table. All night he'd rehearsed a speech to her, a speech in which he would declare that he'd admit to degeneracy only in the matter of having kept a *cher amie*. Since that matter was now in the past, he would say that he deserved to be forgiven, explaining that it was youthful excess. *Even Saint Augustine,* he would conclude ringingly, *prayed, "Oh, God, make me chaste, but not yet."* He could hardly wait to deliver it.

But Jane was not at the table. The only thing waiting for him was a pile of letters at his place. He sat down, let Parks pour his tea, and began to open them. Right on top was an unfranked letter with an unrecognizable seal. "Where did this come from?" he asked the butler.

"It was evidently slipped under the door this morning, my lord," Parks said, looking at it over the Viscount's shoulder.

Luke read the message quickly. "It seems to be from some acquaintance of Miss Simmons," he murmured aloud, frowning. "Says she's ill. Strange . . . she was perfectly well when I saw her just the other day." He pushed aside his other letters and got to his feet. "Tell Hodgkins to ready the carriage at once," he ordered.

"At once? The *c-carriage?*" Parks stammered.

"Yes, I've got to get to Ramsgate." He looked at the butler curiously. The man's chins were quivering. "Is something the matter, Parks?"

"No, my lord, nothing at all." Parks swallowed and started for the door, but he paused before leaving. "Are you certain you w-wouldn't rather take the curricle?"

"Why would I want to do that?" the Viscount asked, eyeing his man suspiciously.

Parks shrugged. "The weather has cleared, you know. It appears it will be a lovely day. I only thought, if you took the curricle, you could drive it yourself and make better time."

"As a matter of fact, Parks, you may be right. I would make better time. Very well, tell him to ready the curricle."

Parks nodded and scurried from the room. Once out of the Viscount's sight, he looked up toward heaven and breathed a relieved thanks to the gods for sparing him the necessity of explaining to his lordship why his groom, his carriage, and his business manager were missing.

Only half an hour after his lordship had departed for Ramsgate in the curricle, the coach and the weary travelers returned. Parks did not require much explanation to determine what had happened. They were all so well besmirched with mud that the reason was plain.

Hodgkins, on learning that the Viscount was out of

town, ordered the stableboys to wash down the horses and the coach, and took himself straightaway to bed. Jane did not permit herself that luxury. With his lordship away, this was the perfect time to take her leave.

She went to her room, shook the dried mud from her boots, cleaned the hem of her gown as best she could, gathered up her portmanteau and Adela's two boxes, and started to make her way down. She hadn't gone far when she realized she could not walk to the coaching inn so heavily burdened. She returned to her room, hastily re-packed only the most important items from all three pieces of luggage into the portmanteau, and left the rest, packed in Adela's boxes, to be sent to her later. There was one item, however, that she did not pack—the leather-bound Caxton Malory that his lordship had given her. That was too precious to trust to the ostlers' rough handling. She wrapped the book carefully in soft paper and put it in the reticule that she hung from her waist. In that way, she would feel it bumping against her with every step she took. A precious remembrance.

Mr. Parks had told the staff that she was leaving. All of them gathered in the foyer to say good-bye to her. One by one they came up to her and wished her well. Mrs. Hawkins embraced her warmly, and Meggie burst into tears. Joseph brought up the rear. Jane threw her arms about him, whispering her thanks for all he'd done for her.

The entire staff looked crestfallen as they returned to their posts.

Only Mr. Parks was left. They embraced wordlessly. Then he picked up her portmanteau and brought it to the door. "I only wish you could have the carriage to take you home," he said sadly.

"I don't mind the stage," she assured him, "or the walk to the inn, either."

"You'd better head for the Swan in Lad Lane," the butler said. "It's the closest. And you'd better hurry. The stages'll all be gone by nine."

She threw a quick glance at the hall clock. "That gives me almost an hour," she said, reaching for the portmanteau. The sound of the doorknocker stayed her hand. She and Mr. Parks exchanged alarmed looks. With a helpless shrug, he opened the door. Sir Rodney Moncton stood in the doorway.

"His lordship is not in," the butler said, trying to block the door.

"I haven't come to see Lord Kettering," Moncton said, pushing the butler aside. "I've come to call on Miss Douglas." He strode into the foyer but stopped short at the sight of her. "Miss Douglas, you're here!"

"How do you do, Sir Rodney," she said with a little bow, noting that the fellow was dressed with unusual care, his white-streaked hair pulled back neatly and his neckcloth immaculate. The only blemish in his polished appearance was a swollen, discolored jaw.

"I've come to ask you to take a drive in the park with me," he said with enthusiastic vigor. "How fortunate you're already dressed for the outdoors."

"I'm sorry, sir," she said firmly, "but I'm about to depart for my home in Cheshire."

His face fell. "You can't mean it! Leaving London?"

"Yes, sir."

He stood for a moment staring at her strangely. "But surely you'll be returning in a few days?"

"No, sir, I shan't." She picked up her portmanteau and tried to pass him by. "If you'll excuse me . . ."

"But I see no coach waiting for you," he said.

"No, I take the stage."

He wrenched the portmanteau from her hand. "You will not take the stage. It will be my pleasure to drive you home in my carriage."

"To Cheshire?" She shook her head and tried to take the luggage back. "That is not possible, sir. I could not accept."

"Why not?" he demanded. "It's but an afternoon's ride."

"It's much more than that," Mr. Parks put in nervously.

Sir Rodney glared at him. "The time means nothing to me."

"Please don't insist, Sir Rodney," Jane said. "We are strangers, after all, and I have no abigail or chaperone. Surely you must understand that I cannot accept such an offer." And she reached again for her luggage.

He held it off from her. "Then at least let me take you to the coaching inn. Are you bound for the Swan? It cannot be more than a few minutes away. What harm can there be in that?"

Jane and Mr. Parks exchanged glances. The butler's look seemed to say that, although Sir Rodney was annoying, the offer was not unreasonable. Jane herself was weary of debating with the man, and time was passing. There was no harm, she supposed, in accepting the brief ride. "Very well, sir," she said with a surrendering sigh,

"I'll accept your invitation with thanks." Quickly, as if he feared she'd change her mind, Moncton ushered her out, gave her portmanteau to his tiger, bundled her into the carriage, and, with a nod to his coachman, jumped in after her. Jane gave one last wave to Mr. Parks, who stood in the doorway watching her, and the carriage set off. She kept looking out of the coach's rear window until the Kettering town house was no longer visible.

If she'd been alone, she could have given way to the tears that had been welling up in her throat for the past half hour, but even this small release was denied her. It wouldn't do to cry in the presence of Sir Rodney Moncton.

She supposed she ought to be grateful to Sir Rodney for his generous escort, but his overbearing manner was not endearing. He had a discomfiting way of behaving as if he were her intimate friend instead of a rather irritating stranger. Even here in the carriage, he'd seated himself much too close to her. She slid over to the farthest corner of the seat, hoping he would not be so rude as to follow. For a few moments he remained where he was, but slowly, almost imperceptibly, he moved toward her until his knee was pressing against her leg again. Squeezed into the corner as she was, she could either submit in silence or complain and make a scene. She decided to submit, for the ride (*thank goodness!*) would be short.

Alarmingly, however, the man moved his arm over the back of the seat and across her shoulders. This she felt she could not ignore. "I wish you'd move over a bit, Sir Rodney," she said firmly. "You're crowding me."

"You don't really mean that," he said with an unctious

smile. "I've seen signs that you're as attracted to me as I am to you."

The remark startled her. "You are much mistaken, sir. I feel no such attraction."

He seemed not to heed what she said. Instead, he slid his hand from her shoulder slowly down her arm. "There's no need to be missish with me, my dear."

"I'm not being missish," she snapped, pulling her arm free. "This sort of attention is the last thing I wish for."

"Perhaps I'm rushing things," he said, unperturbed. Keeping one arm around her, he took her hand into his free one. "I would have liked to make my approaches with more subtlety, but you didn't give me much time." He lifted her hand and brought it to his lips.

She snatched her hand from his grasp. "I'm amazed, sir, at your determination to ignore my words. Please listen and believe what I say. *I have neither the time nor the inclination to indulge in a flirtation with you.*"

"I don't trust words, my dear. I see the inclination in your eyes. And as for the time, we shall have plenty of it. I'm sure that the trip I've arranged will afford us many hours to learn each other's true inclinations."

She froze. "Are you saying you're not taking me to the Swan?"

"My plans," he said with a glint, "are for an inn much farther west." With a sudden movement, he put his hand behind her head and drew her face close to his. "It's located on the coast," he said softly, his lips against her cheek. "At night you can hear the waves lapping the shore."

"I shall not be there to hear it, you may be sure of that," she retorted, pushing against his chest to try to hold herself aloof from him. But his face was still close. She could see in horrifying detail the leering twist of his lips, the nostrils dilated in suppressed passion, the bluish tinge of the skin on his swollen jaw where the Viscount had given him a blow. How she wished Luke Hammond were here now, to give him another. But now there was no help to be had but from her own wit. "Please tell your coachman to stop," she said in her sternest tones. "I shall walk to the Swan from here."

He only laughed and pulled her closer into his arms.

"Dash it, Sir Rodney," she cried desperately, "let me go!"

But his expression of lewd amorousness had changed. "Ooooff!" he grunted, his smile dying and his heavy brows coming together in pained surprise. "What in blazes is hanging from your waist?" He pulled a small distance away from her, and, keeping hold on her with one arm, used the free hand to rub his thigh.

Goodness, she thought, *my book!* The recollection of the Caxton Malory in her reticule combined in her mind with the sight of Moncton's swollen—what had his lord-ship called it?—glass jaw. Without a moment's hesitation she pulled her reticule from its string and swung it, book and all, as hard as she could to the wounded place on his jaw. He gave an agonized howl and fell back against the seat. Released from his hold, she quickly let down the window and shouted to the coachman to stop. By the time it did, however, Moncton had somewhat recovered and was reaching for her again.

She pulled herself free, threw open the carriage door, and leaped to the ground. Moncton followed and made a lunge for her arm. She avoided him and swung her reticule again at the same target. This blow proved too much for him, and he fell senseless to the ground.

She stared down at him for a moment, trembling. She felt both relieved and horrified at what she'd done. When she looked up, she discovered that Sir Rodney's tiger and his coachman were standing beside her, gazing down at their fallen master in awe. "I say," exclaimed the tiger, "that wuz a facer if ever I saw one!"

"Ye tipped 'im a settler, that's fer certain sure," the coachman said admiringly.

"He deserved it," Jane muttered defensively, shaking from head to toe.

"I don' doubt it, miss," said the coachman, grinning at her. "Ye needn't look so shamefaced. There's a good many days I'd like to whop 'im one meself."

"Same wiv me," the tiger said, looking down at his fallen employer with delight. "Many a night I dreamed o' squarin' up to him an' landin' a good 'un right in 'is middle."

"Be that as it may, I'd be obliged if you'd lift him back into the carriage," she said, taking a deep breath in an effort to calm her still-racing heart. "But first, will you throw down my portmanteau? I'm trying to get to the Swan by nine."

"You ain't gonna make it 'less we'll drive ye there," the coachman offered.

"Don' worry, miss," the tiger added. " 'is 'ighness, here, ain't likely to object."

"No, 'e won't wake very soon," the coachman agreed.

"Thank you," Jane replied, watching warily as the two men proceeded to lift Moncton's inert body and hoist it up into the carriage, "but I won't climb into that coach again. If you'll permit me, I'll ride up on the box with you."

"It'd be an honor, miss," the coachman said with a bow. "A real honor."

"Oh?" Jane cast him a look of disbelief. "Why an honor?"

"I cin tell ye that," the tiger said. " 'Cause any lady 'oo could lay Sir Rodney low is a true champeen to us."

THIRTY-THREE

⌒✿⌒

When Luke arrived at Ramsgate and discovered his old governess to be in perfect health, he knew he'd somehow been tricked, but why and by whom was a mystery. All the way back to town he pondered on the problem. No one but Monk would be playing such tricks on him, but if it were Monk who'd sent the letter, how would he have learned of his governess's existence? And what would his purpose have been?

He strode into his house determined to get to the bottom of the mystery. "Has anything untoward occurred while I was gone?" he asked Parks as soon as he stepped over the threshold.

"No, my lord," Parks responded curiously. "Were you expecting something extraordinary?"

"I was expecting some sort of catastrophe." He looked about him, relieved that everything seemed in order. "That letter this morning was a hoax, no doubt to lure me out of town." Handing the butler his hat and riding crop, he headed for the stairway.

"Nothing out of the way has occurred all day," Parks assured him. "Except, of course, that Miss Douglas left for home."

Luke stopped in his tracks. He felt as if he'd been kicked by a horse right in his midsection. "Miss Douglas? Gone?"

"Yes, my lord. She left about half an hour after you departed for Ramsgate."

Luke peered at the butler with an arrested expression. "Did you let her take the carriage? Is that why you were so eager for me to take the curricle this morning?"

"Oh, no, my lord, not at all!" the butler said earnestly.

"You may as well tell me the truth, blast it, Parks," Luke swore. "I shan't blame you. If I'd known she was so deucedly determined to leave, I would've insisted on her taking the carriage myself."

"Yes, my lord, I suspected you would. But she wouldn't hear of it. She took the stage. She was even going to walk to the Swan, but Sir Rodney came by and offered her a lift."

"Sir Rodney *Moncton?*" This was a second blow, and it caused the blood to drain from his face.

"Yes, my lord," Parks murmured, frightened by the Viscount's ashen look.

"And she *went* with him?" Luke demanded tensely.

"Yes, my lord. We didn't think there was any reason not to—"

"Damnation," Luke exclaimed, terror-stricken, "it was *he,* don't you see? Monk, the blasted muckworm! He sent the letter to get me out of the way!" He snatched his hat from the bewildered butler and sped to the door.

Parks ran after him with the riding crop. "Will you be needing this, my lord?"

"No," his lordship snapped, dashing down the stairs. "When I catch up with him, I'll beat the life out of him with my bare hands!"

Luke was not surprised to be told by Monk's man that he was not at home, but he took hold of the fellow's neckcloth in a choking grip. "Where's he gone?" he demanded threateningly. "Tell me at once, if you want to keep breathing."

"Miss Naismith's, I think," the fellow gasped.

"That's a lie! He left in his carriage this morning, didn't he?"

The man nodded. "But it's back. At the stable."

"The carriage is back already?" Suspicious, Luke tightened his hold. "Is that the truth?"

"I swear!" the fellow said, gagging.

Luke let him go. "If he's not at Dolly's," he said over his shoulder as he ran down the stairs, "I'll be back to pull the lying tongue from your head!"

But the fellow had not lied. When Luke burst unannounced into Dolly's sitting room, he found Monk stretched out on a chaise, with Dolly bending over him, applying a wet cloth to Monk's face, half of which was hugely swollen and discolored. But Monk's injury was of no interest to Luke. "Where is she?" he demanded through clenched teeth.

"Luke!" Dolly cried. "What—?"

"What are you doing here?" Monk mumbled through his swollen mouth, sitting up nervously.

"Where is she?" Luke asked again, stepping closer and making a fist.

"Who?" Monk asked innocently, nevertheless raising a hand to protect his wounded face.

"You know damn well who!" Luke snapped.

"What are you talking about?" Dolly asked, looking from one to the other.

Luke ignored her and came closer to the chaise. "What have you done with her?" he asked again.

"Whom are you speaking of?" Dolly insisted. "And what has he done?"

Monk edged to the far end of the chaise. "I didn't do anything with her."

"You damnable liar!" Luke raised his arm, ready to swing. "You tricked her into your carriage, didn't you?"

"Don't hit me!" Monk cried, cowering. He held up both his hands to ward off the impending blow. "I couldn't keep her there," he admitted hastily. "She wouldn't go with me. You won!"

"*Who* wouldn't go with you?" Dolly asked, glaring at the cringing Monk suspiciously.

Luke's arm froze in midswing. "I *won?*"

"Yes, you did," Monk said sullenly. "She got away."

"Did she, indeed?" Luke expelled a deep, relieved breath. "Since you certainly didn't let her go willingly, I can't help wondering how she managed it."

"She hit me with something . . . a brick, I think."

"Do you mean she's responsible for that bruise?" A slow smile appeared on Luke's face as he lowered his arm. "Well, well!"

"Are you speaking of that bran-faced chit Luke's taken on as his business agent?" Dolly asked, looking furiously from Monk to Luke and back again. "You tried to *abduct* her?"

Monk's frightened eyes shifted to Dolly's face for a moment before he turned back to Luke. "Look here, old man, you won the bet. Your Jane is probably safely in Cheshire by this time. So why don't you just take yourself off?" His eyes pleading, he slowly rose from the chaise. "I'll write my vowels for you right now." Holding his bruised face in one hand, he padded in stockinged feet over to Dolly's desk, inked a pen, and scribbled a note. "Here. Your debt to me is paid, and this is my I.O.U. for the other thousand."

"Yes, Luke, do leave," Dolly said, glaring at Monk menacingly. "I have some business with this gentleman that must be transacted in private."

"Very well, I'll go," Luke agreed, pocketing the vowels, "but if I find you've so much as harmed a hair of her head, Moncton, I'll find you out and run my rapier through your black heart."

As he turned his steps toward home, Luke regretted for a moment that he'd failed to give the blackguard a thrashing. But he consoled himself with the thought that Jane had done it for him. She'd apparently administered a very satisfactory blow. And if that weren't enough, there was still Dolly. From the glimpse he'd gotten of her face when he left, she was undoubtedly going to exact a retribution from Sir Rodney Moncton much worse than any he could contrive. If it were anyone but Monk, he might even manage to feel sorry for the dastard.

THIRTY-FOUR

When Jane woke the next morning in her own attic bedroom, it took her a moment to realize where she was. It took another moment—a longer one—to conquer the ache of disappointment. She had to remind herself that her London adventure was over and that she would not, ever again, lay eyes on Luke Hammond.

She made herself rise briskly. She'd sent a message to Lady Martha that she'd be returning to work this morning. It would not do to be late on her first morning back.

She dressed hurriedly and ran downstairs. Adela was already at the breakfast table, reading a letter. She looked up at Jane with shining eyes. "It's a message from Taffy. His groom rode all night to bring it to me. Taffy writes that he'll be driving up again on Saturday with his mother. Isn't that lovely?"

"Yes, it is," Jane said, pouring herself a cup of tea without taking a seat. "Very lovely."

"Mama told me she is feeling so much better that she

plans to be up on her feet to greet Lady Fitzgerald," Adela chirped happily.

Jane finished her tea. Then she planted a kiss on her sister's cheek. "I have to admit it, my love," she said as started for the door, "your Taffy is the best thing to happen to our family in years."

As she scurried down the road and up the hill to Kettering Castle, Jane considered what effect Taffy's impending visit might have on their lives. With his mother visiting, the two lovers might very well become engaged. Before very long, Adela would be wed and gone, and their mother would be without companionship during all the hours Jane was at the castle. It would be a blessing if the two mothers liked each other; then Taffy might invite his mother-in-law to live with them. *Mama would be so pleased,* Jane thought. It would be good for her to live in the luxurious manner she'd once enjoyed. Of course, Jane realized ruefully, she herself would then be alone.

She put the depressing thought out of her mind once she entered the castle. She had to concentrate on the work that lay ahead of her. Lady Martha's accounts must be in a sad muddle after almost three weeks of neglect.

Mr. Massey, her ladyship's butler, greeted her with sincere warmth. "We've all missed you, Miss Jane," he said.

"And I you," she replied with a fond smile. "Is there time for me to have some breakfast, Mr. Massey, or is her ladyship down already?"

"She's awaiting you in the library," the butler said. "She has some sort of surprise for you. I'll see if I can bring up something for you to eat a bit later."

"A surprise? I can't imagine—" Jane flew down the hallway eagerly and threw open the library door. "Good morning, your ladyship," she said as she crossed the threshold. "What's this Mr. Massey said about a—?"

Her breath caught in her throat. The dark-clad figure silhouetted in the window was not Lady Martha. It was a man.

"Good morning, Jane," he said.

Her heart jumped into her throat. "My lord!"

The Viscount strode across the room to her. "Don't you think it's time to stop 'my lord'ing me? The name's Luke."

She could not keep her eyes from his face. He was unshaven and looked weary. He must have driven all night to be here now. Had he come to see her? Moved at the mere possibility, she had to fight the urge to reach up and touch his cheek. "I don't think I should—" she began.

He frowned down at her. "You *don't* think," he scolded. "If you used even a grain of that superior brain of yours, you'd never have run off without a word of goodbye to me. How dared you do it?"

"I didn't think you'd mind."

"Not *mind?* Are you mad?"

"But you yourself admitted that there was nothing left for me to do about your finances—"

He grasped her shoulders in the angry grip she remembered so well. "The devil take my finances! I love you!"

"Luke!" She was so shocked by the words, she didn't believe she'd heard them aright. She could only gape at him.

"You said the name quite adequately," he said, a smile beginning to curve the corners of his mouth, "but my declaration requires a bit more of a response than that. Isn't there anything else you can say?"

With her heart bouncing about in her chest, she had to drop her eyes. "I don't . . . I c-can't . . ."

"You don't, you can't love me?" he demanded, taking her chin in his hand and forcing her to look up at him.

"Oh, Luke," she whispered, wondering if she was dreaming this scene, "surely you must know how I feel."

"How can I know if you don't say it?"

"I gave myself away both times you took me in your arms."

"Did you?" His whole expression brightened, and he pulled her to him. "Let's see if that's true." And he kissed her with all the fervor that had pent up in him since he'd discovered her gone.

This time she let herself respond with unabashed enthusiasm. "There, you see?" she said, smiling, when he let her go.

"My dearest, sweetest Jane!" he breathed, holding her close and pressing his lips against her forehead. "It is almost too wonderful to believe that so brilliant and beautiful a creature can wish to marry me." Suddenly he held her off and looked down at her. "You do wish to marry me, don't you?"

"Marry you?" She gazed up at him wide-eyed. She'd often dreamed of kissing him, but she'd never let herself even dream of marriage. It was too like a fairy tale. He was a viscount, but she was not Cinderella. It couldn't be real. "You want me to *marry* you?" she asked in astonishment.

"Of course! Do you think I'm so depraved as to offer you a *carte blanche?*"

"Well, no, but—"

"I'd be honored to wed you, Jane Douglas," he said, looking down at her adoringly. "Not only will I be taking unto myself a most delightful woman to love but the cleverest of business advisers to manage my newly acquired fortune."

Her head was spinning. "Newly acquired fortune?"

"Yes, my love," he said proudly, pulling a wrinkled paper from his coat pocket. "When I showed Mama this paper this morning, proving to her that I've succeeded not only in maintaining my wealth in the month of my probation but in increasing it, she signed the papers giving me control of the finances and sent them off to Mr. Fairchild."

Jane stared down at the slip of paper he offered her.

Sir Rodney Moncton hereby affirms this I.O.U. to be a valid testament of his debt to Lucian Hammond, Lord Kettering, in the amount of one thousand pounds sterling.

Her head stopped spinning. Reality was asserting itself again. The joyous feeling of the last few moments hung precariously suspended in the air. "Sir Rodney owes you a th-thousand pounds?" she asked quietly.

"Indeed he does." Luke grinned.

She felt herself tumbling from the clouds onto the cold, ungiving ground. "Is it in payment of a gambling debt?" she asked, backing away from him.

His smile faded as he heard the sudden coldness in her voice. "Yes, it is," he said tentatively.

"But I don't understand. Hadn't you just lost a thousand to him?"

"Yes, but this wager was for two thousand. The win canceled my debt to him and left me with this. It will cover all my debts and leave something over."

She felt more than disappointment. She was overcome with anger. "Am I expected to congratulate you for wagering so great a sum?" she said, trying not to show her outrage. "Where would you be if you'd lost?"

"But I didn't lose." He grasped her hands and tried to coax a smile from her. "Don't look at me that way, my love. I was not as rash as it might seem. The bet was a sure thing."

"Evidently Sir Rodney didn't think so."

"But he didn't know you as I did."

"Know *me?* What had I to do with it?"

"We wagered on you. I knew you'd never agree to run off with him."

She pulled her hands from his grasp and stared at him, white-lipped. Her heart plummeted as a kind of rage dissipated whatever was left of the dream. It was he, Luke Hammond, who'd incited Moncton to attempt the monstrous seduction in the carriage. "I can't believe this!" she cried. "Are you saying you wagered on the possibility that I'd go off with him? That he could induce me to become his . . . his *fancy piece?*"

His eyebrows rose, startled by her vehemence. "Well, I would not put it quite that way."

"How would you put it? Is there another way? Sir Rodney told me himself that he planned to take me to an inn by the sea. I would have the pleasure of listening to the waves as he seduced me."

Luke clenched his fists. "Damn him! I should've killed him."

"And what if he'd succeeded in his abduction? He would have, if I'd not had the good fortune to have a weapon on my person."

"I would not have let him succeed."

"You can't be sure of that."

"But, dash it all, Jane, he *didn't* succeed."

"Is that your answer? Do you so easily forgive yourself?"

He looked at her intently. "Is there so much to forgive? I put my money on the soundness of your character, and I was right."

She made a gesture of despair. He didn't even see how immoral his act had been. "You *are* a degenerate!" she cried.

"Jane!" Luke turned white. "You can't believe that."

"I can and I do," she said, turning her back on him so that he would not see her tears.

"That is a terrible thing to say to me," he said quietly.

"It is a terrible thing to be," she retorted in a choked voice.

There was a long silence. "Then I must assume," he said at last, "that marrying a degenerate is not an act you would consider."

"No, it is not."

"I see." His voice was hoarse. "Then I bid you good-bye, ma'am. I'm sorry to have troubled you."

She did not turn until she heard the door close behind him. Then she went to the window. In a few moments she saw his curricle make off down the drive. Only then did she collapse onto the window seat and clap a trembling hand to her mouth. It was a gesture meant to hold back the torrent of tears swelling up in her chest. But a hand is an inadquate barricade against such a flood of emotion. The suppressed sobs shook her shoulders and made her chest heave until, finally, they burst through the dam with a force that shuddered her whole body. She let them come, knowing all the while that they could not do much to ease the pain of the sudden shattering of a lovely dream.

THIRTY-FIVE

⚜

"Jane Douglas, what have you done?"

Lady Martha asked the question from the doorway, but Jane's gasping sobs kept her from hearing it. Nor did she hear her footsteps crossing the floor. She was not aware of another presence in the room until her ladyship laid a hand on her shoulder. She jumped. "My l-lady!" she cried in a hiccoughing gasp.

"My poor, sweet child," Lady Martha murmured with sincere sympathy. But then she repeated her question: "What have you done?" There was something more in that question than sympathy. There was a decided note of disapproval in it.

Jane made a brave attempt to suppress the heaving of her chest. Brushing at her cheeks with the back of her hands, she said, "I've s-sent him away."

"Yes, I know. I listened at the door."

Jane stiffened. "Are you saying you . . . you heard it *all?*"

"Yes. Every word." Without a smidgeon of shame in her eyes, her ladyship looked down at the girl sitting before her. "I am an unscrupulous old woman. As degenerate as my son."

"No, you are not." Jane met the older woman's critical gaze with a reproachful one of her own. "Eavesdropping is deplorable, but not degenerate."

"I could use those identical words about gambling," Lady Martha retorted.

Jane shook her head. "When I called your son degenerate, the word did not refer to gambling in general. It referred to a very specific wager: a wager on a libertine's ability to rob me of my virtue. To engage in such a wager sounds very much like degeneracy to me."

"But, my dear girl," Lady Martha argued earnestly, "Luke's money was on you! He was wagering on the strength of your virtue, not on your capitulation. And he was certain of the outcome. The degeneracy was all on the other man's side."

There might be some logic in that argument, Jane thought. She wanted with all her heart to believe it. But her brain was not easily convinced. If she were too eager to believe the best of Luke Hammond, how could she trust herself to think clearly? "You're his mother," she said, putting up a hand as if to ward off any vindication of the man she'd so severely convicted. "Naturally, you'd wish to interpret his actions in the most favorable light."

Lady Martha smiled down at her. "And you're the woman he loves," she pointed out. "Shouldn't you, too, try to see him in the most favorable light?"

The woman he loves! What a miracle of joy those words would have created in her breast a mere hour ago. Now, however, there was only this almost unbearable ache. She turned away from the kindly woman standing over her and rested her fevered forehead against the window-glass. "I wish I could," she said brokenly, the tears beginning to flow again.

Lady Martha slipped down on the seat beside her and took the girl in her arms. "There, there," she said, rocking her gently, "cry it out. My grandmother used to say that tears are like midnight—it's dark, but there's always the promise of morning coming."

"I don't think m-my morning will ever c-come," Jane sobbed.

"Nonsense." Lady Martha stroked the girl's hair soothingly. "In time, you'll find the perfect man for you . . . a young man who's proper and bookish and mathematical, and you'll—"

"Like F-Ferdie Shelford," Jane said, sitting up and snuffling back her tears.

Her ladyship seemed to stiffen. "You've met such a man already?" she asked, peering at Jane intently. "How . . . er . . . delightful!"

"Not at all," Jane said, pulling out a handkerchief and blowing her nose. "He's a dreadful bore."

"Is he indeed?" She smiled in relief. "Well, no one can say that of Luke."

"No, that's true. He's anything but a bore."

"Just think of it," her ladyship remarked with a distinct twinkle in her eyes. "You were bored with the young man who was perfect, and you fell in love with the young man who was full of flaws. Doesn't that suggest anything to you?"

"It only suggests that Shakespeare was right," Jane said bitterly. "He said that love is a madness and deserves a dark house and a whip, as madmen do."

Luke's mother continued to smile serenely. "It suggests to me, my dear, that your heart is wiser than your head. Would you wish Luke to change his character and be more like this Ferdie you spoke of?"

"Good heavens, no!" Jane exclaimed. The words had no sooner left her tongue than her eyes widened. "Are you saying I love Luke *because* of his flaws?"

"I'm saying you love him *with* them. His flaws as well as his virtues—and he does have virtues, you can't deny that!—are what make him what he is."

Jane stared at the lady beside her, a terrible awareness slowly dawning in her eyes. *His flaws and virtues make him what he is.* The words echoed in her head like a flourish of orchestral music. To love him was to love *all* of him!

When the full import of these words burst upon her, she dropped her head in her hands. "Oh, my lady," she moaned in abject misery, "what have I done indeed?"

THIRTY-SIX

It was not yet nine when Luke returned from the club. He'd never before come home so early. He'd gone there to try to recover from the dismals that had enveloped him since his return from Cheshire, but he'd found the company and the activities not at all congenial. The gaming seemed a dreadful bore, and Taffy, whose companionship had always been so satisfying, was tonight so repetitious in his effusions about his forthcoming betrothal—and to the sister of the woman Luke was trying to forget!—that getting away from him seemed a necessity.

All the way home he'd berated himself for the weakness of his character. To feel so wounded by a woman's rejection seemed to him to be unmanly. But no amount of self-reproach relieved the unhappiness that weighted down his chest like the stone of Sisyphus. *Blast you, Jane Douglas,* he cursed inwardly, *you have unmanned me!*

More blue-deviled than he remembered ever having

been before, he entered the house and absently handed his hat and cane to Parks. He was so absorbed in his own misery that he didn't notice the butler's quivering chins. But Parks could not contain his excitement. "She's here, my lord," he whispered urgently. "Our Miss Jane. She's been waiting for you in the library."

Luke, on his way to the stairs, froze in mid-motion. Then he turned slowly, as if his butler were holding a gun to his back. "Jane *Douglas?*" he asked in a voice so hoarse he did not recognize it.

"Yes, my lord," Parks said, agog with all sorts of promising speculations, "she arrived just after you left for the club."

Luke's brows rose, and he peered at his butler for a moment as if the man had spoken in a foreign language. Then, without a word, he turned and strode quickly toward the library.

Parks ran after him. "She would not say if she's staying," he said. "I don't know if I should have a room prepared for her or order the carriage."

"Later, Parks," Luke said shortly and, crossing over the threshold of the library, closed the door in the butler's eager face.

Jane was standing high up on the library ladder, reaching for a book. His pulse began to race at the charming sight she made, but he warned himself not to let down his guard. She'd probably come on a mundane matter of business, not for any personal reason. "I seem to remember discovering you this way before," Luke remarked, studiedly casual.

Jane gasped and, clinging to the side of the ladder, blinked down at him. "I did not expect you so early, my

lord," she said, breathless and discomposed. "I was trying to find something to read while I waited."

"What? Had you no accounts to review?" the Viscount asked coldly.

"I . . . did not come to work on your accounts."

"Indeed? Then perhaps you should come down and
tell me why you're here." He took the few steps necessary to bring him to the ladder. "Do you wish to fall
down into my arms again, or will you climb down on
your own?"

"Since you said, the last time, that I was too fat to
hold, I shall climb down on my own, thank you."

"I never said you were too fat." He reached up, lifted
her by her waist and set her down on the floor. "I said
you were an armful. Quite another thing."

"Oh?" She looked up at him, blushing. "A more flattering thing?"

Not in the mood for badinage, he turned away from
the flirtatious glint in her eyes. "If not to do the accounts,
ma'am, why are you here?" he asked.

"I would like to tell you," she said timidly, "but not
to your back."

"I'm sorry," he muttered, not turning, "but I haven't
the courage to face any more of your frontal assaults."

She put a light, imploring hand on his shoulder. "This
is no assault, Luke, I promise you."

"I hope not," he said, turning to face her, but with
obvious reluctance. "I've not yet recovered from your
last broadside."

"Was my refusal really so painful to you?"

"Good God, woman," he said in disgust, "how do you
think a man feels when, for the first time in his life he

declares his love for a girl, and that declaration is thrown back in his face because she finds him degenerate?"

"I would think the blow would be softened by his realization that she loves him anyway."

He gulped. "Does she?" He grasped her shoulders and fixed her with a look of frightening intensity. "Don't play with me, Jane!" he commanded. "My emotions are too raw to endure these no-I-don't, yes-I-do games. What are you trying to tell me?"

"Oh, Luke"—she sighed—"I do love the look of you when you're angry."

He glared at her. "That is no answer!"

"Yes, it is. Part of the answer. I love the look of you when you laugh, too." She loosed one arm from his hold and lifted her hand to smooth the frown from his face. "I love you so much I don't care if you're degenerate or not."

He expelled a long, deep breath. He wasn't sure she'd said what he thought she'd said, but something inside him had heard the words well enough, for the stone of Sisyphus rolled off his chest and melted away. The sudden lightness made him dizzy. He pulled her into his arms. "Did you say you loved me?"

She hid her face on his shoulder. "Yes, I said it. I love you. My very words. I've been saying them to myself from that very first day, when I was an armful to you."

He made her look at him. "I can't believe it!" he exclaimed, studying her face as if he'd never seen it before. "All that time? Through all my excesses, my gambling, my drunkenness, my stolen kisses?"

"Especially the kisses," she said, reddening again.

He had to kiss her then. And then once more. The

third kiss was so fervent they were breathless when he let her go. Weak in the knees, she had to lean against him for support. He held her with both arms and put his lips on her hair. "I'm not really so degenerate, my love," he said softly. "I know I'm not worthy of you, that my life has been wasteful and frivolous and wild, but even at my worst I would never lie to you or use you ill. And I can change. I'm ready and eager to become anything you wish—a proper squire of my estates, a member of the Lords where I might do some good—anything to make you proud of me. But one thing is certain: if you wed me, I promise I shall never make a wager again, on anything."

Her head came up abruptly, and a look of alarm crossed her face. "No, no," she cried, "don't say that! I don't want to change you. Forgive me for calling you degenerate. You are no more a degenerate than I am a prude, although we seemed so to each other for a time. I don't want you ever again to think of me as a bad influence."

"How can my brilliant beloved speak so foolishly? You surely must have understood that, even when I called you a bad influence, I knew you were exerting the very best influence on me."

"No, you mustn't go on like this!" she begged, placing her fingers on his mouth to stop him. "Why should I wish to alter what I love so dearly? Please, Luke, let me be a loving wife to you, not the arbiter of your morals, and not your Constable of Finance."

Overwhelmed by her words, he gently took her face in his hands. "Very well, my love," he said, kissing away the worried look in her eyes, "I promise never again to think of you as my Constable of Finance. And I'll go to the club occasionally and drop a few hundred pounds at the gaming tables, to prove to you I'm still the reprobate you evidently want me to be—although I'm certain that I'll always prefer staying at home with my enchanting wife. And I'll hire a man to do the accounts. Of course, I imagine you'll look over the books occasionally, to make sure I'm not being diddled. After all, of what use is it to have a wife who's a genius with numbers if she never puts that talent to use?"

Jane threw her arms about his neck in delirious relief. "Oh, Luke," she said with a sigh, "I do love you so!"

He responded to this very satisfactory declaration with a passionate embrace. In the midst of it, however, they heard a discreet knocking at the door. He lifted his head. "It's Parks," he muttered in annoyance. "I suspect that everyone in this household is speculating on what is occurring in this room at this moment. Of course, Parks will only ask where you are to sleep tonight."

"Tell him I'll go to my usual bedroom."

"I don't see why the Rose Bedroom won't do. You are a special guest—my betrothed, in fact—not my business agent. And you needn't fear that I'd do any nighttime wandering until we are safely wed."

Jane, aglow at the word *betrothed,* felt incapable of sensible thought. "The Rose Bedroom? How lovely that would be! But then the whole staff would guess—"

"Let 'em!" Luke laughed. With a quick kiss on her hand, he went to the door and threw it open.

Parks stood in the doorway, his eyes flitting curiously from Luke's face to whatever he could see over his lordship's shoulder. "I regret to interrupt you, my lord," he said in exaggerated obsequiousness, "but Hodgkins doesn't know if he should keep the carriage in readiness. Is Miss Jane returning to Cheshire tonight?"

Luke gave the butler a bland, noncommittal and very small smile. "I wouldn't wager on it," he said.

EPILOGUE

⌒✻⌒

Jane's heart thumped rapidly she ran up the stairway leading to the visitors' gallery of the House of Lords, the thumping caused not by her dash up the stairs but by fear—fear that she might be late. The baby had been fretful, and she hadn't been able to tear herself away from him until he'd settled down. *I can't be late!* her inner voice cried as she lifted her skirts to race up the last few steps, *not today!* Luke was about to make his maiden speech before this august body, and the occasion was something she would hate to miss. It was too important an event not to be shared by both of them.

She found the narrow gallery more crowded with visitors than she'd expected. About two dozen strangers were crowded at the railing, looking down at the rows of peers seated on long benches in the hall down below. A quick glance along the row of visitors, and Jane spotted Lady Martha, with Taffy standing next to her. She edged her way over to them. "Am I late?" she asked breathlessly.

"No," her mother-in-law assured her. "They haven't called him yet. Lord Gavin has been prosing on for the past half hour. Is little Benjy all right?"

"He's fine," Jane said. "He was just a bit peevish. Meggie was putting him to bed when I left."

Taffy, who'd been scanning the faces of the hundreds of peers seated below to find his friend, identified him at last. "*There* he is!" he cried, pointing. "Look at him! He seems cool as ice."

Jane looked down at her husband, her breast swelling with pride. Luke was quite impressive sitting there among the formally clothed peers, his arms crossed over his chest, his eyes fixed on the speaker with rapt attention. Relieved that she'd apparently not missed anything important, Jane slipped her cloak from her shoulders and looked about. "Who are all these people?" she whispered to Taffy. "Are they here to hear Luke?"

"Most of them," Taffy replied. "Those fellows over there are a contingent of the Corinthian set. They've heard that Luke is to speak today, and they've come out in support of one of their own. And those elderly fellows grouped at your right are members of Brooke's club."

"Really?" Jane glanced over at them in surprise. "I shouldn't have expected gambling gentlemen to interest themselves in the arguments about the corn laws."

A bewhiskered gentleman standing behind her laughed. "No, that doesn't interest us," he declared, not at all embarrassed at having eavesdropped. "A number of us at Brooke's have wagered on the possibility that Kettering'll make an ass of himself, and we want to see the outcome for ourselves."

"Indeed!" Lady Martha whirled about and fixed a cold

eye on the gentleman's face. "If you've put money on *that* possibility, my good man, then *you're* the ass!" she snapped. She'd traveled down from Cheshire especially to hear her son's first public address, and she did not enjoy learning that some of the observers were hoping he'd fail.

Taffy glared at the fellow, too. He'd also come a long distance to be on hand for this occasion, despite Adela's objection. (His wife had called him cruel to leave her behind in Devon when she was just barely recovering from the birth of her second daughter, but he'd pointed out that, in the first place, he could not be expected to miss the debut in the Lords of his very best friend; that, in the second place, it wasn't his fault she'd given birth a full two weeks before the anticipated date; and, thirdly, that he would, in any case, be gone from her side for only two days.) "Seems to me, Colonel Foster," he scolded the gambler, "that we, fellow members of Brooke's, ought to stand together."

"Nothing personal, old man," Foster replied with a shrug. "We're all fond of Kettering. But any excuse for a wager, y'know."

Jane was paying no heed to this exchange. She stood at the railing with her hands clenched at her breast, gazing down at her husband, her eyes alight in anticipation. Her only regret was that her ten-month-old son was too young to be present at this significant moment of his father's life.

When Lord Gavin concluded his remarks, and the Lord High Chancellor rose to call Luke's name, Jane's chest tightened. She wondered if Luke, too, was clenched in his innards. After all, he intended to express opposition to the popular view of the corn-laws question—an extremely difficult stance to take in a maiden speech. But he rose to his feet with apparent calm, and his voice was firm as he stated at the outset that he was strongly opposed to the corn-laws proposal. Ignoring the shouts of disapproval that came from all around him, he proceeded to explain how the laws had, in their four-hundred-year-old history, produced more harm than good, proving his point with facts and figures so specific that, for the moment, the opposition was silenced. "History proves," he declared, "that the benefits would accrue only to the landed gentry at the expense of the farm laborers."

This bald statement enraged the peers, and they let the speaker know it by hooting, hissing, and stamping their feet in angry disapproval.

Jane wanted to slay them all. *Let him speak!* she cried to herself. *Open your selfish minds and listen to him!* She wanted him to shout them down, to assert himself, to express some of the fury she was feeling. But Luke only paused, held a hand out for silence, and waited with calm patience for the uproar to subside. Then he went on, giving a graphic description of the plight of a typical farm laborer, citing in exact numbers the dismal effect the new proposals would have on this bleak situation. "Yet if we vote *against* the corn-laws proposal," he suggested, "we'd give evidence to the entire population that we, for once, are concerned more for the welfare of the country than for our own selfish gain."

A wave of murmured dissents filled the room. Luke ignored it. "Must we continue to uphold bad laws?" he asked, a quiet conviction underlining his remarks. "There is nothing noble in maintaining a superior position over powerless men," he concluded. "True nobility comes in being superior to our previous selves."

There was silence as he took his seat. Then a lone voice somewhere in the rear shouted, "Hear, hear!" and, as if the cheer had broken through a dam of resistance, an enormous wave of applause swept the room. Although a number of derisive hoots were mixed with the approbation, Jane sighed with relief and pride. Considering the unpopularity of his views, that swell of applause was very satisfying.

"Thank you, Lord Kettering," said the Chancellor, "for that enlightening and, I might add, very brave speech. And, since whatever follows is bound to be an anticlimax, I declare that we stand adjourned."

In the gallery the Corinthians cheered in pride, while the gamblers who'd expected Luke to fail paid off their debts. Jane, Lady Martha, and Taffy embraced each other in joyful triumph before hurrying down the stairs to the foyer to find their hero. They discovered him standing helplessly in the middle of the room, completely surrounded by House members eager to shake his hand. "Good speech," Lord Gavin was saying, "even if it won't change many votes."

"Damn if I don't change mine," the Earl of Hanley declared, clapping Luke on the back.

It was several minutes before Luke was able to make his way over to where his wife stood waiting with his mother and Taffy. His eyes went immediately to Jane's face. Her answering glance—sparkling with love and exultation—told him at once all he needed to know. "Let's get out to the carriage," he whispered and tried to usher them toward the doorway. But just then the

Lord Chancellor approached him. "I must compliment you, Lord Kettering," he said. "It's not often that a speaker in the Lords supports himself so well with statistics. You gave an excellent speech, with a superb conclusion."

"I don't deserve the compliment, my lord," Luke responded, taking Jane's hand and bringing her forward. "Whatever statistical information I used was supplied to me by my wife."

The Chancellor's eyebrows rose in disbelief. "Indeed?"

"It's quite true," Luke assured him, lifting his wife's hand to his lips. With his eyes smiling into hers, he added softly, "but, more important, she inspired the concluding remark as well."

"Made you *superior to your previous self,* is that what you mean?" the Chancellor asked as he raised his pince-nez to his nose and peered at Jane with an admiring smile. "I've heard that this husband of yours was a ne'er-do-well before you took him in hand, ma'am. You are to be commended on the improvement."

"He was always the man you see now," Jane said with a gleaming glance at her husband. "He just didn't bother to show it."

The Chancellor laughed. "Well, well, Kettering, then I compliment you on your marital choice. Your wife has beauty, brains, and modesty, too. You seem to be fortunate in many ways."

"Yes, my lord," Luke said, putting an affectionate arm about his wife and leading her off, "more fortunate than I can ever deserve."

They managed to find their carriage at last. Lady Martha climbed into it, and Jane was about to follow when Colonel Foster came up to them. "I say, Kettering," the Colonel asked loudly, "why ain't we seeing you at the club these days? Don't tell me marriage has changed you so much that you don't enjoy a good game of cards anymore?"

Jane laughed up into her husband's face. "*Has* marriage changed you so much, my dear?"

"I believe, my love, that I promised it would not," he said, grinning back at her. Then he turned to the Colonel. "Very well, Foster, since I apparently have my wife's permission, let's have a game at the club tomorrow evening. Shall we say about nine?"

Colonel Foster's eyes narrowed as he watched Luke climb into the carriage. "Needs his wife's permission, does he?" he asked Taffy with a disdainful smirk. "He's changed all right. Perhaps I'll be able to beat him at last."

"Beat Luke at cards?" Taffy retorted with a snort before jumping up into the carriage. "I doubt he's changed as much as all that."